	DATE DUE		

Every Woman for Herself

Every Woman for Herself

Trisha Ashley

Thomas Dunne Books
St. Martin's Press ✺ New York

For Alfred Wilson Long,
With love.

Chapter 1

Alien Husbandry

Got up at the crack of dawn to kill the Fatted Breakfast before driving Matt to the airport, only to discover that aliens had stolen my husband during the night and substituted something incomprehensibly vile in his place.

I expect their replicator was having a bad day. I distinctly remember marrying a gentle, long-haired, poetry-spouting Jason King lookalike with a social conscience, but what was facing me over the breakfast table was a truculent middle-aged businessman, paunchy, greying, and flaunting a Frank Zappa moustache edged seemingly with egg yolk: but I know better. The alien snot was the clincher.

It was not a pretty sight, but fascinating for all that.

I went and peered into the kitchen mirror to see if *I'd* changed as well: but no, I still looked like a miniature Morticia Addams.

'Charlie,' the Matt creature said impatiently, 'did you hear what I said? About wanting a divorce?'

I certainly had; what did he think had ripped the veils of delusion from my eyes? But I was temporarily deprived of speech as a quarter of a century of married life flashed before my eyes in Hogarthian vignettes: Flake's Progress.

The inner film came to a jerky halt. 'Yes,' I said finally, nodding. I understood.

Unfortunately my memory was not of the selective kind, a cheery sundial remembering only the happy hours, so my recollections were freely punctuated with loss. Lost mother, lost virginity, lost babies, lost husband, Lost In Space.

Charlie Rhymer, this was your life.

Matt seemed disconcerted by my reaction, for some reason.

1

'We've grown apart since I've been taking these foreign contracts, and I've come to realise that this will be best for both of us. In fact, we can divorce right away, since we've been separated for more than two years.'

'How can we be separated when you're here?' I asked, trying to get my head around this concept.

'But I'm not *really* here, am I?' he said impatiently. 'I'm in Saudi.'

'But you're back for quite long holidays between contracts – and you said it would be better if *I* stayed here.'

'You would have hated it – you know you don't even like leaving the house, let alone the country.'

'But that's just York – it's got the wrong sort of outside. I'm fine at home.'

'This is your home.'

'I meant Upvale, and Blackdog Moors.'

'You seemed eager enough to run away from it with me.'

'That was love, and unplanned pregnancy, and Father.'

Matt said earnestly: 'Charlie, it isn't that I'm not still fond of you . . .'

'Oh, thanks,' I said. 'In fact, thank you for having me.'

He ignored that; I'm not sure he even heard it, like most of the things I say.

'It's just that I'm not getting anything out of this marriage,' he continued.

'You make me sound like a bank. What were you expecting to get out? More than you put in?'

'At least there are no children to complicate things,' he said, which was a very low blow. He was starting to make me feel quite sick.

'I'm sorry it's come to this, Charlie, but we really can't go on. I've been offered a long contract in Japan, and I can't afford to continue maintaining two households.'

'But the house . . . the mortgage?' I said, my brain starting to limp onwards a bit now the first shockwave had broken over my head. 'What will happen?'

'The divorce will go through quickly if we are both in agreement – my solicitor will send you things to sign. Then I'll pay you maintenance every month, so you won't have anything to worry about. The solicitor will get in touch with you and explain everything.'

'Will he? Is that what you've been doing this week, organising our divorce? Why didn't you talk to me about it, instead of suddenly handing me a fait accompli on your last morning home? After all, I haven't done anything, have I?'

'No, you haven't done anything,' he agreed curtly. 'Perhaps that's just it. I've moved on, and you haven't. Other women have families and careers and interests. Perhaps it's time you got out there in the real world.'

I've been cocooned for the twenty-odd years of my married life, and now suddenly I'm to be ripped from my chrysalis and told to make like a butterfly?

He rose from the table. 'I'll ring you from Saudi, once you've had time to think it over.'

Questions were already beginning to bubble scummily to the surface, like: when did he see this solicitor? How long had he been planning this? What does he mean, he'll give me maintenance? Was there some other woman behind this? Who on earth would want him?

'Hurry up and get the car out,' snapped Alien Nation in a reasonable impersonation of my husband, 'while I get my bags.'

'What?'

'I've got a plane to catch. It's time to go.'

It certainly was. I went into the conservatory, locking the door carefully behind me. Although it's so tiny, once I'm in the middle where my easel and table are, you can't see me for jungle plants.

Palms, bamboo and bananas, and a fig tree in a big pot ... Dense foliage and warm, slightly steamy, air.

Matt banged on the glass a few times like a deranged moth, shouting, but I disconnected, picking up a brush and carrying on painting the tiny, naked, cowering figure at the heart of the rampant forest. It looked like Steve, the handsome young gardener at the park, and something threatening was *definitely* lurking in the undergrowth.

Probably me: I often have lustful thoughts about him when I go there to sketch in the greenhouse, but in reality there is not enough cover to drag him behind even were he willing – and it is one of those ironic twists of fate that as you age you lust after fewer and fewer men, and those are the very ones who wouldn't look twice at you.

I really should have sown my wild oats before I got married; I fear it is now too late.

Sometimes, too, I wonder if my body wouldn't have rejected each pregnancy if they hadn't been fathered by Matt? Perhaps our genes are incompatible?

Too late for that, as well.

Much later I resurfaced to the sound of a familiar loud thud and yelp as Flossie (my spaniel) attempted to walk through the glass door again. But at least if she'd come out of hiding it meant Matt had gone.

Flossie is not big on brains, but she *has* grasped that Matt hates her, and it's safest to keep out of his way. Of course she forgets sometimes, especially when overcome by greed, like yesterday morning when she was drooling over his feet at breakfast, and he kicked her when he thought I wasn't looking.

Later I went up to the bathroom and gave *all* my big silver rings a vigorous cleaning with his toothbrush and a bit of powdered floor cleaner. The rings came up a treat and I expect his teeth did, too.

Flossie now sat in the dining room outside the conservatory door, looking dazed. (But this is not unusual.) She wagged her tail happily when she saw me coming.

The breakfast debris still littered the table, and Alien Nation had left a note pinned down by the teapot that said he'd had to call a taxi, and if he missed the connection it was my fault.

There was also the name and address of the solicitor who would explain everything to me.

I wish someone would.

Why do I never seem to grasp anything until a couple of years after it's happened? I never know where I'm going, only where I've been.

As Joni Mitchell says, you don't know what you've got till it's gone. I only know what I had to start with.

Or do I only know what I *think* I had to start with? Or did I have what I thought I had, but somehow swapped it for an alien? Could living with me for so long have *turned* him into an alien?

He was right about one thing – he's changed, but I don't think I have very much.

Clearly that was my mistake.

I took stock of my innermost feelings and discovered there weren't any: I'm a blown egg, all shell and void.

You might hear the sea if you put your ear to me, but that's about it.

Chapter 2

Wrong in the Attic

Lay awake all night with my mind doing hamster-in-wheel impersonations, then came groggily down this morning to find a letter from Matt's solicitor.

Isn't this indecently fast? The letter said that since Matt and I were in agreement (*are* we?) and there were no children of the marriage, I did not need to have my own solicitor: just sign on the dotted line when asked to, and don't make a fuss.

The only good thing Matt's sudden bombshell did was make me look at him and realise that he *had* turned into this alien, and an elderly one at that. Otherwise, who knows how long it would have taken for me to realise that I was beginning the slow trek through that long, rocky hinterland before fifty, hand in hand with a grumpy old man? (And as Sherpas go, he'd have been no Tensing.)

A day or two later Matt phoned, his usual bossy self, and instructed me to just do as I was told, basically, and he would see me right financially.

That will be a novelty.

And there was definitely an underlying threat there . . .

I've finished the painting: miniatures of looming menace my speciality.

When I lived on the moors among all those vast spaces I painted long, narrow landscapes where tiny figures were set like random jewels. But once transposed to the claustrophobia of a city (even one as beautiful as York) I began painting ever-smaller canvases in which the minute figures cower under threatening jungle foliage.

7

They sell quite well through Waugh-Paint, a local gallery. Vaddie Waugh, the owner, says it's because they are so small they are easily portable. Or maybe people just like having something small, dark and threatening hanging on their walls?

I haven't told anyone about the divorce yet because it doesn't seem real. And anyway, there's only really the family to tell, and frankly I do not want to phone home and confess that not only have I failed in the motherhood stakes, I've also failed as a wife. The solicitor *has* explained everything to me, but it all slid away from my grasp immediately. All I understood was that financially we are up Shit Creek without a paddle, so there is no point in my fighting for half the house or a huge chunk of maintenance. The maintenance Matt does propose giving me is a pittance, though combined with my painting earnings I expect I will survive: Remittance Woman.

I know I won't be able to keep the house, but the only thing I regret is my conservatory. I will have to return home to the Parsonage at Upvale – but where can I put my jungle? I can't paint without it any more.

I suppose I will have to find some kind of job, and a house of my own if I can afford it, because much though I love going home, it would be difficult to do it permanently after having my own place for so many years. I *could* live on my painting, but it would not pay a mortgage.

Having looked around the house, it is amazing what Matt removed without me noticing before! Still, I do not wish to keep ninety-nine per cent of the household contents anyway, since they were never my choice, and in fact are as alien to me as Matt now is.

Perhaps everything could go to one of those auction houses that take anything? I suppose I'd better ask Alien Nation if he wants to keep any of it first – if he ever phones again. He's gone from checking up on me every other night (although after all these years he must know I'm either here or in Upvale) to one solitary, admonitory phone call.

A couple of weeks after the discovery that Matt was an alien, I opened the door to a most unwelcome visitor: Angie, raddled bride of Matt's best friend and colleague, the revolting Groping Greg.

'Angie! What are you doing here? I thought Greg's contract didn't end for another three weeks?'

Of course, had I known she was home, I wouldn't have opened the door without checking who it was first, from the upstairs window.

She pushed a bundle of magazines and a box of chocolates into my arms. 'These are for you,' she said in the hushed tones of one visiting the sick. Then she trailed past me into the house exuding a toxic effluvium of sultry perfume and nicotine.

If you dipped Angie into a reservoir it would turn yellow and poison many cities.

I followed her into the living room where she draped herself into one of the minimalist white leather and birch chairs. She looked surprisingly comfortable, but then, she is all sinew and leather herself.

'I had to leave Greg out there and come home early, because the cleaning service said we had weird noises in the attic. But anyway, after Matt told us about the divorce, I just *knew* you'd fall apart! And since you've got no friends except us, I said to Greg: "I'd better get back and help poor Charlie."'

Angie is not, and never has been, my friend. I disclaim her as a friend. Her presence is about as welcome to me as a tooth abscess.

'I'm not falling apart,' I assured her, which I wasn't, because nothing lately seemed at all real. I wasn't sure if I'd been living in a dream world for years and just woken to reality, or vice versa. Sleeping Beauty in her jungle. 'Actually, I feel more as if I'm imploding – hurtling inwards on myself. There'll be a popping noise one day, and I'll have vanished, like a bubble.'

'You poor thing! There, I knew I was right to come back. But look on the bright side, darling – you and Matt are having a *friendly* divorce, so it will go through really fast. Then he's going to pay you maintenance, although I don't suppose you'll need much because you will just go back to that insane-sounding family of yours. Did you see your sister, Anne, on the news last night? There were bullets flying around her head, and she just kept on talking.'

'Emily – my older sister – has second sight, so she knows Anne's invincible to bullets. And I don't know why you say my family's insane. Matt was keen enough to marry me once he found out who Father was, even if he can't wait to get rid of me now.'

'Anne, Emily – and your brother's called Branwell, isn't he? What were your parents trying to do, breed their own Brontës?'

'Yes – well Father was, anyway. He thought if he recreated the hothouse environment and we *didn't* become literary geniuses, or *Branwell* became the literary giant, it would prove his point. You know – like in his book: *Branwell: Source of Genius?*'

From her puzzled expression, clearly she didn't know.

'And Charlie's short for Charlotte, of course. When the experiment palled on Father he sent us all to the local school, and although Em didn't mind being known as Effing Emily, I got very tired of being Scarlet Charlotte the Harlot. My family always called me Charlie, anyway.'

'Weird!' she muttered again. 'I suppose you *will* go back there?'

'I'll have to, but I can't just return as if the last twenty-odd years never existed.'

Though, mind you, when I do visit home it feels as if I'd never left. Everything's the same: Em running the place and striding the moors composing her lucrative greeting-card verses, Gloria and Walter Mundi haphazardly doing the work, Father writing his infamous biographies and installing his latest mistress in the Summer Cottage, Bran and Anne turning up on visits.

And the moors. Nothing ever changed on Blackdog Moor except the seasons, that was what made me feel so safe there and so very *un*safe here in York.

'You can get a little job, can't you?' suggested Angie. 'You're not too old.'

'What as? Besides, I might make enough from my paintings if I exhibited more.'

'A London gallery, that's what you need.'

I shuddered. "Oh, I couldn't go to London! All those people, and the dirt, and the noise . . .'

'Don't be such a wet lettuce,' Angie said impatiently. 'It's time to stop being such a shy, mimsy little wimp once you're past forty.'

I gave her a look. I may be reserved, stubborn and quiet, but I plough my own furrow, as she should know by now. I'm an introverted exhibitionist. Why should I like crowds? I'm simply not a herd animal.

No one could accuse Angie of being mimsy or shy. She's at least ten years older than me, but her hair is dyed a relentless auburn, she wears eyelashes like tarantula legs, and her face has had every cosmetic art known to science applied to it at one time or another. Her body is lean, brown, and taut, except for the crêpe-paper skin.

Flossie wandered in from her basket in the kitchen, wrinkling her nose at Angie and sneezing violently, before climbing onto my lap and regarding my unwelcome visitor with the blank expression only Cavalier Queen Charlotte Spaniels can assume. I'm convinced they are the result of an early failed cloning experiment.

'At least there are no children to dispute custody of,' she said, staring at Flossie.

I'd learned not to look upset when people say this sort of thing to me, as if I hadn't desperately wanted children. 'No, there is that, and Matt has always hated Flossie, so we won't be disputing over *her*.'

'So everything's all right? Matt says the first part of the divorce will go through in a couple of weeks, and six weeks after that, it's finalised. Isn't it quick?'

'That's because I didn't contest anything – I haven't even got my own solicitor – and we can't go for mediation because we are in different countries.'

'Matt says you don't *need* a solicitor, because the house is in his name, and remortgaged to the hilt anyway, and there are lots of debts, so there isn't much to share. But I'm sure he will be generous with maintenance. You will be fine.'

'Yes, though I do suspect any mildly generous impulses he has now will dwindle away, like in *Sense and Sensibility*.'

She looked blank.

'You know, Angie, where the widow and her daughters were going to be looked after by the son who inherited everything, only the allowance sort of dwindled away to the present of the odd duck?'

Angie isn't much of a reader. She carried on staring at me with her mouth open for a full minute.

'The odd duck?'

11

'Not literally, in Matt's case. How could he send me a duck from Saudi? Or Japan, which he's supposed to be going to next. What an awful lot of students want to learn English.'

'Just as well – and Greg's been offered a Japanese contract too. I quite fancy it.' She looked around her vaguely. 'What are you doing with everything? You can't take it all back with you to Upvale, can you?'

'No, but I wouldn't want to anyway – I've never thought of most of the furnishings as mine. They are all Matt's choice, and most of them were already here when we married. There's very little we chose together. Unless Matt wants any of it, I expect I'll sell it. There are places that come and pack it all up and take it to an auction for you.'

'Yes, but I don't think you get much for it. Doesn't Matt want it stored?'

'Apparently not. He must have been plotting this long before he came home for his last holiday, because he'd already removed all his personal stuff into storage without me noticing.'

'You're not the most observant of women are you? Head in the clouds. Or the plants.'

'I might want a few bits and pieces, because I don't think I could live at home again for very long, not after living in my own house for years. And I need somewhere to put my plants.'

'I don't think Upvale sounds very exciting. Matt said it was just one steep cobbled road like a Hovis advert, with three street lights, half a dozen houses, your Parsonage, and a lot of dirt tracks leading to farms.'

'There are a lot more houses than that in Upvale, but they are spread out. And the only cobbled bit is about a hundred yards in front of the pub.'

'I didn't know there was a pub. Civilisation!'

'Yes, the Black Dog, after the local legend. There's Blackdog Moor, too haunted by this huge, hideous fanged creature, with blood-red eyes and jaws dripping with—'

Angie shuddered. 'No more, please. What with noises in the attic and demon dogs I won't sleep a wink tonight all on my lonesome.'

'Oh yes – the noises in the attic. Are you haunted, Angie?'

She should be, by the ghosts of all the creatures who died in animal experiments on cosmetics.

'No, it's squirrels.'

'Squirrels? You've got squirrels in your attic? What colour? Those nice little reddish Squirrel Nutkin ones, or the big grey ones?'

'What does it matter? They're all vermin, and they've chewed the furniture I'd stored up there to bits! Squirrels! They've eaten all the wooden parts of the chairs and the grandfather clock, and a nice tallboy. I suppose I'm lucky it wasn't rats, which is what I thought when I got back on Wednesday and heard all those funny thumping noises. Isn't that what you'd have thought, Charlie?'

'What?' I said, dragging my mind back from my own problems with some effort. *'I'm* the madwoman in the attic, I think, or will be. Perhaps I should join your squirrels.'

'Who mentioned madwomen?' she demanded crossly. 'Do concentrate, Charlie. The little tree rats have eaten all the lovely furniture Mother left me. I mean, what am I going to say to the insurance company? "Squirrels ate my furniture"?'

'"Weasels Ripped My Flesh"!' I exclaimed, perking up. 'I'd forgotten all about that song. Wasn't it Frank Zappa and the Mothers? Or no – maybe it was Jethro Tull.'

Angie sighed. 'Not weasels, *squirrels,*' she said in cold, clipped accents.

What a matron she would have made if she hadn't got off with Greg and left the nursing profession! Or a wardress.

'Sorry, it just reminded me of that song and . . . but do go on. Squirrels ate your furniture?'

'Yes. Grey ones.'

'How did they get in? There must have been a hole somewhere.'

'A tiny one, but they found it. Still, I expect the insurance will pay up in the end.'

'Unless squirrels are an Act of God, Angie.'

'Don't be silly. How can squirrels be an act of God?'

'You never know. When our garden wall fell down that time, they said it had been undermined by moles, and *that* was an act of God, so—'

'You *are* joking, aren't you?' she asked warily.

I smiled encouragingly: 'I expect they will pay up – and what a shame about that furniture. I really liked some of it, especially that knobbly triangular chair. Although bottoms aren't that shape, are they? And with all those bits sticking out it wouldn't have been very comfortable, and although it would fit right into a corner of a room, you don't usually want to sit right in the corner, do you? So I expect you can replace it with something more practical when you get the money.'

'You do go off at a tangent.'

'I'll have to go off altogether, Angie – I've got my hairdresser's appointment.' Which I absolutely *loathe*; but my roots were showing.

'That dead-black Goth look with the dark eye make-up and purplish lipstick is very out of fashion,' she said, scrutinising me severely.

'I know, but Matt insists, and—'

Suddenly I realised that it didn't matter any more what Matt liked or didn't like. He wouldn't be here to throw a major wobbler if I stopped dyeing my roots, wearing heavy black eye make-up and vampire-style black clothes . . .

It was a look that seemed less and less *me* as I got older. I mean, it was what I was into at seventeen, but I didn't think I'd be stuck in a timewarp forever afterwards.

But now I could do what I liked.

'I can do what I like,' I told Angie.

'You always did,' she said sourly. 'Wasn't that part of the problem?'

'Only in the major things, the ones that mattered, like the painting. In little things Matt had it entirely his own way. And I hadn't realised we *had* a problem.'

I was about to add that until the morning Matt asked for a divorce I hadn't realised how *old* he was either, but just managed to stop myself in time: like Matt, Angie and Greg are a good ten years older than me.

Greg is an awful, red-faced old roué who tries to jump on women the moment he's alone with them. He's Father's type, I suppose, but without the leonine good looks – and Father does go in for his mistresses one at a time, as a rule.

'Greg will be home in a couple of weeks, if you want any help,' Angie offered.

'Oh, no thanks Angie,' I said hastily. 'I'm sure I can manage.'

Her eyes fell on the stack of magazines she'd brought, and she pounced on the top one. 'Now what's that doing there? I didn't mean to bring that old copy of *Surprise!*. I only kept it because it had photos of that gorgeous Mace North in it.'

'Who?'

She exhibited the magazine, and I scanned the man on the cover with no recognition whatsoever, although it was a very distinctive face. His slightly oblique, hooded dark eyes seemed to be staring back at me assessingly. (And probably finding me wanting.)

'You must know him! He's a well-known actor, and he's got this deliciously plummy voice, a bit like Jeremy Irons.'

'You know I don't watch much TV. But it sounds an unlikely combination with that face,' I commented. 'He looks a bit – barbaric.'

'It's the Tartar blood.'

'Oh? I thought tartar was something you found on your teeth,' I said disagreeably.

'Not that sort of tartar – it's a place in Russia. Mongolia? The High Steppes, or Chaparral, or something? His great-grandmother was a Tartar and that's where those fabulous cheekbones come from, and the come-to-bed eyes . . .' She gazed at the magazine and sighed. 'He's sort of like a young Bryan Ferry crossed with Rudolph Nureyev.'

'Rudolph Nureyev's dead.'

'You must have seen photos.'

'Yes, but I don't find men in tights very appealing. I'd never have made Marian.'

After a minute she smiled weakly: Sunrise over Yellowstone Canyon.

'You will have your little joke,' she said, hoisting herself to her feet and tucking the copy of *Surprise!* firmly under her arm. 'I'd better go and sort out the roof rats. I'll have the little buggers out of there.'

Her car was parked opposite, outside Miss Grinch's, who would not be pleased: she likes the front of her house kept clear so she has a better view of what her neighbours are doing. Had Angie been a man visiting me while my husband was away she would have been straight across with a milk jug or sugar bowl to try and catch me out in some imagined misdemeanour.

I don't think I've ever done anything yet to surprise her – I must be *such* a disappointment. You'd think she'd have lost interest by now. Apart from Angie and Greg, Matt's friends don't bother me

15

when Matt's away, and if Greg comes to the door when I'm on my own I pretend I'm out.

I always check from the landing window first, after one nasty experience soon after I married Matt, when Greg found me on my own and was horribly overfriendly in a near-rape kind of way. He's even like that in front of Angie at parties, and she doesn't seem to mind particularly. Maybe she thinks he's all mouth and no action. Maybe he *is* all mouth and no action when it comes to the crunch – I don't intend finding out.

When she'd gone I finally phoned Em, the Ruler of Upvale Parsonage, told her about the impending divorce, and asked if I could come and live at home for a while.

'Okay,' she said.

'Will you tell everyone? Father?'

'He always thought Matt was a waste of space. Anyway, he won't be very interested – he's got a new mistress.'

I groaned. 'Is she in the Summer Cottage yet?'

'Not yet. She's renting a house down in the valley. But she's always round here, and they're all over each other. It's revolting. And she's got twin little girls who sit about giggling. She leaves them here when she goes out with Father.'

I suppose it's better than leaving them in an empty house, but not much – Em doesn't like children, so she will not see their presence in the house as being anything to do with her.

'He's never had one with children before has he?'

'No, unless you count Bran's mother, and that was un-intentional. He'll probably get tired of her, if she won't move into the cottage. You know how he likes everything convenient.'

'Flossie says hello,' I told her.

Em's voice immediately softened to a medium baritone that was positively sugary. 'Give her a big kiss on her shiny black nose from me, and tell her Frost can't wait for her to come and live here.'

Flossie is petrified of Frost, a giant grey lurcher with question-able habits (a bit like Father, really), but I appreciated the sentiment.

'I will – and thanks, Em.'

'I haven't done anything.'

'You're just – there.'

'Where else would I be?' she asked, sounding puzzled.

16

Chapter 3
All Panned Out

I didn't turn up for my hairdresser's appointment yesterday, which made me feel like I was bunking off school. I need never sit in one of those foul-smelling torture chambers again. Things are moving so quickly now that I've decided to start packing things up. I'll put the things I don't want in the small spare room: it's half-decorated as a nursery, a place of abandoned hopes, so entirely suitable. The things to take with me can be stacked at one end of the living room.

I've been looking at the heap of magazines left by Angie, and I'm feeling extremely irritated: none of them seem to have *any* connection with reality as I know it. They might as well all be called 'Rich Young Brain-Dead Anorexic London-Based Fashion Victim Magazine', and have done with it. Where are the magazines aimed at women like *me*? 'Skint Old Northern Woman', perhaps? I'll have to write my own:

SKINT OLD NORTHERN WOMAN: ISSUE 1
Our motto is: Every Woman For Herself!

Welcome to our new magazine for the older, more frazzled reader. While written primarily for the Northern woman, it may also prove invaluable for those Southerners harnessing their huskies ready to brave the Frozen North, containing as it does many cultural hints.

To any peripheral Skint Old Southern Women, why not write your own issue, addressing the topics you find important?

We welcome readers' letters, except those sycophantic ones

17

*saying how wonderful our magazine is: we already know that,
so for God's sake write about* something. *If you have an embarrassing personal problem write in to Sister Charlie's 'In
Confidence' page: she will only share it with the entire reader-
ship* . . .

I think I've discovered a fascinating new hobby.

The house is now on the market, and Matt, via his solicitor, has
said he will give me half of any profit, but I can see that it will all
be eaten up by these mysterious debts and the overdraft. It's never
felt like my house anyway, so I don't care.

He says he has stored everything that he wants from the house,
and he doesn't mind what I do with the rest.

What a busy boy he must have been during that week at home
– and how unobservant of me not to notice.

He is going to carry on paying the mortgage and utilities
until the house is sold, but for some reason he has not trans-
ferred any extra money across this month for food, etc. Is this
a mistake, or have I already dwindled to the present of the odd
duck?

Seeing that I would have to start selling the furniture *now*
(however odd an appearance that will give to prospective house
purchasers) I went out to the supermarket and removed as many
cardboard boxes as I could fit into my ancient 2CV.

I also laid in a large supply of long-life consumables, like baked
beans, jars of olives, red wine and dogfood, before the money ran
out altogether.

Em phoned: the mistress has got into the house, and is laying
waste like Angie's squirrels.

None of the others have managed to sidestep the Summer
Cottage like this, and Em has begun an offensive against the
invader. Em does offensive very well. She hopes to have them out
before I move back, but in the meantime the mistress is domiciled
in *my* room! I was highly indignant, even though Em has removed
all my personal belongings from it and stored them in one attic,
and the two little girls in another.

She would have much preferred squirrels, and so would I.

Why did it have to be *my* room? Why not Bran or Anne's?

18

Having foreign bodies in my only remaining sanctum is the last straw. Think the aliens are now taking over Yorkshire.

'Don't worry, I'll get them out,' Em said grimly. 'Father won't be able to stand them around all the time once the sexual novelty's worn off – you know what he's like. Then I'll put your room back as it was.'

'But it will never be the same again,' I said sadly, for now I really do feel like a dispossessed person. I'm blowin' in the wind.

I told Em about *Skint Old Northern Woman*, and she said it was a wonderful idea, and she would write some inspiring verse for it, or maybe cookery hints, like: *In Yorkshire We Eat Faggots*.

Em has a knack for writing doggerel verse, which is very saleable: practically every greeting card seems to contain one of hers. Now she reminded me that we all had old portable typewriters. Father bought them when it became clear that we weren't going to write Gondal-type stories in the minute notebooks he kept giving us. Perhaps he thought we needed a bit of twentieth-century apparatus?

When I found mine, the ribbon had dried to paper tape, and trying to buy a new one proved to be a vain quest, for the computer age had overtaken me.

When I eventually did track one down it was the wrong sort and I had to hand-wind it onto the old spools. I may have red and blue hands for the rest of my life. Still, it works.

Skint Old Northern Woman
In this issue:
   Tart up that skirt
   Normal women bulge
   Superfluous hair
   Bulimia for beginners: what to do if your body doesn't want
   to part with the food

My roots are turning slowly silver as the divorce proceedings trundle tumbrel-like towards the final division. I've always had long hair, but I don't think all that dye will come out. It looks quite interesting, though – more badgerish than Cruella.

My clothes I can't do much about at the moment, since they are all black; mostly culled from charity shops and jumble sales. And there are one or two floaty Ghost things, purchased at who-knows-what-price or with what credit card by Matt in London, but they are black, too.

Since I'm not the same person who eloped with Matt, it doesn't seem right that I should look the same, especially if I'm moving back to Upvale. I'm going full circle on my life, but surely it should be a different me that returns?

New To You.

It's melancholy packing up the house, and my dreams with it. And there was that moment when the auction van removed the marital bed . . . Very symbolic.

Not that I ever liked it.

Angie has been ringing continually, offering to help, but that's just nosiness. And Greg is back, but he hasn't got in, even though he phoned first to make sure I was here. That should have got the message through.

Soon he'll be flying off again – they both will – and I need never see them or any of Matt's other friends ever again, so there's at least *one* good side of divorce.

Skint Old Fashion Victim: Part One
  Criteria for buying second-hand clothes:
1. It fits you
2. It has no noticeable holes or stains
3. You can (just) afford it
4. It doesn't say 'dry clean only' on the label
5. The colour doesn't make you look like a dead Martian
6. It conceals/reveals all bulging bits in a socially acceptable manner.

Phoned Anne's London flat, and for once found her home. Her normal manner of answering the phone is so indistinguishable from the answerphone that I'd started to leave a message when she broke in.

'Anne, this is Charlie—'

'And you think I can't recognise your voice after all these years?'

'Oh, you're there! Good. Is Red there, too?'

'No. Bosnia.'

'I didn't think anything much was happening there at the moment.'

20

'It isn't; he's coming back.'

'Has Em told you I'm getting divorced?'

'Yes. Bloody good idea.'

'It wasn't mine, but I'm getting quite used to it. I've discovered that although I'm deeply shocked and upset, I'm not heartbroken. Mostly I'm annoyed that I stayed faithful all these years when I needn't have bothered.'

'Em says you're selling the house and going home.'

'Yes – I won't have much money, so I'll have to live at home for a bit, until I can rent a place of my own. But to do that I'll need to either sell more paintings or get a job of some kind.'

'The mistress has got in the house.'

'She's not only in the house, she's in *my* room. If Em doesn't get rid of her soon I'll have to stay in the Summer Cottage.'

'You might like it. Home but sort of independent. Eat in, live out.'

'Yes . . . Oh, I saw you on the news a few days ago. Nice waistcoat – khaki suits you.'

'Just as well; never wear anything else. Like you, with your black.'

'I might have a change.'

'Em's thinking of having a change, too: turning to the Black Arts, or maybe greyish. The darker side of Wicca, anyway,' Anne said non-committally.

'Yes, but is it a good idea?'

'Who knows? No one can stop Em doing anything she's made her mind up to do.'

'That's true. I expect she's got the measure of the mistress by now, too. Do you think you might be visiting Upvale soon?'

'Might do, in a few weeks. Depends.'

She rang off after a few bracing words about getting a solicitor and a better settlement, but I don't think Matt's got very much to settle, so it would be pointless and tiring.

Came back from the supermarket with a whole lot more boxes, and had to kick the front door closed behind me.

Flossie was still snoring in the kitchen, lying just as she was when I went out: on her back in her furry igloo, with her head hanging out of the opening and her ears on the floor. She didn't wake up even when I started clattering unwanted cooking-ware in the boxes.

It was as I was standing on tiptoe on the very top of the high kitchen steps, unhooking the cast-iron frying pan from the ceiling rack (so convenient for Matt, who never cooked, so inconvenient for me, who did), that I was seized extremely familiarly from behind.

'All alone at last?' gloated a horribly familiar voice. 'You can't know how long I've wanted to get my hands on these!' And he squeezed painfully, like an over enthusiastic fruit tester.

These were, I fear, the last words ever spoken by Angie's husband Greg. Had he known, perhaps he'd have thought of something a little less trite: but then, everything he uttered was straight out of a Victorian melodrama, so perhaps not.

Startled and off-balance, I couldn't stop the weight and momentum of the pan I'd just grasped from swinging down and connecting with his head.

What an odd, strangely meaty, but hollow noise it made against his skull! A sort of watermelon-hit-by-a-cricket-bat sound which I don't think I'll ever forget as long as I live.

It *was* only the smaller frying pan, but unluckily he turned out to have a very thin skull. Mind you, even with a two-handed swing I would probably have dropped rather than swung the bigger pan. Bad luck all round.

As I stepped carefully down, Greg twitched like a dying insect at my feet, then lay still.

Not dead yet? Not dead?

Someone let out their breath in a long exhalation, and when I looked up, Miss Grinch was standing in the doorway, her bony fingers to her choppy lips, as Shakespeare has it. An empty milk jug hung from the lax fingers of her other hand.

'I mustn't have locked the door,' I said inconsequentially. 'I'm always careful, especially when I know Greg's home – but it was awkward with all those boxes.'

Naturally Miss Grinch would have been so consumed with curiosity she'd followed Greg in. Probably tiptoed up the hall right behind him.

'Is he dead?' she enquired, stepping into the room just as I dropped the pan from nerveless fingers. (It landed on Greg's foot with a crunch, but he was beyond caring by then.)

'Did he fall, or was he pushed?' I quavered.

'Not that he doesn't deserve it, behaving in such a disgusting way to a defenceless woman,' she said severely. 'Find a mirror and hold it to his lips.'

I began to giggle helplessly: 'A mirror? Why would he want to see himself at a time like this?'

'Pull yourself together, girl,' she snapped. 'A mirror will mist up if he's breathing. Here, I'll do it.'

She unhooked the small pine square from the wall under the clock. 'You phone 999.'

I managed that, even though my fingers felt even deader than Greg looked.

'Ambulance – accident – emergency!' I babbled. 'There's no mist on the mirror!'

'Where are you speaking from, please?'

'This is Miss Grinch,' that lady said, taking the receiver from my hand. 'I don't think there's any rush. He's dead.'

She gave my name and address to the operator, then added: 'We just need the ambulance, no police. This is such a nice neighbourhood, and none of the Grinches have ever been mixed up with police.'

'Except the one who stole Christmas,' I said helpfully.

Of course, we did get the police, much to her indignation, but never did I think I would be so glad to have a nosy neighbour!

Were it not for Miss Grinch I'm sure I'd be facing a murder charge right now. But she described how she'd followed Greg right into the house and had seen the whole thing, which was an unfortunate accident.

If Greg hadn't suddenly assaulted me just as I was reaching down the pan, with no idea that I was not alone, it would not have occurred.

The frying pan was impounded, but I wasn't, although I felt so guilty at having taken a life I'd have gone without a struggle.

Flossie finally awoke at one point during the noisy and exhaustive debacle, took one look out of her igloo and retired back in, until everyone was gone except Miss Grinch and me. She's easily confused by loud voices and big feet.

Later, Miss Grinch gave me a small glass of colourless fluid and insisted that I drink it. I'm positive she said it was gin and laudanum, but surely that can't be right?

Whatever it was, it put me out like a light.

Chapter 4
Sheared Off

Late last night Angie came to the door and beat on it, screaming hysterically: 'Bitch! Whore! Murderess!'

The last was the only one I felt truly applied.

Fortunately I was sitting in the upstairs bay window, sleep now being something I've lost the hang of, and my legs had gone too numb to go down, otherwise sheer guilt would probably have made me go and let her in.

After a while lights went on in several neighbouring houses, including Miss Grinch's, and shortly after that a police car coasted quietly up and removed Angie.

There was a faint, receding cry of 'Pigs! Pigs! Arrest the murderess!' and then the street slowly sunk back into dark silence.

I'd been wondering how I could break the news of the accident to Matt, but in the end I didn't have to, because Angie'd done it for me.

He phoned today just to tersely inform me that henceforth all communication would be through the solicitor, and put the phone down.

I suppose murdering his best friend *is* a pretty irreconcilable marital difference?

Miss Grinch continues to be my comfort and guide throughout this nightmare. I don't know what I would do without her, which is a far cry from the way I felt about her before she became the star witness for the defence.

She is now my bestest friend. Not so much a mother figure, as an acidulated spinster figure – everyone should have one, but they are a dying breed.

Em would have come to stay for a few days, but Father's latest mistress is still infesting the house.

The housekeeping is, and always has been, Em's preserve, and she won't stand interference, let alone a takeover bid. Outright war has been declared.

Normally this would have all interested me extremely, especially since one of the combatants was occupying the hallowed ground of my bedroom, but now I moved through the days like an automaton. I signed everything the solicitor sent me; Matt, true to his word, having ceased personal contact.

I'll be lucky if I even get the duck now.

Miss Grinch, like Anne, urged me to get my own solicitor and a better deal, but so far as I could see there wasn't anything but debts and an absent husband, and I don't want half of either of those.

Anyway, I don't feel I deserve anything any more now.

All I can think of is that ghastly thud as the pan connected with Greg's head, and I'm tortured with wondering whether I could have prevented it: I mean, when I hit him, I *wanted* to hit him – so was it really an accident? Was there a moment when I could have diverted the fatal downward swing?

I don't think so, but I'm not sure. And I *feel* like a murderess – I *have* killed someone.

Miss Grinch doesn't understand that. She says God will look into my heart and judge me, but I'm afraid He already has. He just hasn't told me the outcome.

We have had several people round to view the house, though how many are motivated by the thrill of blood I don't know. Miss Grinch has been conducting the sightseeing tours with a brisk efficiency reminiscent of Anne and Em. Perhaps that's why I like her so much?

She has also helped me pack most of the house contents up, and everything except a few necessities has now gone to auction. I didn't keep a lot – I feel a certain revulsion at the things that remind me of Matt (and through him, Greg), which most things do. Anything unsaleable has gone to the nearest charity shop or in the bin.

I sent a small van of things to Em to store for me: the driver was cheap, but he certainly wasn't willing, especially when it came to my plants. He said he had hay fever and wouldn't take *any* of them, so I will just have to fit as many of them as I can into my 2CV when I move, with the roof open, even though it is pretty cold to be transporting tropical foliage. I gave a lot of the smaller ones to Miss Grinch, who was delighted, so at least they've gone to a good home.

Eventually there was just me, Flossie, and a few vital odds and ends left. Like the survivors of a shipwreck, we were marooned until after the inquest.

Angie has made banshee late-night appearances twice more on my doorstep, but been removed much faster than the first time.

I have been buying head-sized melons.

Skint Old Gardening tips: 1
  Always keep margarine tubs of compost on your window sills, and whenever you eat fruit, push the pips or stones in. Water daily, and eventually something will come up. The novelty of this method is that you won't have the faintest idea what it is.

Even in my current numb state – which now seems part of me, like permafrost – I found the inquest appalling, although but for Miss Grinch it might have been a murder trial, which would have been very much worse.

The kindly coroner treated me like a frail little flower, and Miss Grinch with respect, but was firm about having Angie removed from the room when she became hysterical and demanded the death penalty: my death, that is.

She was still screaming: 'Murderess! Murderess!' as she was escorted out.

I knew in my heart of hearts she was right, even though the coroner assured me it was not my fault at all, and urged me to put it behind me. It was brought in as accidental death.

The coroner added a little speech to the effect that people who succumbed to the current craze for heavy cast-iron pans would do better not to hang them from the ceiling, and I'd have to second that one.

By the time I got out of the hearing the reporters from the local paper were encouraging Angie to stage the scene of her life.

She spotted me. 'Murderess!' she screamed with a certain

27

monotony, tossing her black veil over her shoulders and then lunging at me with blood-red talons like a deranged harpy.

'Murdering harlot!'

Well, that was different – but why harlot? Surely it was because I had resisted her lechering husband that he was dead today? And she knew what he was like.

One or two people were holding her back, fortunately, since I was transfixed to the spot by all the avid stares.

'I'll never let this rest until my poor Greg has justice!' she howled. 'Wherever you go I'll find you, and make sure people know the sort of woman you are!'

I wish *I* knew what sort of woman I am.

'You'll *never* be able to forget it.'

Well, that was certainly true.

'Wherever you go, I'll follow you,' she added, sounding suddenly exhausted, and dangling limply from the hands that a moment before had been restraining her. 'You'll never escape.'

Nowhere to run to, nowhere to hide . . .

'Why, Angie?' I asked. 'You must realise by now I didn't mean to kill him. Don't you think I feel badly enough about it already?'

'No, but I'll make sure you know what it's like to suffer – to be friendless and alone . . . like me.' She drew a dramatic hand across her eyes and gave a broken sob.

'But Angie, Greg walked into my house uninvited and indecently assaulted me! And you must have known he was serially unfaithful?'

'Yes, but none of them ever *killed* him!'

Well, there was that. And the more I protest, the guiltier I feel. Could I really not have diverted that fatal downward swing?

'Besides, whatever his faults, he loved me,' declaimed Angie, looking tragic.

'Maybe he did, but he slept with anyone he could get,' I pointed out.

'They weren't important.'

The voices of the listeners now rose in a babble of questions, but Miss Grinch popped up suddenly at my side, seized her chance, and hurried me through a gap to the waiting taxi.

'How tall?' I whispered as we climbed in. 'Did you find out?'

'Five feet, ten inches, dear,' she replied.

Looking back, I could see Angie still holding forth on the steps like Lady Macbeth.

'I wish I was dead,' I said dully. 'There doesn't seem any point to living any more.'

'Clearly God still has a use for you,' Miss Grinch said placidly.

'Compost?' I suggested.

'We are all God's compost, if you like,' she said. 'Interesting – I've never thought of it like that before. However, I am sure he has something in mind for you before that. He moves in mysterious ways.'

'Like the frying pan,' I agreed, and we were silent until we reached the house.

Miss Grinch bought the local papers, and thankfully I hadn't merited the front page. Even with Angie's theatrics I suppose they can only get so much story from a domestic accident without insinuating anything libellous.

I was described throughout as Mrs Charlotte Fry (although I've always called myself by my maiden name), and there were several photographs of me looking very small and weird, like a glaze-eyed rabbit cowering under the menacing overhang of Angie's bust.

My hair was now a clear white for about an inch at the roots.

'I always wondered about that very dense blue-black shade,' Miss Grinch said, scrutinising a particularly hideous photo.

'It was my natural colour.'

'Believe me, it is a mistake, once a woman reaches forty, to dye her hair a dark colour. Your skin has lost the fresh bloom of youth and the contrast is too severe.'

'I know, but Matt wanted me to keep it black. He liked this sort of Goth look with the long hair and the dark eye make-up because he thought it made me look young. He was so much older, so I was a sort of a Trophy Wife, you know?'

'You can do what you like now, dear.'

'I don't think I care.'

'I'll have my hairdresser come round and do something with it – have it made as God intended.'

'God intended my hair to turn silver at thirty, like my mother's, but my eyebrows and eyelashes to stay dark.'

Mother is Lally Tooke; when I see her on the jacket of one of her radical feminist books, or on TV, she looks a bit like she's wearing a powdered wig, but she looks good. We have the same big dark eyes, the purplish colour of black grapes.

Matt was always impressed by Father's fame (or notoriety), dragging his name into conversations like a dog with some malodorous and grisly find. 'My father-in-law, Ranulf Rhymer.'

He never felt the same way about my far-flying mother, but then, neither do I: *that* hand did not so much rock the cradle as break off shards and wage a bloody battle with them before leaving the field forever.

'You could start wearing prettier colours than black,' suggested Miss Grinch, who had been pursuing thoughts of her own.

'I don't have anything else. Most of my clothes come from charity shops and jumble sales anyway.'

'Time for a change.'

'I can't afford a change.'

'My hairdresser's very cheap,' she assured me, and looking at her frizzed ginger-grey curls I could believe it.

She was right: her hairdresser was cheap. In a moment of madness induced by receiving the decree nisi in the post, I summoned her and had all my hair chopped off: very cathartic.

It is now clipped short and close to my head like a convict, but at least it is all silver. I left off the heavy eye make-up, which made me look like a marmoset in combination with the cropped head, but the loose black clothes (I've lost weight) and big boots now look ridiculous.

I have forgotten how to eat as well as sleep, which is why my clothes hang on me, but there is no more money so the escaped fugitive look will have to remain for the time being.

A rare phone call from Mother in America.

The last time she called me was after I married Matt, when she said that I was a pathetic, downtrodden negation of everything the women's movement had ever fought for.

Perhaps I was. And perhaps I might have turned out differently had she taken us children with her on her flight from Father; but then again, maybe not.

This time it was a congratulatory phone call, she having now heard about Dead Greg.

30

'Well done!' she said. 'A blow struck right at the heart of male oppression.'

'More the head, Mother. And I'm not proud of it. I'm finding it very hard to live with the idea that I've killed someone.'

'The guilt was his: it was his own fault.'

'True, but somehow that doesn't seem to make it feel any better. Mother, did you know Matt and I are divorcing? We're waiting for the final bit to come through.'

There was a pause. 'I'd have loved to have you stay with me,' she said eventually, as though I'd asked. 'But I'm afraid I'm about to go on a lecture tour for my next book, and – wait, though! – you could come with me, and tell everyone about—'

'No thanks,' I said hastily. 'I'm going home to Upvale.'

'You can open the cage door, but you can't force the animals out,' she said cryptically, sighing.

31

Chapter 5
The Prodigal Daughter

It is strange to be going home for good and yet not to be going back to my square, high-ceilinged bedroom, with the teenage-timewarp decor.

Of course, I've escaped back from time to time over the years, usually alone. Among so many big, self-assured people Matt always felt very much the small Fry in the pond, I think. (Which he was.)

Father, Em and Anne petrified him, but Branwell I don't think he found threatening, just loopy. When I asked Bran soon after I was married if he liked Matt, he just replied vaguely: 'Who?'

Matt was always jealous of the stretched but uncut umbilical cord that connected me – and all of us Rhymers – to Upvale, though strangely enough I hadn't even realised it existed until I tested its limits by running away with Matt.

Even Anne, globetrotting TV correspondent that she is, returns from time to time to recharge her batteries on Blackdog Moor, before going back to foreign battlefields. Wherever in the world there's trouble, there also is Anne in her khaki fatigues and multi-pocketed waistcoat. Wars don't seem to last long once she's arrived – I think they take one look and unite against a greater peril.

Since the Ding of Death I'd tried to phone Anne a couple of times at her London flat, (stark, minimalist, shared with her stark, minimalist, foreign-correspondent lover, Red) but there had been no reply other than the answering machine. Em said she'd managed to get hold of the lover once, but he'd just said Anne was away and put the phone down.

Anne, Em and Father are all big, handsome, strong-boned, grimly purposeful types, with masses of wavy light hair: leonine.

Maybe that's why they make Matt nervous – he thinks he may be the unlucky zebra at the waterhole.

I'm small and dark – now small and silver-haired – like Mother, but I'm not the fragile little flower I look. Bran is slight too, but wiry, with dark auburn hair like a newly peeled chestnut, and strangely light brown eyes. We think he must take after his Polish mother's side of the family, but we barely remember her brief tenure as au pair, mistress, and oh-so-reluctant mother; even Em, who is the eldest.

Em has run the house as far back as I can remember, with the help of Gloria Mundi and her brother Walter. Funnily enough, housewifery didn't sort of seep into me by osmosis – I had to go out and buy a book. But you can't say I didn't try; it's just that nature intended me to be an artist, not a housewife.

Upvale Parsonage never saw a parson in its life – that's just Father being Brontëan. It stands four-square in stone, with a small formal garden of mossy gravel and raddled roses dividing it from the road. Behind it the ground falls away steeply down to the stream, so the kitchen and sculleries are built into the hillside below the road level, facing across the valley.

And even below *that* is the undercroft, which we call the Summer Cottage, also partly built into the hillside, and linked to the house by a twisting and rather dank spiral staircase with an oak door top and bottom.

The Summer Cottage gives on to the narrow, rough track that leads down to another cottage, derelict last time I saw it, but recently renovated and sold to some kind of actor, according to Em. Then there's Owlets Farm, where Madge and her old father, Bob, live.

Em's always kept the hinges on the Parsonage door to the Summer Cottage unoiled, so she'd know by the squealing when an alien invader (i.e. one of Father's seemingly endless string of mistresses) was entering her territory.

But this time the invaders had sneaked in behind her back.

Kitchen Pests
1) Your Father's mistress
2) Your Father's mistress's children
3) Your Father . . .

*

34

'The van got here okay,' Em said when I phoned her from my strangely naked house. 'I had everything put into the cottage, including all the stuff from your bedroom that I'd stowed in the attic. Walter took it all down.'

'It seems odd coming back to the cottage. Still, I suppose I do still have a lot of things and I'm going to have a car full of plants, despite Miss Grinch having taken some. I don't know where I'm going to put them, but I'll need them if I ever paint again. I can't do it without the jungle round me, now.'

But would I ever paint again? I've had painter's block since the Great Swing . . . and if I did paint, would I revert to the old style at Upvale, or perhaps evolve something between the two?

'You *will* paint again,' pronounced Em, like the word of God – or maybe the Word of Wicca – 'and Walter is making you a conservatory in front of the cottage, only of course he calls it a verandah.'

'Out of what?'

'Someone gave him some old doors and windows, and he's using clear corrugated plastic for the roof. I told him you needed somewhere like his friend George's pigeon loft, only much lighter, and he got the idea immediately. He's been at it a week – I can hear him hammering now.'

'Father's been complaining, but he isn't working – too busy banging away himself. That woman's so insatiable it's embarrassing. I caught him carrying her up the stairs the other night, which won't do his back much good.'

'He was always like that, though, Em.'

'This one's different. She's got into the house, for a start, with her brats.'

Like Angie's squirrels. Let's hope Angie doesn't follow me here and get in the house, too.

'Does he mind my coming home for good?'

'He doesn't care, just says you'll have to pay for your keep, so the mistress must be expensive.'

'He's right, though, Em – and I can't stay in the Summer Cottage forever. He is bound to want it for the next mistress. I'll have to find a job of some kind, and rent a place. Matt hasn't sent me any money since I dinged Greg. I *knew* it would be the odd duck, and that only if I was lucky, but I don't think I want his money any more anyway. I don't deserve it after killing his best friend.'

'It was an accident, and you're entitled to some maintenance – we all keep telling you. You've got to live on something until you paint again, so—'

'*If* I ever paint again,' I said pessimistically.

She ignored that. 'So I've got you a part-time job, starting Monday.'

Panic clutched me round the midriff with sharp talons. 'A job! What on earth as?'

'Helper in the Rainbow Nursery down the road. You don't know it – they started a sort of self-sufficient commune in Hoo Hall, and there's a progressive nursery attached.'

'Montessori or Steiner or something?'

'Something. They don't keep their staff long, probably because they don't pay much, so they're always desperate.'

'Do they know I'm a murderess?'

'You're not a murderess, and the accident didn't make the national headlines, so probably not.'

'Oh Em, I don't think I can do it. I don't know anything about children and—'

'You can try. Then maybe something else will turn up, or you'll start painting again.'

'Vaddie at the gallery keeps asking me for more – but they've got everything I'd finished.'

'You need to get back here and let the moors cure you, and Gloria will brew you up a tonic. You'll see – everything will be okay.'

Gloria is a wisewoman, and taught Em everything she knows, but she brews the most god-awful tasting potions.

'It'll be odd living in the mistress's house.'

'Gloria Mundi's cleaned it till it squeaks, and I've oiled the kitchen door so you can come and go as you like without anyone knowing.'

'Thank you Em,' I said gratefully, 'I've put you to a lot of trouble.'

'No you haven't – you know I like organising. It's that Jessica woman who's making trouble – you'll have to help me to get her out.'

'They never last long,' I assured her. 'Bran's mother was the longest, but that was only because she wanted to have Bran before she went back home. I don't think she and Father were communicating in any way once Bran was conceived.'

'Ah yes – Bran. He phoned me the other day from outside the university. Apparently the High Priestess of Thoth manifested herself, and informed him that he shouldn't use mobile phones any more because evil spirits escaped from them into his head. I couldn't hear him very clearly because he was holding it away from his ear, and then he threw it into the river.'

'Ah.'

'Yes, so I've put Rob's taxi on stand-by to go and collect him. I don't suppose Bran's students will notice his absence if he has to come home for a break. He doesn't remember he's got any half the time, and when he does he probably lectures them in some ancient tongue they can't understand. But apparently the book's going to be brilliant.'

'There has to be a good reason the university is prepared to put up with his little ways, other than his having an IQ greater than the sum of all the other staff.'

'He also has a whanger bigger than any of the other staff,' Em said, which was true; even skinny-dipping in the icy beck as children he'd been impressive in that department. But unless the high Priestess of Thoth manifests herself in a more solid form and draws him a diagram, I fear that asset will be entirely wasted.

'I don't think that would particularly impress academic circles,' I said.

'Perhaps not. I've asked them to phone me if he doesn't calm down in a day or two, and Rob can set off.'

Rob knows Bran's little ways and is always quite happy to drive all the way down to Bran's ancient and hallowed university (which had proved surprisingly accepting of his eccentricity) and transport him back without mishaps.

'Well, I suppose you couldn't put *Bran* in the summer cottage,' I said, though it still rankled that I'd been the one ejected for the mistress.

'I had one of my visions – about Anne,' Em said, reading *my* mind too. 'She is in difficulty, and she'll be coming home soon, for healing.'

'Spiritual or otherwise? She hasn't been shot, has she? I thought you said she couldn't be shot?'

'I don't think it's that sort of wound,' Em said doubtfully. 'But I can't tell clearly – my predictions are getting more and more fuzzy: I think the vertical hold's gone. Really, what is the point of hanging on to my virginity in order to retain my powers, when all I ever see is the boring and mundane? I've never clearly seen *anything* wildly exciting. I really think I might as well explore the darker side of witchcraft.'

'Well, don't do anything hasty,' I begged her. 'Especially anything . . . Aleister Crowley.'

'That poseur! Certainly not. No, I'm thinking more of joining the local coven and fully embracing the Ancient Arts – and perhaps a suitable man. Lilith's running one.'

'What, a suitable man?'

'No, a coven.'

'And just what do you mean by a *suitable* man?'

'Big, strong, silent and malleable.'

She could add 'courageous' to that list of qualifications. I've seen strong men turn and run when they see Em coming.

'That actor's quite dishy, up at the cottage,' she mused. 'And Gloria said his reputation with women stinks, so he'd be terribly suitable.'

'Em! You wouldn't really.'

'What time are you arriving tomorrow?' she asked, changing the subject.

'Early afternoon, I hope, but snow's forecast, which will make negotiating Ramshaw Heights and Blackdog Moor tricky. I don't know why, but that's the only way I *can* come back.'

'It's because you left that way the first time with Matt, and so you must describe the full Circle of Return,' Em said.

'It'll be dicey if it snows heavily.'

'You'll make it – the 2CV will glide over the top. Wrap Flossie up well, though. These little spaniels are inbred; she catches cold too easily.'

'Yes, and the plants, too. They are all a bit tropical for a winter spin on the moors with the roof down.'

'You will arrive safely. I would at least know if that were otherwise,' Em said deeply, then added more prosaically: 'See you then. Drive straight down to the cottage. The key is in the frog, and Walter will unpack your stuff for you while we catch up with things.'

When I came over Ramshaw Heights I could see Blackdog Moor – transformed into Whitedog Moor – glittering like quartz below me. I felt inwardly cleansed by the bright light bouncing off the vast whiteness.

I'm a bit of a dog at the moment: a Heinz 57. Cropped white head and black clothes hanging long and loose ... more Uncle Fester than Morticia.

And speaking of dogs, bubbling snores were coming from the depths of Flossie's fake-fur-lined igloo, which was on the floor at the front passenger side. The passenger seat itself, and all the rest of the car, was jammed with all my favourite huge plants – figs and lemons, palms and bananas – wrapped in newspaper and layers of bubble wrap, and sticking up out of the open top of the car like so many extras from *Invasion of the Body Snatchers*. My driving visibility was almost nil.

We had received some strange looks when we set out on our journey, but the closer to home we got the less notice anyone took. Yorkshire folk can absorb every last detail without looking directly at you.

Externally I was freezing, my hands stuck to the wheel. Inside, too, I still had the feeling that all my organs had turned to ice, which I'd had since the moment Greg died, only now there was just the faintest tinge of warm hope.

'You're nearly home, Charlie: everything will be all right now,' I encouraged myself as we slid down Edge Bank.

But the Snow Queen whispered in Angie's voice: 'Nothing will ever be right again.'

'Maybe it won't, Angie,' I said aloud. 'But at least it will be all wrong in the right place.'

Chapter 6

Pesto in the Kitchen

Skint Old Crafts: Stick it, Stitch it, and Stuff it

Hint One: for those of you living south of Luton, I suggest you shred this magazine and reassemble it in a different order with Sellotape, since it will give you hours of fun and make just as much sense afterwards.

I turned down the snowy track behind the Parsonage and slid to a halt, more by luck than judgement, next to the wall of the unseasonably-named Summer Cottage.

It's more of a Hobbit hole in the hillside than anything, with the heavy bulk of the Parsonage threateningly poised above, ready to toboggan down the hill sweeping all before it.

The front of the cottage now sported a ramshackle, half-glazed appendage, painted a vivid shade of Mediterranean blue. The door was in need of a second coat, for the word LADIES could still faintly be seen, although I thought the heart-shaped cut-out very tasteful.

Walter had excelled himself.

I was just sniffling a few sentimental tears away when a voice as mellow and melodious as a cello suddenly addressed me from behind, making me jump and whirl around like a Dervish.

'Are *you* responsible for that excrescence on the beautiful face of Upvale?'

Icy fingers of Arctic wind undulated my numerous layers of loose black drapery, and I had to claw a web-fine woollen scarf out of my eyes before I could see the man who'd spoken.

41

He was very tall, even taller than Em, and his dark, heavy-lidded eyes regarded me with a sort of weary wariness, as though I was a surprise gift he didn't want. He was also carrying a giant teddy bear.

'I don't think a man who walks about wearing a red duvet and a jester's hat has any right to criticise my cottage,' I informed him coldly, although his strange garments did not actually look quite as ludicrous on him as they might sound, while my verandah, as Walter would call it, certainly did.

I didn't mention the teddy bear in case he was sensitive about it. Bran always takes his soft toy, Mr Froggy, everywhere in his pocket with him, but at least it is small.

'It's ski-wear,' he said, looking down his remarkably straight nose at me.

'Not in Upvale it isn't. You might as well have "Oft-Comed 'Un" stamped across your back; but I suppose you're the actor – Em said we'd got one in the cottage down the track,' I said, making him sound like a disease. 'I don't think she mentioned your name.'

And the bit of him I could see, between upturned collar and pulled-down hat – high sculptured cheekbones and slightly slanting, droopy-lidded eyes – did look vaguely familiar, even to someone who rarely watches TV or films.

'I'm incognito.'

'It's all right with me. I don't expect the urge will come upon me to boast about meeting you. Or your teddy bear,' I added, throwing caution to the winds.

'My teddy bear?' he echoed, looking at me strangely, but that might have been because my knitted coat was flying up behind me like black bat wings.

'Am I not supposed to mention the teddy bear? It's moving,' I added, fascinated.

Indeed, it was now not only moving, but muttering. The head turned and I saw a little face screwed up in sleep, framed by honey-brown fur and round ears. Then it snuggled back into the red duvet.

What with that and the Mediterranean verandah I was starting to feel quite freaked. Upvale had always previously stayed the same, my one fixed constant in a threatening world. It was a relief when the actor edged past me without another word (unless you count what sounded like a muttered 'crackers!') and strode off up the lane with his little furry friend.

I prised *my* little furry friend out of her warm nest in the car, and she looked around her with a sort of vague surprise: the world had moved while she slept, *again.*

The door key was in the mouth of the stone frog as usual, together with some small wooden tablets inscribed with what looked like runes, and a bunch of dried herbs. I left those.

We went through Walter's Folly, and I opened the door of the cottage to be met and embraced by a warm miasma of lavender, furniture polish and bleach. There was no leftover redolence of mistress here, for Gloria Mundi had clearly excised every last iota of their existence. It simply smelled like home.

Flossie pattered across the flagged floor behind me as I climbed the stairs up to the Parsonage kitchen and opened the strangely silent door.

There was a delicious aroma, easily identified as steak and kidney pie with suet crust, and Em was sitting coring baking apples at the kitchen table, and plopping them into a big earthenware bowl of water.

'You've come, then,' she stated, without looking up from her task. 'Put the kettle on – you must be frozen. Where's Flossie?'

With a wheeze like a small pair of bellows Flossie hauled herself up the last step, looking vaguely around, then made straight for the wood-burning stove in the corner, a shaggily-upholstered heat-seeking missile.

'She must be cold,' said Em fondly. 'I'll warm her some milk.'

'She isn't cold – she's been fast asleep in her igloo all the way here. I'm the one who's absolutely brass-monkeyed, because I had to have the roof open for the plants. Where's Walter?'

As if on cue the door swung open and in hobbled a gnarled and cheery little goblin. The bridge of his over-large glasses had been bound with a great wodge of Sellotape, and his baggy corduroy trousers were held up with Father's old school tie.

'Hello Walter,' I said, giving him a kiss.

'I've got no eyebrows.'

'I know. How are you?'

'No eyebrows. No bodily hair what-so-ever!' he proclaimed happily. 'I've made you a verandah, and now I'm going to put your plants in it and make a jungle.'

'It's a wonderful verandah, Walter – it's the best one I've ever seen. Thank you!'

Beaming like a lighthouse he hobbled off towards the cottage stairs, muttering, 'No eyebrows . . . no bodily hair what-so- . . .'

Em plopped the last apple into the bowl and got up. 'There we are, now we'll have a hot drink. Don't worry about your stuff,' she added, as ominous Burke-and-Hare dragging noises wafted up from the cottage. 'Walter will bring it all in, and you can arrange it as you like later. I've put a couple of greenhouse heaters in the verandah to take the chill off, because there's no electric in it yet, of course, and the floor's just the old paving stones. Do you like the colour?'

'Yes. It's very bright.'

'Walter's choice. Gloria wanted dark green, but I thought that was a bit municipal. You can do your own thing with the inside of the cottage.'

Gloria is Walter's sister, and they do not so much work at the Parsonage as inhabit the space at odd hours between dawn and dusk, as the fancy takes them.

'Where *is* Gloria? Where is everyone?'

'Gloria is turning out Bran's room, in case. Father's in his study composing another epic.'

'Oh God – who is it this time?'

'Browning. Apparently, he didn't produce much good work while he was married to Elizabeth Barrett Browning because he was actually busy writing all her poetry for her.'

'The same line as usual then?'

'He doesn't change. But at least it's lucrative; everyone loves to disagree with him. Otherwise, the mistress has gone out shopping, and then she'll probably be picking up the two sprogs from school. Do you know, she wanted them to have Anne's room because she didn't like them sleeping in the attic? I told her that Anne locked her room between visits and even Gloria only cleaned when she was there, and that shut her up.'

'Any word from Anne?'

'No, but her answering machine's changed: it just says "this is Anne Rhymer, leave a message" and doesn't mention Red at all.'

'Perhaps they've parted? Not that they ever seemed to be in the same country simultaneously anyway.'

'Something's happening – I can feel it.'

'She will tell us if she wants to.'

'Yes, or simply turn up. I'm starting to get the idea she might be coming home soon,' said Emily, her eyes getting that strange, faraway expression. Then it was gone and she was saying briskly: 'Funnily enough, I've had much more interesting foretellings since I made up my mind to embrace the Dark Arts than ever before, but I think I'm going to go ahead anyway. I've got three friends coming round soon to tell me about their coven. You know one of them – Xanthe Skye.'

'I don't remember *anyone* called Xanthe Skye.'

'She was Doreen Higginbottom until The Change.'

'Oh yes? That will be nice,' I said dubiously. 'Didn't she have a brief fling with Fa—'

I stopped dead for the man himself, possibly attracted by the smell of freshly brewing coffee, had wandered in: big and broad-shouldered, in corduroys and a shirt rolled up to show muscular arms. He still had a full head of light, waving hair like Anne and Em, and though his face was looking a bit pummelled by time, the general effect was large, virile and handsome.

'Hello Father.'

'Oh God! Keep the pans locked up, Em,' he said resignedly.

Silently she poured out a mug of coffee and handed it to him, and he took two Jaffa cakes out of the Rupert Bear tin and went back out without another word.

The study door closed behind him with a snap.

While I unburdened my soul to Em she baked a batch of sultana scones and made the biggest treacle tart you could fit in the oven, intricately latticed over the top.

She didn't say much, but it was comforting all the same, as were the two hot, buttered scones she insisted I eat.

It was quite a while later before the front door slammed and a woman's voice shrilled: 'Hello everybody!'

Silence answered her. Even the zooming noise of Gloria Mundi's Hoover stilled momentarily.

'That's her – Jessica. Can't hear the sprogs, perhaps they're out for tea or something.'

A woman staggered in and dumped a couple of bulging carrier bags on the table with a sigh of relief. 'There you are!'

She was fortyish, with a firmly repressed dark downiness and an aura of elegant sexuality – a sort of hungry look about the shadowed eyes. Her body was diet-victim skinny, and the rather bird-billed face perched on top made her look like a duck on a stick.

'Hello. You must be Charlie?' she said, smiling.

'Charlie, Father's tart – Father's tart, Charlie,' introduced Em.

'Fiancée,' Jessica said, her smile going a bit fixed. 'Is that your sweet little dog? Is she all right? She isn't moving, is she?'

'She isn't dead, if that's what you mean. She's a Cavalier Queen Charlotte. They go into suspended animation at regular intervals.'

'King Charles?'

'Not unless he was a bitch.'

'Take this stuff off my table, Jessie,' Em ordered. 'I'm trying to get dinner ready.'

'I thought we could have something a bit different tonight,' Jessica said, with a sort of determined jolliness. 'The girls don't really like all this meat and stodge, and I'm sure it's not healthy for a man of Ranulf's age. And there *are* vegetables other than mushy peas, you know! So I've got some pasta, and sun-dried tomatoes and pesto . . .'

With one sweep of her muscular arm Em cleared the table, and Flossie found herself under a sudden rain of cellophane packages. She sat up, looking vaguely surprised.

'Sod off out of my kitchen,' Em said. I was relieved she was taking it so well.

Jessica laughed and began to retrieve her goodies. 'Now, Emily, I know your bark is worse than your bite, so—'

'No it isn't,' I assured her earnestly. One of Em's bites from a childhood disagreement we had still aches in cold weather, and I certainly don't come between her and anything she wants, any more than I'd come between a rabid dog and a bowl of water.

'Perhaps we could have pasta tomorrow?' persisted Jessica. 'I'll just put everything in the cupboard, shall I?'

'You can put it anywhere you like, as long as it isn't in my kitchen,' Em said.

'I – I think I'll go and see Ran,' Jessica said, backing towards the door.

'Do that,' Em said, and added: 'Frost's behind you.'

The great grey lurcher had indeed silently approached up the hall, and was now looming with his sad yellow eyes fixed on her.

Jessica gave a squeak of terror and shot off into the study, slamming the door.

They didn't emerge until dinner was ready, when Father looked excited and exhausted in equal measure, which I don't think was the book.

The two giggly little twins, Chloe and Phoebe, were decanted by someone's mother at seven. They looked about nine, and were attenuated versions of their mother, with legs like liquorice laces. The presence of Father and Em seemed to subdue them, but once they were sent off to bed they could be heard giggling for ages.

Gloria Mundi (whose only comment on seeing my shorn, silver locks had been: 'Well, I'll go to the foot of ower stairs!') stayed for dinner, but Walter had eaten a coddled egg and several scones in the kitchen and gone off to the pub.

Gloria would generally have gone too, by now, but had stayed in order to make sure I ate enough for ten people, and went to bed early: but then, I always was her favourite – probably because I was the runt of the litter.

She sat opposite smiling at me, her pale bright eyes glowing in her crumpled face like stars in a net. She's about as close to a mother figure as we've ever got, and it was comforting tonight to have someone trying to mollycoddle me, even if, as predicted, she did make me drink a herbal brew that tasted as if it had been strained through an old sock.

Miss Grinch had been an absolute tower of strength, but Gloria was glorious.

Skint Old Cook: Part One

How to tell your Mushy Peas from your Pease Pudding.

These two northern delicacies are easily distinguishable from each other. Mushy peas are simply, as the name suggests, peas cooked until they go mushy and give off liquid. Much runnier than pease pudding they are often served with chips or pies. The canned variety can be an interesting shade of green – try them with potatoes and gravy for an enticing mixture of colour combinations. Your dinner guests will never forget it!

Pease pudding is a solid, grey-green stodge, sometimes sold in little tubs. It's cheap, filling and full of fibre. For the desperately hungry and/or hard up, use it as a sandwich filling.

It tastes better than it looks, as so many regional delicacies do: after all, weren't jellied eels once memorably described as looking like a bad cold in a bucket?

Chapter 7

Enlightenment

Chivvied by Em I walked reluctantly down to Hoo House to meet Inga early next morning before all the children arrived at the nursery. I was worried that she wouldn't take me on, and worried that she would, but I needn't have bothered; I suppose if I had two heads or something she wouldn't employ me, but after seeing some of the other members of the commune with their feet in the trough at breakfast, I wouldn't bank on it.

They can't know I'm a murderess yet – but they might well regard it as a sort of minor peccadillo when they do find out.

The nursery is called 'Rainbow of Enlightenment', which is as close as they can get to the Japanese original. I've never heard of it, so it obviously didn't take off like Steiner or Montessori.

Inga, a squat, damp limp Scandinavian (no, they're not all tall, blond ice maidens) gloomily took me around the two big, square front rooms of the house that formed the nursery, pointing out the arrangement of the equipment: apparently the children have to complete a series of tasks in their right order. 'Building the Rainbow of Endeavour to the Further shores of Enlightenment . . .' or something.

Susie, the other helper, was setting out paint pots and brushes.

'We have sixteen childwen,' lisped Inga, 'including my own – Gunilla – who is in the gawden, being at one with Natuwe.'

'Natuwe?'

'Ja, Gunilla loves Mama Natuwe.'

'Oh, right. Does she also love the Rainbow of Enlightenment?'

'Gunilla is being bwought up by obsewving the behaviouw of The Gwoup. But it is also impowtant that she mixes with other

49

childwen. She often chooses to join in with her fwiends as they complete their tasks.'

'I see,' I said, and so I did; no wonder staff didn't stay long, if Gunilla was doing her own thing while the other children were put through their very structured hoops. I mean, I know nothing much about nursery education, but it sounded a recipe for disaster.

Still, maybe Gunilla was a sweet little thing, and it would all work beautifully? Yes, and I'm Pollyanna and everything comes up roses.

I left just as the first children were arriving in a series of mammoth people carriers driven by Mummy or the nanny. The Rainbow must be trendy.

Inga greeted the children by name in the same gloomy tones: China, Poppy, Zoë and Josh were just a sample. I expect I will get them all hopelessly mixed up.

'Ah, Caitlin,' Inga said, her voice warming up to blood heat. 'You awe eawly. Is Daddy hewe? I wanted to speak with him.'

'Gone,' Caitlin said succinctly. She was wearing a teddy-bear suit, the head, which I now saw was a hood with ears, pushed back. On her feet she wore flowered wellingtons, like a frivolous Paddington. 'Daddy wants to be left alone, because he's writing a play. And resting. And looking after me, while Mummy's in a film. Then she's going to marry Rod, and I've got a bridesmaid's dress. Daddy says it makes me look like a meringue.' She eyed me curiously, especially the limp black drapery and lace-up boots, then informed me: 'My Daddy's a famous actor – he's Mace North.'

'Face North?' I echoed, puzzled.

'*Mace* North.'

'Of course,' I said, trying to sound impressed, which is not easy if you don't watch films very often, although the name *was* ringing bells faintly somewhere. 'Then I think I met him behind my cottage yesterday. I'm Charlie Rhymer, and I live at the Parsonage.'

'I know Em. And Frost. Em gave me a gingerbread dragon with chocolate drop scales.'

'Em's my sister.' And she's not usually prone to like children. What *is* she up to?

Caitlin gave me a look of disbelief for which I didn't blame her. I can hardly believe I'm related to three such enormous entities myself.

'Daddy's frightened of Em, but I'm not.'

'I'm suwe youw daddy isn't fwightened of anyone!' Inga said. 'Wun along in; we awe neawly weady to begin.'

I took the hint and left as yet more expensive dinosaurs trundled up the drive to decant their small passengers, and as I walked home through the mushy, melting snow I tried to remember if I'd ever seen Mace North in anything. (Other than a red duvet.)

I don't go to the cinema (just the idea of being shut in the dark with all those strange people gives me the shudders!) and although Matt was wont to hire videos, they were of the violence, sex and nastiness kind, which were not images I wanted stored in my subconscious forever.

However, that made me think of the actor's barbarian cheekbones, so at odds with his rather posh, mellow voice, and then I remembered where I'd seen him before: the cover of *Surprise!* magazine, the one Angie'd whipped away again.

Tartar blood, that was it.

When I got back to the Summer Cottage Flossie was just waking up, so I took her for the hundred-yard stroll she considers a strenuous trek, which got us as far up the track as the actor's cottage (no sign of life) but not quite as far as the farm, although Madge waved from the doorway. Then I set to work to try and turn the cottage into a home.

It's just two rooms, really, built into the hillside, and partitioned off to provide a bed-sitting room and the usual facilities. The decor is a bit flowery – the last mistress's taste, presumably – and if I'm going to be here for any length of time I will have to paint it.

I set up my easel in the verandah, a gesture of hope, and arranged my plants around me, though there now weren't enough of them to quite give me that being-towered-over-threateningly feeling. I'd brought the tall ones, it was just the thick jungle effect that was missing.

I would have to take a big chunk of the auction money, go to the nearest garden centre – and hope they deliver.

It wasn't very warm, either. The two paraffin heaters were only there to stop the plants freezing, and they gave out a pleasant but strange smell all of their own (a bit like Walter).

I could do with some coconut matting over the stone flags, and electricity so that I could have lighting, and some heating . . .

51

Which sort of presupposes I'm ever going to spend some time in here painting; but Em and Walter have done their best to encourage me.

I went up the stairs to the kitchen to see if Em fancied a trip out plant-hunting, and Flossie trailed wearily after me, wheezing. I'm sure all this exercise will do her good.

The kitchen was deserted except for Frost, who lifted his head and gave Flossie a leer.

Walter was in the small front room, watching TV and carving a walking stick. He grinned, but didn't say anything. His wig, never worn, occupied its usual place of honour on the mantelpiece, draped carefully over a polystyrene head.

Father's study door was shut with his Do Not Disturb sign on it, though if anyone was already disturbed it was Father.

There was no sign of the Treacle Tart, and the children must be at school, but the sound of hoovering was still audible from above, where Gloria Mundi was singing Gilbert and Sullivan in a falsetto.

She was a very model of a modern major-general.

I found Em eventually in the sitting room, the curtains half-drawn, which is why I was well into the room before I saw that she had company.

'Sorry,' I said, 'I didn't know you were entertaining, Em. I was just going to tell you I was off to the garden centre.'

'That's okay – you know Xanthe, don't you?'

Xanthe nodded graciously at me; she did look vaguely familiar from her days as Father's Flavour of the Month.

'And this is Lilith Tupman and Freya Frogget.'

Lilith looked like she'd been blanched under a pot. Freya was large and clad in billowing white like over-exuberant ectoplasm.

'I'll leave you to it, but let me open the curtains first,' I offered, taking hold of the heavy velvet drapes.

There was a gasp from Lilith, who held her hands to her temples and exclaimed hysterically: 'No! No! The light must not touch my face!'

I hastily unloosed the curtains. 'Sorry.'

Maybe she was a vampire? But then, how had she got here?

'Would you like me to make you some coffee or something before I go?' I offered in atonement.

'Thanks, Charlie,' Em said. 'There's a tray ready in the kitchen – just fill the pot with boiling water and bring it in, will you?'

'You could join us,' said Lilith, recovering. 'If you wished?'

'No, no, her aura is *blue!*' Xanthe cried. 'I cannot have blue near me . . . it drains my psychic energy.'

If Father didn't manage to drain her powers, I can't see how my blue aura would

'Ice, I must have ice!' gasped Freya, in a parched voice.

'A bowl of ice from the freezer, too, please,' said Em. 'Do you want a hand?'

What, the Hand of Death? The Hand Of Glory? The Hand of the Baskerv—

'No, that's okay,' I assured her, backing out, and starting to puzzle over the ice. Still, Em's friends all appear to be women of a certain age: Freya might be having a hot flush of mega proportions.

I brought the tray, which contained all sorts of home-baked goodies, plus a pot of some disgusting-smelling herbal brew reminiscent of Gloria's best, then left them to it.

Flossie was now snuggled up to Frost, the hussy, and showed no interest in accompanying me, to the garden centre or anywhere else.

Tips For Southern Visitors, no. 1:

It is possible to have any variety of Northern accent in conjunction with an intellect.

At dinner it emerged that Father had also inadvertently crashed Em's tea party, barely escaping without being ravished by Freya, Lilith and Xanthe. (Well, that was *his* version, anyway.)

'Congratulations, Em,' he said through a mouthful of home-made chicken pie. 'Not one of your friends is normal.'

'Speaking of normal,' Em said coolly. 'Your son is coming home tomorrow for a rest.'

Jessica helped herself to a lettuce leaf, looked at it doubtfully, and put half back again in the bowl. 'I haven't met Branwell yet,' she said. 'Is he as dishy as you darling?'

The two little girls, who were doing full justice to the despised stodge, giggled.

'He's nothing like me,' he said tersely. 'Charlie's nothing like me, either.'

'I'm like Mother, though, and I expect Bran takes after his.'

'Your mother's very famous, isn't she?' Jessica asked. 'Big in America. But I do think all this writing books and talking about feminism does more harm than good, don't you?'

'Someone's got to speak out, especially when men are trying to claim great works of women's fiction as their own,' Em commented pointedly, but Father refused to rise to the bait.

'Yes, wasn't Elizabeth Barrett Browning lucky, having such a clever husband to write her work for her?' I said innocently. 'I wonder how on earth she managed before he came along? Perhaps one of her brothers?'

'You mustn't tease,' Jessica said earnestly. 'Ran researches very thoroughly. He works very hard.'

'He has to research thoroughly to find scraps of evidence that can be twisted into proving what he wants,' Em said.

'And you, of course, are a great writer and know all about it?' he said sarcastically. 'My dear Em, I don't think writing doggerel for greeting-card manufacturers quite qualifies you as a literary critic.'

'No, but I don't just write for greeting cards – I'm also Serafina Shane.'

While this was a bit of a damp squib as far as Father and myself were concerned, Jessica laid down her fork and stared.

'What, Serafina Shane out of *Women Live!* magazine? *Womanly Wicca Words of Spiritual Comfort?* I've ordered the book!'

'Advance orders *have* been very brisk,' Em said complacently, and bestowed a slightly warmer gaze on Jessica than I had ever seen before. She might just live, after all.

'Well done, Em,' I said. 'If I'd known I'd have read them, but I never buy women's mags – they're all New Woman, and Never Admit You're Forty Woman, and Rich Bored Bitchy Woman, when all I ever wanted was something like *Skint Old Northern Woman.*'

'You're right,' Em said. 'Weren't you going to start one?'

'Yes, in fact, my hobby during the last few weeks has been writing articles for the sort of magazine I'd really like to find. I've got quite a lot.'

'Do I understand, Emily,' Father broke in, 'that you've been writing your ghastly doggerel for a women's magazine, and it's now coming out as a book?'

'Yes – inspirational verse and prose. I'm very popular.'

'Serafina what?' I asked.

'Shane.'

'At least it isn't Rhymer!' Father said.

'Well done, Em!' I enthused.

'So what were you plotting with your abnormal friends when I came in this morning?' enquired Father.

'We were trying various means to discover where Anne is. There's something the matter with her, and I can't get any reply from her flat. Xanthe tried the crystal pendulum.'

'And Xanthe knows everything?' He frowned. 'And why does she look so familiar?'

Em ignored this. 'The crystal showed us where she was – somewhere near her flat. Then Freya did a reading, and discovered that Anne's had an operation, but she'll be here soon to recuperate.'

'I suppose you know this because Anne's phoned,' he said sceptically.

'No. You know Anne, she'll phone when she's nearly here. Gloria Mundi's turning out her room, now she's finished Bran's.'

'What makes you think the Three Witches got it right?'

'They always get it right. That's why I'm joining their coven. I've been pussyfooting round the mealy-mouthed edges for long enough, and now I'm going to wholeheartedly embrace the Ancient Arts.'

'Prostitution?' suggested Ran. 'I hear it's very well paid.'

Em gave him a look. 'The Ancient *Black* Arts,' she said.

Jessica gasped, her eyes widening in alarm. 'You mean – black magic? Oh, my God! The children!'

But the little girls, bored with the conversation, had crept away unnoticed. One of the dishes of meringues from the sideboard had gone too.

'Oh, Emily – promise you won't say anything about it in front of the girls! Don't they sacrifice little children, and sell their souls to the Devil?'

'Hands up all those present who've read the entire oeuvre of Dennis Wheatley and believe every word?' I said. 'Really, Jessica, grow up!'

'Charlie's quite right. I wouldn't harm *any* animal, even your children,' Em assured her.

'Thank you!' Jessica said, slightly hysterically. 'Ran are you going to sit there and—'
Father stood up abruptly. 'No, I'm off to the pub. Coming?'
'How can I leave the girls?' she shuddered.
'I'll listen out for them,' I offered.
'But *you* killed someone . . .' she began
'And I'm Spawn of the Devil,' Emily finished for her.
Father sighed. 'Lock up the pans, Em, and don't sacrifice the children. Satisfied, Jess? Come along!'
There was a brief internal struggle as Jessica's maternal feelings fought a losing battle, and then she hurried out after him.
'Tell me more about this *Skint Old Northern Woman* magazine,' Em said, passing the port.

In the woods the wild violets bloom.
From a distance,
the crumpled cigarette packet
is no less beautiful.
        'Words from the Spirit' by Serafina Shane.

Serafina Shane's first book: Womanly Wicca Words of Spiritual Comfort *is available, price £5.99, from the Fishwife Press.*

Chapter 8
Dangerous To Melons

Skint Old Northern Woman: The Love Quiz

Would you exchange your husband/boyfriend/significant other for:
1. A box of chocolates
A) Yes   B) No   C) A big box

2. A bag of pork scratchings
A) Yes   B) Snatch your hand off   C) No, I'm Jewish, but try me with pistachio nuts

3. A night with Robert Plant
A) Yes   B) Never heard of him, but yes anyway   C) No, never liked blondes/heavy metal/men even older than me, but try me with George Clooney

I am afraid our resident thespian caught me taking a swipe at a large yellow melon with a frying pan this morning, so now probably thinks I'm demented, which I'm not: merely obsessed.

It was not the *fatal* frying pan, because Miss Grinch cleaned that up once the police had finished with it, and sent it off to a jumble sale.

Let's hope it isn't haunted by the red, bloodhound face of an elderly roué. I mean, imagine *that* materialising by the cooker, just as you were getting your omelette all puffy.

The melon was balanced on the gatepost, and I was standing on a large crate. It wasn't ideal – the relative heights were wrong, and the melon kept trying to roll off the perfectly flat surface as though possessed.

I'd just started the downward swing on a ripe yellow honeydew when I caught the glint of weak sunlight on raven's-wing hair above the stone wall that separated my strip of garden from the track, but by then the momentum was unstoppable: the pan connected with a meaty *thunk!* and the melon bounded past me and ricocheted off the verandah.

Mace North stopped by the gate, and surveyed me briefly with unsurprised, world-weary dark blue eyes. (Funny, I sort of expected them to be brown.) His black hair looked as if it had been casually hacked off with a sword – something fancy in gold, with a jewel in the end – and covered his head with feathery artlessness.

Then there was just the clatter of loose pebbles as he headed for home.

Good morning to you, too.

From my vantage point on the box I'd seen becoming strands of purest silver among those black locks, so he's no spring chicken, though I don't think the weary look is an age thing – he's probably always looked like that.

Isn't it odd how much you can notice about someone in the briefest moment, even when you're not particularly interested in them?

He certainly made off quickly enough, probably afraid I'd fling myself on him pleading for his autograph, or something. But he can be permanently incognito as far as I'm concerned, and I don't expect he will be bothered by crowds of admiring followers up here unless he's in a popular soap.

Still, as an actor I don't suppose he found my behaviour in any way unusual.

Last night Father, who has got acquainted with Mace up at the Black Dog, warned me that he liked to be treated just like everyone else (although not, perhaps, to the point of being struck by a frying pan). That is fine by me – I was not about to follow him around with an autograph book clutched in one sweaty hand and my tongue hanging out, and he will probably keep a healthy distance from me, too, now he knows I'm armed and dangerous, if only to fruit.

But the most interesting thing about our encounter was that I'd noticed him just as I'd lifted the pan above my head ready for the swing, and I still didn't manage to stop it or even divert it. If I could try that again with the heights properly measured . . .

It would be a bonus if the sound was right, too. If I could hear it once more outside my head instead of in. It's all pretty cathartic, but I feel that if I find one that makes the right sound, I'll be exorcised to the point where I can at least paint again, especially if I can convince myself without doubt that it really had been an accident.

I'll never be able to forget I've killed someone, but at least I will know I didn't intend to do it.

I tried melon number three, a smallish watermelon, but it still didn't make quite the right hollow, meaty noise. Then I took the battered fruit upstairs to the Parsonage kitchen and put them on the table.

'Canst tha not bash something more useful than a melon?' demanded Gloria Mundi. 'A turnip, maybe? There's none here will eat melon.'

Em, who was removing perfect loaves from the oven, said over her shoulder: 'I've got a recipe for melon and ginger jam. I'll make it later. We all like ginger – and you're forgetting, Gloria, that Bran likes melon.'

'Yon Branwell's one on his own.'

'The university phoned, Charlie. Bran needs to come home for a little rest. Rob's set off to get him. I told him to make sure Mr Froggy doesn't get left behind this time.'

'How is he?'

She shrugged. 'Talking a bit fast. Then yesterday he told one of his students that a spirit ordered him only to speak in ancient Amharic from now on.'

'Not too bad then – he'll be right as rain after a little rest at home.'

Jessica stuck a cautious head through the doorway. 'I'm just off to school with the girls and . . .' she stopped, and looked from the battered melons on the table to me. 'You know, when I looked out of my bedroom window just now, I could have sworn I saw you hitting one of those with a pan.' She laughed uncertainly.

We stared at her. Gloria gave an audible sniff and went out past her with her mop and bucket.

'Well,' said Jessica into the silence, 'I'd better be off and – oh, that's what I came to say: Ran says he'd *love* to try a pasta dish tonight – perhaps with a big salad, and some garlic bread and—'

'He'll get what he's given,' Em said shortly.

'If you don't know how to cook it, I've got a recipe book you could borrow.'

'Hark at Lady Muck!' said Gloria, briskly and sloppily swabbing down the flagged passage round Jessica's feet so that she jumped back. 'She'll be giving out the household orders next!'

'Mummy!' shrilled the girls. 'We'll be late!'

With another uncertain look Jessica went, skidding on the damp floor with a certain coltish grace. I bet she can ice-skate.

'I wonder if we could put something in her food?' mused Em.

'Not unless you can coat a lettuce leaf in it – she doesn't seem to eat anything else.'

'Well, I'll have to take some action – our Ms Tickington-Tingay's getting on my wick.'

'Is that her real name? Jessica Tickington-Tingay?'

'Oh aye,' said Gloria. 'Double-barrelled names are breeding up here.'

'Look at the time!' Em exclaimed. 'You should be on your way to the nursery. You're supposed to be there well before the children, to set things up, aren't you?'

I shifted uncomfortably. 'Em, I don't really think I can do this. I mean, they can't know about the Greg thing, and I've had no experience with children.'

'Forget about the accident with Greg, and as to the experience with children, you will pick that up as you go. You need the money they will pay, until you start painting again.'

I glared at her a bit resentfully. She's never had to go out and earn her living, although she does run the house like clockwork, cooks wonderfully, and makes what money she needs writing her verses . . . and now the book.

Okay, that's all working, I admit.

She also does a little magic and fortune-telling, too, when asked, but she doesn't take money for that, just trade goods.

'Off you go; Inga's expecting you,' she said firmly.

'That Inga's a miserable bugger,' said Gloria, now giving the kitchen floor a sort of third-degree water torture. Frost, sighing deeply, got up from his rug and jumped onto the safety of the settle, where he sat looking resigned.

'She's Scandinavian,' said Em excusingly. 'They all sound like that, even when they're telling jokes. It's to do with only having two hours of daylight a year, or something.'

60

'Couldn't you come with me, Em?' I whined cravenly.

She sighed. 'I suppose I could walk down there with you. We'll take the dogs, and I'll bring Flossie back for you.'

'Flossie's still asleep. She doesn't usually get up until lunchtime.'

'She's not a dog, she's a cushion on legs. Go and get her, it will do her good.'

Flossie was disgusted, but consented to accompany us down the long, winding road to Hoo House, though whether she would walk back up it again was a moot point. Perhaps Frost would pick her up in his long jaws and carry her home like a puppy?

We were the only walkers; a series of immaculate four-wheel-drive vehicles passed us, all converging on the nursery, each giant petrol-eater containing one adult and one mutinous infant.

Em strode through the decanted parents and offspring, grunting at anyone who dared to wish her a good morning, and dragging my reluctant self and the dogs with her.

Our resident Luvvie, exiting too hastily from the doorway, fell over the entwined dog leads, gave me a look of surprise and then, collecting himself, strode off with a nod and a grunt as brusque as anything Em could produce.

'Morning,' said Em affably. I stared at her in amazement.

A small, bun-faced woman in riding breeches and hunter wellies cantered out in hot pursuit, crying shrilly: 'Oh, Mr North! Hef you got a minute?'

'He's incognito,' I said to her helpfully.

He was certainly fit – he was halfway down the drive already. And he didn't come in a car, though I wouldn't put a four-wheel-drive past him.

'Incognito? He's gorgeous!' muttered bun-face, drooling after the retreating actor. (Tall, broad-shouldered, expensively hacked hair – no jester's hat today.)

'You can't call someone wearing a bright red duvet gorgeous.' I objected.

'It's vintage Kenzo,' she said absently.

'Is that sort of like judo kit?'

'Judo? No,' she said, getting a grip on herself and really looking at us for the first time. 'Ah, Emily, is this your sister?' she said graciously. 'Inga said she was going to be the new helper.'

'Charlie,' Em said shortly, 'this is Elfreda Whippington-

Smythe. Bought that half-ruined farmhouse up by the Donkers. Husband looks like Monet on a bad day. One sprog.'

'Er ... yes, Satchel,' agreed Mrs Whippington-Smythe nervously, but then, Em often has that effect.

'Satchmo? Good name!'

I'd have expected something more stolid, like John or Charles, or even Ethelred or Wolfbane.

'No, not Satchmo,' she corrected me. '*Satchel* – like Woody Allen's son.'

'I thought Woody Allen's aura was a bit tarnished round the edges these days?'

'Oh no – he's such a genius! You simply can't believe all those fairy tales Mia was putting about; she's the jealous, unbalanced one.'

Genius? Enough people seem to think so, although I've never been a fan. Maybe I just don't have an ear for that sort of thing, like understanding classical music, or opera.

'Satchel . . .' I mused. 'It's pretty odd as a name when you think about it, isn't it? I mean, I wonder what made him think of *Satchel*? Why not Handbag? Or Portmanteau if he wanted to be posh: "Come on, our Portmanteau." Or even Bumbag.'

There were limitless possibilities to luggage names.

'Tea Bag?' suggested Emily, interested.

Then I noticed Elfreda's fixed stare of offended incomprehension and got the giggles, which offended her even more.

'What's the matter with *her*?' asked Em, as the small figure strode away in her green wellies like an outraged plum duff.

'I expect the thought of Tea Bag Whippington-Smythe was too much for her.'

It had made *me* feel better, though.

It was a bright, cold day, the kind I like best, the children were all milling about in a non-threatening sort of way, and anyway they were all even smaller than me. So when Em said a brief 'See you,' and loped off, I didn't feel too bereft.

Flossie gave me a look of entreaty as she was towed along behind. Bet Em ends up carrying her.

Resolutely I passed through the portals to the sound of small voices raggedly singing.

Chapter 9

Nature In The Raw

How good it was to see Bran again, even if at the moment he is more one *with* us rather than *of* us. Were any of us able to speak in Amharic, I'm sure we could have many interesting conversations, but I expect he will descend to our level soon, even if only through the translation skills of Mr Froggy.

He has brought his manuscript and reference books, which took up most of the car, and refused to come down to breakfast this morning until he had rebuilt them into a wall of Frantic Semantics across the floor of his bedroom, in exactly the same order as they were in his college room.

Tips for Southern Visitors, no. 2: Lancashire

Contrary to popular belief, a Coronation Street-style conurbation does not cover the entire county.

After breakfast I went down to the nursery alone, trying to convince myself that it hadn't been *too* awful yesterday. I could survive it.

Resolution – that's what I needed – and money. I'd put melons on Em's shopping list again, and they're dear just now, although I'm sure I'll hit on the right one soon – literally.

Walter is kindly making me a pole on a stand, exactly five feet ten inches high, to impale them on. If I can just get the sound right, as well as the relative heights . . .

'Good morning, Inga! Isn't it a lovely day?' I said, coming into the light, sunny classroom.

Inga was kneeling, trying to coax a pencil from between the floorboards with the pin of her edelweiss brooch.

The sun seemed to have leached the colour out of her so that her sad, beige hair dripped down her shoulders like a frozen waterfall, and her pale eyes reflected dully back like a dead fish.

'Ja,' she agreed mournfully, with a voice that held the long, dark despair of centuries of Scandinavian winters. 'It is a beautiful day. The sun is shining, but you can nevew be suwe. Later it may wain, and the stowms come, and the big, black clouds, heavy, heavy! And the lightning and the big wolls of thunder – and then I must get into the cup-bowd.'

'In the cupboard?'

'Ja. Always, since I am a little giwl, I must go in the cup-bowd.'

'Any particular cupboard, Inga? Just so I know where to find you if necessary?'

'Is the cup-bowd under the stairs – dawk and safe. When the lightning stwikes and the house falls down, the staiwes will stop the big stones fwom falling on my head.'

'Right. And Gunilla? Does she go in the cupboard, too?'

It was only my second day, and already I was wishing that Gunilla would go in the cup-bowd on a permanent basis.

'No-o,' sighed Inga heavily. 'She will not go in, though I plead with hew and say it is the only safe place. But she is excited when the thunder sounds and the lightning cwackles, so she likes to wun about, scweaming.'

'Sounds like fun.'

'Ja. It is her natuwal way of expwession. And when the wain is heavy she must take off hew clothes and wun outside.'

'Must?'

'Must.'

Since Gunilla was supposed to be modelling her behaviour on that of the adults – The Group – around her, it poses the question: which members of the community run about in the rain, naked? And surely not in the winter?

'Is that a good idea, Inga?'

'Ja. If you twy to stop hew she bites. Sometimes she does not put hew clothes on again for the west of the day, because she must be as one with Natuw. In the summew,' she added heavily, 'we awe all at one with Natuw, but only when school is finished. Some of the pawents, they do not feel the need to be at one with natuw.'

'No, I can imagine.'

Mrs Whippington-Smythe, for instance, is only at one with large, hairy, four-legged creatures that neigh.

'The childwen come now,' she murmured unnecessarily, as a tide of shrieking banshees raced towards us.

'Stop!' bellowed a male voice from the hall. 'Sing!'

Sudden silence was followed by the ragged, reluctant, voices of fifteen children droning something unintelligible.

'What *is* that song?'

'It is the Wainbow song – to inspwire them for the wowk.'

'Funny, it sounds a bit like Japanese.'

'Ja. that is so. They awe singing: "Build the wainbow, bwidge the world with coluw, and walk acwoss into the clouds of happiness. Go fwom flowuw to flowuw, and sip the knowledge of life thwough natuw."'

The roar began again and the door bounced back on its hinges with a crash.

'Here they come for a taste of that, then, Inga.'

Gunilla, predictably, was first in. Snot streamed from her nostrils like twin green pennants as she made for the easel and paints. Or rather, paint: only pots of liquid black were supplied, and big bamboo brushes.

'Aren't they supposed to start at one side of the room and then move around in a big arc, from task to task?' I said, baffled by the milling tots. Yesterday I'd observed rather than joined in, but hadn't managed to make a lot of sense of it.

'Ja – see, Susie has them beginning with the thwee discs of logic now.'

Indeed, some of the children were slapping multicoloured discs onto a pole, with the fierce concentration of those desiring to progress quickly to something more interesting.

'But Gunilla is—'

'Gunilla is mowe at one with Natuw than the othews; she is beyond this stage and must be allowed her fwee expwession. Besides, she is being bwought up puwely thwough Natuw.'

'I think she has a cold.'

'Ja, it is because she wuns awound naked in the wain in winter, as in Natuw,' agreed Inga.

Nature in the raw. 'Right. Er . . . what do you want me to do?'

'I think today you can help them to build the Wainbow of Happiness. That they always find hawd – always it falls down befowe the Key of Enlightenment is insewted into the Hole of Stability.'

'My whole life's been like that,' I said, and she nodded a sad agreement.

That morning was the first time that I felt almost glad that I hadn't got any children, although one or two were quite appealing in an untrammelled sort of way.

En masse, of course, they were all monsters; but none more so than poor, natural Gunilla. (Or Godzilla, as I kept accidentally saying.)

Gunilla was everywhere, pinching the other children, screaming with rage if she couldn't get her own way, and shoving in anywhere she wanted.

'I want to put the Stone of Enlightenment in!' she declared, using her elbows to break into my group, who were laboriously constructing the rainbow, eyes crossing with concentration.

I smiled at her: 'Sorry, Godz—I mean Gunilla, this is Josie's turn. But then you can help to build the rainbow back up and put the stone in.'

Gunilla stared at me incredulously. 'I'm putting the sodding stone in *this* time!' she declared, stamping her foot.

'No, Gunilla,' I said patiently. 'It's Josie's turn this time, but you can do it next – we will build a very special rainbow just for you.'

'Do it fucking *now!*' she screamed, trying to shove the large, stolid, Josie aside.

'No, Gunilla. Why don't you go and find a hankie and blow your nose, and then it will be time to build your rainbow?'

Josie inserted the central stone of the arch while Gunilla stared at me with a sort of malevolent incredulity.

Goblins are alive and well, and living in Upvale.

Then, turning, she bit Josie, who overbalanced, screaming, onto the rainbow arch, which collapsed.

Gunilla threw herself to the floor and went into a paroxysm of rage, and Inga hurried over to snatch her infant to her bosom, which instantly became smeared with viscous green.

She rocked, crooning in lightly fractured English: 'What is the matter with my baby? Tell Mama, and she will make it all wight again.'

Gunilla darted a glance at me, as I tried to comfort poor

Josie, who now sported a crooked circle of bite marks on one hand.

'Horrible cow wouldn't let me put the stone in the rainbow!' she whimpered.

I looked up. 'No, because it was Josie's turn – she'd built the rainbow. Gunilla could have had her turn next.' I turned back to Josie worriedly. 'Inga, Gunilla's teeth have pierced the skin – I think I'd better put some antiseptic on the bite, if you'll tell me where the first-aid stuff is.'

Inga rose to her feet, cradling her four-year-old to her chest like a baby. 'Nevew, nevew must you cwoss Gunilla! How could you? She is lewning thwough fweedom to be one with Natuw.'

'But surely during the Rainbow Nursery sessions she must fit in to some extent with what we are doing with the other children? With the Rainbow ethos? Is it fair to teach them a rigid structure, and then let Gunilla come in and disrupt everything by doing just what she wants?'

'I want my mummy!' sobbed poor little Josie. 'I want to go home.'

'I want the nasty lady to go away!' screeched Gunilla.

'Mamma will build the winbow for you, and you can put the stone in now,' soothed Inga, pushing her jumper up to reveal a breast like an elephant's ear. She proceeded to breastfeed her hysterical child, ignoring both the wounded infant and the small circle of watchers, one with a thumb in her mouth and a couple noticeably damp round the edges.

'Big baby!' Caitlin commented critically, standing stolidly on the bylines watching play, with her hands thrust into her dungaree pockets, rather like a miniature Em.

'Quite right,' I agreed, picking Josie up and going to look for the antiseptic.

Gunilla's little yellow teeth gave promise of tetanus if not rabies, and I only hoped the little girl's inoculations were up to date.

When I returned her to the class later (much happier, due to the fortunate discovery of a rather strange tin of biscuits and a story book, which I'd read to her three times) Gunilla ran up and kicked me hard on the shin.

With a gasp of pain I picked her up so that she was nose to nose with me and said furiously: 'Don't ever, *ever*, do that to me again!'

Her eyes were two startled discs – Discs of Enlightenment, I hoped. 'Mama!' she screamed.

But Mama had already flown to the rescue like a virago. Not to *my* rescue, though: frothing at the lips she seized Godzilla and pointed at the door.

'Go!'

'Go?' I bent down, hitched up my skirts and peered at a promising bruise. It was unfortunate that my assailant had been wearing clogs with wooden soles when she'd committed her onslaught. 'Yes, you're right. I'd better put some antiseptic on this, too. I'll be in the kitchen when Gunilla is ready to apologise, Inga.'

Susie popped her head into the kitchen a few minutes later and winked. 'Good for you! But they won't let you come again, you know, if Gunilla's taken against you. Keith will be in soon to tell you, in a deeply understanding voice, that it's all your fault. Make sure they pay you for the two days before you go.'

'Right. Thanks, Susie,' I said.

Keith, a tall, skinny man with a head like a lightbulb, duly informed me in hushed tones of reproach that Gunilla's behaviour that morning was entirely due to my own aura of hidden aggression, which the poor sensitive creature had sensed, and therefore he unfortunately did not feel that I should work with the children any more.

'I'm not aggres—' I began indignantly, and then stopped. Maybe I was? Maybe I'm wearing a permanent aura of Frying Pan Murderess? But aggressive ... I don't think so. And certainly not towards children, even poor little Gunilla. Firmness isn't aggression, and the other children seemed to like me.

'I don't agree with you.' I said politely. 'I think Gunilla is simply confused by being allowed total freedom, while attending a nursery with a very rigid structure that the other children have to stick to. It isn't fair to her or the others.'

'The lesson that life isn't fair will benefit them all,' Keith said deeply.

Little twerp.

'It's a pity Gunilla hasn't learned that one yet, isn't it? Still, if you'd like to pay me for the two mornings I've worked, I'll be off.'

He looked taken aback. 'But surely after what's happened you don't expect—?'

68

'The labourer is worthy of her hire. And look on the bright side: I won't claim any money from you for this top, which Gunilla ruined by wiping her paint-covered hands up the back. It's got poor little Josie's blood over the sleeves, now, too.'

He stared at me, chewing his moustache, then grudgingly dipped into his pocket and counted out my measly wages in small change. 'There. Now, perhaps you could go to Gunilla before you leave and make peace with her? Her sensitive nature has been troubled by your aggression, and—'

'No,' I interrupted firmly, 'but if Gunilla would like to come to me and apologise before I go, you could fetch her now?'

'Apologise? Gunilla?'

Seeing we had reached an impasse in understanding I left the house, jingling my money and limping, and Inga and Gunilla glowered at me silently from the schoolroom door.

For a moment as I turned away I felt like a horrible, evil, child-eating witch, but really, I don't want to hurt anyone, and would never have struck Gunilla however hard she kicked me.

But Natuw has a lot to answer for.

Then a small figure in an unzipped teddy-bear suit wriggled out between Inga and the door frame, ran up and hugged my legs fiercely – and painfully. Caitlin stared up into my face with her usual pugnacious expression and then ran off ahead of me to where the parents were gathering.

The actor swung Caitlin up into his arms as I walked past down the drive, and he did it with such infinite grace that I half-expected someone to roll out of the bushes on one of those trolley things with a camera shouting: 'Take two, scene one!' or something of that kind.

But nothing happened except for my very nearly being flattened by Mrs Whippington-Smythe's big red off-roader hurtling up the path.

Skint Old Cook, no. 2

Savoury Ducks aren't.

Chapter 10
Small Change

When I looked at the paltry coins Keith paid me, three were French and one German, which were of no earthly use to me, but perhaps my Feng Shui money frog would like them? I could sort of heap them round him like a dragon's hoard.

One by one the little gremlins passed me, homeward bound in their monster carriers. The only ones walking up the hill were the actor and Caitlin, and they didn't catch me up until I was nearly home.

I heard the thump of small feet behind me, and then Caitlin was embracing my legs again. I nearly fell over. When she held her arms out to be picked up I did, and hugged her, though I didn't know what I'd done to deserve it. Still, it did make me feel a bit less of a witch, and also suffer a sharp pang of regret for my lost chances of motherhood. A sort of strange, low pain inside.

Maybe my heart's in the wrong place.

'Are you crying?' asked Caitlin anxiously.

I smiled. 'No, it's the cold making my eyes water.'

She peered into them alternately from two inches away. 'They're a very funny colour.'

'Em says they're the colour of black grapes.'

'Trodden-on-black grapes,' amended Caitlin. 'The insides are sort of purply.'

'Caitlin seems to like you,' her father said, catching us up.

She looked at him severely. 'She's okay, Daddy. Gunilla bit Josie, and then she kicked Charlie, and Charlie sorted her out. She calls her Godzilla, and I'm going to call her Godzilla too, because she's a monster.'

71

'She's just a confused little girl,' I said to the actor, who was raising one eyebrow.

(How did he do that? I can never do it, even though I've spent hours in front of a mirror trying. It's both, or nothing. I can twitch the end of my nose without moving my lips at the same time, though, and I bet he can't.)

Mace had to be older than me, but he'd worn in a sophisticated, lounge-lizard sort of way. Nature, as well as artily silvering the odd strand of hair, had given him interesting lines around his dark eyes to map out what he'd been up to for the last forty-odd years. He also looked fit (as far as you could tell from someone wearing a duvet) without giving the impression his personal fitness trainer flew in by helicopter every day to put him through his paces.

Caitlin slid down again and took his hand.

'So we meet again,' he said, with more resignation than enthusiasm. 'Em says you're her sister?'

I didn't blame him for sounding surprised. (And just when did Em get on chatting terms with him?)

'Yes – Charlie Rhymer. I'm living in the Summer Cottage because my husband's divorcing me and Father's mistress has taken over my bedroom.'

'Now why doesn't that surprise me?' he mused.

'Which bit?'

'The divorce.'

'Like you and Mummy,' commented Caitlin, swinging on her father's arm like it was an exercise bar.

'Mummy's marrying Rod,' she told me. 'He's very nice but *thick*, and he can't be my daddy, because I've already got one. He says I can just call him Rod.'

'That's nice,' I said weakly.

A faint spasm of something that might have been either pain or annoyance passed across the actor's face, and he abruptly changed the subject.

'I still think that lean-to is an excrescence on the beautiful face of Upvale,' he said, his lovely posh and mellow voice at odds with his exotic face.

'Like that duvet you're wearing,' I said shortly.

'It's Kenzo.'

'So I've heard from Elfreda Whippington-Smythe.'

'Which one's she?'

'Small, bun-faced, always wears jodhpurs, talks from up her nose.'

He shuddered. 'Oh, God, that one. She rides past every day, and lingers. And if I go for a walk, she always just happens to be crossing my path.'

'I expect she keeps her binoculars trained on you from the other side of the vale. You should wear something more inconspicuous. My sister Anne's an expert in camouflage, and she's coming home soon – you could ask her.'

He looked down critically at himself. 'Perhaps you're right – this does look worryingly at one with your lean-to. Garish.'

'Verandah. But don't worry. I expect good taste is optional for the acting profession.'

'Speaking of good taste, that's the biggest garden gnome *I've* ever seen,' he said blandly, pointing behind me.

I turned. Walter was standing just inside the verandah, wearing a red woolly hat and his usual voluminous corduroy trousers. He was beaming and pointing at where his eyebrows would have been had he got any. I blew him a kiss.

'Walter made the verandah as a welcome-home present,' I said, 'and I think it's perfect!'

We stared at each other, then a most disconcerting smile appeared on his even more disconcertingly beautiful pinky-brown lips.

Wow.

I could probably have prevented my own plebeian mouth smiling back had I coated my face in concrete.

Caitlin, tired of jumping up and down waving at Walter, tugged his arm. 'Come on, Daddy – I'm hungry.'

She turned to wave as they carried on up the path, but Mace didn't.

Walter's presence in the Summer Cottage was easily explained: an electrician was just putting the finishing touches to the socket and lighting he'd installed, probably illegally, in the verandah. Walter doesn't trust any tradesmen not to make off with the family stainless steel.

'Anne's come,' he informed me over his shoulder before escorting the electrician up the stairs to the Parsonage.

I changed and tidied up. There was no sign of Flossie, so she was probably up with Frost in the kitchen.

*

Anne was striding up and down the kitchen in her usual fashion, in khaki cotton trousers and a camouflage waistcoat that would have blended the actor into the woods quite nicely.

'They entered from the left and circled—' She broke off briefly to thump me on the shoulder and say: 'Hi, Chaz.' 'Circled the enemy before attacking.'

'Where have you been? Which battle is this?' I demanded.

'Hospital,' Em informed me. 'Anne's fighting the Big C.' She carried on shearing chickens into pieces and tossing them into a big pot.

I recognised nourishing chicken soup in the making, and looked at Anne more closely. She did look fine-drawn and tired.

'You don't mean . . .?'

'Cancer,' Anne said. 'Lump – left breast. I was just telling Em – they circled the little bugger, and whipped it out before it could invade.'

'Oh, Anne! Why didn't you tell us? We could have been with you.'

'Enough on your plates already. Fight my own battles,' she said.

'Did Red go with you?'

'Spineless git. Couldn't face any of it – cleared off.'

'Is – is that it, now? Do they think the cancer's gone?' I asked, worriedly.

'So they say. Took a lymph node, too, and it wasn't in that. Got more puckers than Bride of Frankenstein. Just as well I've got no boobs to speak of anyway.'

I sat down at the table next to Em, feeling limp.

Em tossed the last chicken piece into the pot with the vegetables. 'They took the gland from under her arm to check if it had spread, but there was no sign of it,' she interpreted. 'So she's clear.'

'Left arm's a bit sore,' Anne admitted. 'Got to go over to the hospital every day for six weeks for treatment – back-up stuff. Then back to work.'

'Have you told them?'

'Told them it was a small op on my dodgy knee – rest up, back right after Christmas.'

'What about Red?'

'Break *his* knees if he says any different.'

'Why don't you go and lie down for a bit?' suggested Em daringly.

'Fall back, regroup, and fight another day,' she agreed, to my astonishment. 'You'd better not have put that tart with the see-through blouse in my room: where does she think she is, the bloody Cannes Film Festival?'

'No, she's in Charlie's room.'

'Bad luck, Chaz.'

'Never mind – I quite like it in the Summer Cottage,' I said. 'Did Em tell you Bran's home too?'

'Seen him – didn't know he spoke Croatian.'

'I've put your stuff upstairs, our Anne,' Walter said, hobbling in. 'Outside the door.'

'Good man. See you've got no eyebrows yet.'

'No bodily hair what-so-ever,' he agreed, beaming.

Tips for Southern Visitors, no. 3: Fashion

1) It is socially acceptable now, and always has been, to wear white stilettos with jeans.

2) If going out for the evening in a big city, remember, even in winter, that one *layer of clothing is enough. Coats and tights are for wimps.*

3) If you are wearing a bra you do not need a handbag.

'Well,' said Father sarcastically, gazing at the complete family circle around the breakfast table next morning. 'All my little chickens come home to roost?'

'Cluck,' said Anne, who was eating French toast lovingly prepared by Em, who was inclined to hover over her – but then, we'd never seen Anne looking ill before. She moved stiffly, and there were dark circles under her eyes.

Bran stared across at her and smiled. 'There's no reason why we can't *all* use the click language,' he said in perfectly intelligible English, before resuming the creation of a strange triple-decker sandwich that involved a lot of marmalade and bacon, watched with fascination by the two little girls.

Frost came in with a mouthful of letters and spat them onto the carpet.

'Must all my post be covered in dog saliva?' demanded Father distastefully.

'Beats me why folks bother writing to you at all, you great lump of nowt,' Gloria said, coming in just then with more toast and the teapot.

'Thank you for that vote of appreciation,' he said. 'Do you think you could ask Walter if he'd take a look at my desk? One of the legs is a bit wonky.'

He and Jessica exchanged fleeting but meaningful glances.

'I'm not surprised,' Gloria commented cryptically, and patted me on the head like an infant in passing as she went out again.

Jessica was rather daringly eating a boiled egg, but I didn't think she would make it through the whole gargantuan repast; she'd already had one spoonful and a bite of dry toast.

'Well, it's nice to meet all Ran's family at last,' she said, 'even if Anne and Em do rather dwarf poor little me!'

'Bran and I aren't much taller than you, 'I pointed out.

'No – you two certainly don't take after Ran, do you? In fact, it's hard to believe you are related!'

'Charlie looks exactly like her mother – Lally Tooke,' Ran said, looking up from his paper.

'And does Bran look like *his* mother?' asked Jessica slightly waspishly.

'I don't know. I can't remember,' he replied calmly. 'It was all a long time ago. Aren't those girls going to be late for school?'

Jessica looked up at the clock, squawked, and dragged her protesting children away. I peeled the rest of her boiled egg and tossed it to Frost, who ate it in one gulp.

Not having to go to the nursery ever again made me feel inordinately happy – until I discovered the hate mail from Angie, dewed with dog drool, under the table.

... better start looking over your shoulder, Charlie, because I'm coming to Upvale. Soon everyone will know you're a murdering whore, leading men on and then turning on them ...

Life is just a rollercoaster of pleasure lately.

Chapter 11
Parting

Health Check

There are few minor ailments that cannot be alleviated by the application of two large gin and tonics.

'Get your coat,' Em said, appearing on the stairs after dinner.

'Why, where are we going?'

'Freya's house – it's her turn.'

'What for?' I asked, obediently pulling on my coat and hurrying after her. Flossie's snores reverberated up the stairs behind me.

'The discussion group. It was a reading group, but now we just meet and discuss – stuff. And anyway, Freya's husband's coming back tonight to collect his things, and he has a violent temper.'

'I didn't know she had a husband.'

'Had's the operative word. She's thrown him out and got an injunction against him, but a fat lot of use that is. Still, she's being fair – she's letting him come round tonight to remove his half of their belongings.'

'But I thought she had magic powers. Can't she just do something nasty to him?'

'You've never seen so many boils on one man's neck,' Em said. 'But that was Xanthe Skye – Freya's powers lie in other directions.'

I didn't ask what. Already it sounded like a fun evening.

'Who else will be there? I'm not feeling very sociable.'

'Madge comes, and she isn't terribly sociable either – and Susie from the nursery, and Xanthe Skye and Lilith, of course. Madge's old father is driving her mad – and ours is driving *me* mad. And

77

you can have a good moan about Matt. We could get Freya to do something nasty to Matt, if you still have any of his belongings.'

'I think I already did, killing his best friend, and I've cleared out everything to do with him.'

'Purged,' she agreed.

'In every way.'

We trudged up the hill in icy darkness, lit at irregular intervals by the small yellow circles grudgingly cast by three old street lamps. The Black Dog looked terribly warm and inviting; Father and Jess were probably in there already. The last bus up from town stopped just ahead of us and decanted Inga and Godzilla before chugging slowly onwards.

Inga gave me a sad, pitying smile as she passed us, but Godzilla lingered pulling faces at me and capering, until she looked at Em instead, and suddenly ran off crying: 'Mama! Wait!'

Freya lived at the end of a terrace of old stone weavers' cottages right at the top of Upvale. The bus passed us again on its way down, a brightly lit and empty *Marie Celeste*.

The tiny sitting room, already full, became crammed to bursting point with our arrival.

Freya pushed past us gasping: 'Ice, ice – I must have ice!' in a parched voice, but she came back fairly soon with coffee, gin, and crackers smeared with something that probably only *looked* like road-kill hedgehog.

All the time we were drinking and chatting heavy footsteps thumped about overhead, with muffled cursing. From time to time something bumped down the stairs and was dragged out.

Then the footsteps and creakings from above were replaced by the sound of frenzied sawing, and flakes of plaster drifted down into my cup.

'What's he doing?' enquired Madge.

'Sawing the wardrobe in two,' replied Freya calmly.

'Isn't that taking the "his half" business a little too seriously?' I said.

'He's taking it to the letter, but I don't know what he thinks he's going to do with half a wardrobe. I'll use mine for firewood. Mind you, if he'd asked I'd have given him the whole thing. I don't want it. I was never big on white melamine.'

'I know what you mean,' I agreed. 'My ex-husband liked angular modern furniture, all cream and white, with no colour or pattern.'

'No wonder your aura is still faintly blue,' Xanthe said, edging a little further away.

'Sorry. Is there some way I can clean it off? Sort of Magic Flash?'

'Are you joking?' Xanthe asked, looking at me severely.

'No, she's serious,' Em explained. 'She just doesn't know much about that sort of thing. I'm the only one who ever listened to Gloria Mundi.'

'You have a natural talent for the Ancient Arts,' agreed Lilith. 'Far beyond Gloria, who is a mere wisewoman.'

'Oh, nothing's beyond Gloria,' I assured her. 'Em's just gone in a different direction.'

There was more frenzied sawing from upstairs.

'The dressing table?' suggested Lilith, and Freya nodded.

'Yes – he's taken it very hard; but then, so did I when he tried to slap me around.'

'Your having already found a much younger lover seems to rankle particularly,' said Xanthe.

'Have you?' I said with respect. 'Who is it?'

'He's new – a teacher from the valley – but I'm teaching *him* one or two things. He lives on that new Mango Homes estate – Raspberry Road, just off Strawberry Street. You've just bought a house there too, haven't you, Susie?'

'Yes, but mine's Galia Gardens, up Honeydew Hill.'

'Fruity,' I commented.

'Well, I drew the line at Passionfruit Place, but otherwise I don't mind,' Susie said. 'They renamed my old road Mandela Street, and every time someone forgot to put the town on my mail it went on a Round-Britain Tour. There's a Mandela something in every town in the country.'

The halved furniture descended the stairs in a series of crashes, and a few minutes of dragging and swearing later the van drove away.

'I'll just pop out and perform a protection spell for you,' Lilith said. 'In case he tries to come back.'

'And I'll go round with the Bowls of Cleansing,' offered Xanthe. 'Mix us a large G&T, dear, for afterwards.'

Rituals accomplished, things got quite merry, and after some urging from Em I told them all about *Skint Old Northern Woman* magazine.

79

Everyone came up with suggestions for more articles, some so rude I'd probably be prosecuted if it came to anything.

'You should publish it,' suggested Madge. 'Everyone would love it. It would go down a treat at the W.I.'

'Publish it? I couldn't possibly do that – it would take a fortune to start up a magazine.'

'Yes, but you could try it as a one-off issue, and see how it went.'

'It would be great!' Susie said. 'My sister Jen works for a small publishing company. I'll ask her how much it would cost.'

I shook my head regretfully: 'I can't afford anything at all.'

'It should be published!' Em said, as if she'd just received Divine Revelation. 'Anne thought so too, when I told her about it. Perhaps we could pay for the first print run?'

I shook my head. 'No, you'd just lose your money – but it's fun writing the articles. Anyone got any more ideas?'

'How about an 'Are You a Victim' quiz?' suggested Freya.

Are You a Natural Victim? Try our quiz and find out!

Your partner slaps you around, and then goes out. Would you:
A) Put up with it, because it was your fault after all, and he won't ever do it again, will he?
B) Balance a large heavy item on top of the half-open kitchen door and await events
C) Leave (May be combined with answer B)
D) Fell the bastard with a large heavy object as he turns to go, thus giving you plenty of time to pack.

On the way home Em and I stopped in at the Black Dog, where we found the new vicar playing darts with Walter, Bran and Father, with Jessica sitting in the corner looking bored over a Martini.

Bran, surprisingly, can throw a mean dart. You just have to remember not to stand between him and the board when he's got the darts in his hand, because he throws them fast.

I was introduced to the vicar, whose name was, entirely suitably, Christian, although he likes to be called Chris. He was a different species from our last one, being very tall, rangy, fortyish, and with a long, iron-grey ponytail and drooping moustaches, like a handsome but slightly melancholy Wyatt Earp. He wore small gold rings in his ears with dangling crosses, and a T-shirt with a dog collar and waistcoat printed on it.

The moment he set eyes on Em he dropped his darts and assumed the unmistakably sheepish expression of the seriously smitten male, but I don't think she noticed.

She looked especially nice tonight, I thought. The red T-shirt under her dungarees had washed out to a flattering faded rose, and her light blue eyes with their blacker-than-black pupils looked like a very intelligent goat's.

Em joined in the game while I took my drink and sat with Jessica, who seemed pitifully grateful for any company, even mine.

'God, this is boring!' she confided. 'I thought Mace North might come in – he does sometimes when Madge babysits for him – but not tonight.'

'Madge was at Freya's house for the discussion group.'

She yawned. 'Then Mace won't be coming. The vicar's quite dishy, but he won't flirt – that's the trouble with vicars. I think I'll go home.'

'I'll walk back with you,' I said, draining my pint of bitter and blackcurrant. 'I'm pretty tired – it's been a long day.'

'I'm going home, Ran,' she called, and pouted when Father just smiled and waved a hand at her before taking careful aim with his next dart.

I think lust's first bloom has rubbed off already. But it will be a bit worrying if Jessica leaves, because the next mistress will probably need the Summer Cottage, which is just starting to feel like home.

Chapter 12

Jumbled

'Chris – the vicar – gave me a message for you, Emily,' Jessica said a couple of days later. 'Did you ask him to find you a plumber, or something? God knows, the bathrooms are still in the last century, and none of the locks work. I walked in on Bran the other day while he was showering. He's a big boy,' she added thoughtfully, a faint smile crossing her face.

Oh well, I don't suppose she really registered on him. If he's got a sex drive he hasn't found the on switch yet.

'What was the message?' Em demanded curtly.

'The message?' she echoed blankly. 'Oh yes, the message – silly me! Chris said to tell you that Barkis is willing. Willing to do what?'

'Barkis is willing?' I repeated, staring at Em in astonishment, and she went a faint but becoming shade of pink.

'Chris is quite dishy,' Jessica said, 'for a vicar. He invited me round tonight.'

'He can't have done,' Em said shortly. 'It's the jumble sale.'

'Yes, he invited me to that.'

'You don't invite people to a jumble sale, you just tell them about it,' I informed her. 'Are you going?'

'Oh no – I get all the girls' stuff from Gap, and *I'm* so petite—'

'Skinny,' interpreted Em, but Jessica was impervious.

'That I have to buy most of *my* clothes from children's departments too!'

So *that's* why the shops are so strangely full of sexy clothes for little girls – they're really meant for all the tiny stick-women like Jessica. I'm glad to have that explained to me.

'I wouldn't say it like it was an asset being a bag of bones – *bag* being the operative word,' Em said disagreeably, but Jessica just laughed.

Her bones must be rubber, because she always bounces back. Or maybe she doesn't take in everything Em says? She certainly seems immune to her little whitish spells – let's hope Em doesn't call in the Black Dogs of War in the shape of Freya, Lilith and Xanthe.

I'm getting to sort of like her a bit, but I must try not to, because of loyalty to Em.

'I'll go to the jumble sale,' I said. 'I'm tired of black, and nothing fitting. I might find some jeans or something.'

'If you lost another stone, you'd probably fit into my clothes,' Jessica offered.

'if she lost another stone she'd be even more skeletal than you,' Em said. 'We're trying to build her back up again. Anyway, she doesn't wear tart clothes.'

'Thanks, though, Jessica,' I said hastily. 'Fashion's a funny thing, isn't it? Remember all those transparent dresses women wore with just knickers under? I mean, people went *out* wearing those and no one much said anything. It was just like the Emperor's new clothes.'

'Which Emperor?' Jessica said, puzzled.

'In the fairy tale,' Em said. 'You're right, Charlie – no one dared to tell the Emperor he was totally nude and the family jewels were on public display, because he'd been brainwashed into thinking he was wearing a magic suit.'

'Except for a little boy, who didn't understand, and shouted out that the Emperor was in his birthday suit – and then the crowd all got the sniggers,' I finished.

Anne came in, looking exhausted. Even the multi-pockets on her battle fatigues looked limp, although her light hair still stood out round her face like a dandelion clock.

'Clear off,' she said to Jessica, although not with her usual energy.

'You Rhymers!' Jessica said, laughing, but getting up all the same. 'I told Ran he'd made a bad job of bringing you up. All that isolation has warped your social skills.'

'Go to bed, Anne,' Em said tersely. 'Charlie will bring your tea up in five minutes.'

'It's no wonder you're tired, if you keep going out when you're supposed to be convalescing after an operation,' Jessica babbled. 'I suppose it was a hysterectomy or something, and that's why you're not telling us what it was?'

'Telling *you* what it was,' Anne said pointedly, and Jessica gave up probing and went off to pick up the girls from school.

'Was it okay?' I asked when I took Em's lovingly prepared tray upstairs to Anne. It was odd seeing her in bed during daylight hours, but she did look exhausted.

'Quite bearable. Only for a few weeks.'

'Your hair's not going to fall out, is it?'

'No, different sort of treatment.'

'Will you have to have anything else done?' I ventured, since this was talkative for Anne.

'No. This is a back-up – they got the bugger. Gave up before the battle began. Like Red – one mention, and he cleared off. No guts.'

Even cancer's got more sense than to tangle with Anne twice.

'Doctors wanted me to take some drug for ten years. "Just in case". Told them to stuff it up their jacksies.'

'Should you do that?'

'What, stuff it up their jacksies?' She sniggered.

It's all that hanging around with soldiers. Anne's language sometimes has to be heard to be believed. I'm always afraid she's going to slip up when she's broadcasting live, but she hasn't yet.

There was a familiar wheezing noise as Flossie appeared in the doorway, wagging her tail in a mildly pleased way. Then she scrabbled up onto the bed next to Anne.

I stared at her in surprise. She doesn't usually take a liking to people; I'm not even sure she can distinguish *me* from everyone else half the time.

'Do you want me to take her away? She'll cover the bed with hair.'

'No, leave her,' Anne said, leaning back and closing her eyes. 'She's company.'

That's another thing Anne's never sought much before. I backed out feeling a bit ruffled, but leaving the door slightly open for Flossie when she remembered food and attempted to find the kitchen.

85

Anne's hand was on Flossie's head, in a touchingly dying-Brontë way, but Flossie's tongue was just starting to explore the perimeter of the tea tray.

I put my head into Bran's room on the way down. He was standing by the window, saying something calmly, but in an obscure-sounding tongue, to Mr Froggy.

'Tea, Bran? Hot cheese scones?'

His light brown eyes regarded me amiably. 'Buttered angel cake?'

'Yes,' I agreed. Em always has to make angel cake for Bran. He interpreted this for Mr Froggy, and then stuffed the toy unceremoniously into his pocket before picking his way through a drift of books and papers. Someone, either Em or Gloria, had put new leather patches on the elbows of his corduroy jacket.

I led the way down. 'There's a jumble sale tonight at the church hall, Bran. Do you want to come? Books?'

'Books,' he agreed.

Jumble Sale Etiquette

Step one: queue in an orderly fashion in front of the door, peering in to see where the best-looking tables are, if you get the opportunity.

Step two: as soon as the doors open, stampede in, jostling for a position at your chosen table with your elbows. (As Mae West once so memorably put it: 'He who hesitates is last.')

Step three: grab anything that looks remotely interesting without stopping to examine it until you have an armful and can't grip any more. Then retire to a corner of the room and sort through them, returning to put the rejects back on the table and pay for your chosen items.

Stow paid-for items in a bag and repeat step three.

Em, Gloria and I formed a cordon around Branwell to prevent him wandering into the hall and rifling the books until the doors officially opened. Walter had somehow managed to insert himself at the head of the queue, and could be heard informing Madge that he had no eyebrows, and, probably, that he had no hair anywhere else either.

86

It was a good jumble sale, and well attended, since word had got out that Lady Hake-Hackett had been having a major clear-out. Word had also got out that the vicar was including some of the obscure volumes left behind by the previous incumbent, but no one except Bran was showing much interest in those: I had to go back and get the car at the end and load them in.

The vicar helped. He seems drawn to Em like an unwary moth to the flame.

'Barkis is willing to what?' I asked her later while we examined our booty in the kitchen, Bran having retired to his room with his books.

Jessica and Ran had gone to the pub in our absence, leaving the girls in the nominal care of Anne, but they'd gone to bed when we got home. Anne said she'd told them a few stories first, which seemed unlikely, because the only stories I've heard her tell usually end something like: '. . . and bugger me if the next second he didn't tread on a landmine and get himself blown to smithereens!'

Em shrugged, pulling a voluminous mass of tawny crushed velvet out of her bag. 'Marry me, presumably,' she said off-handedly, holding the dress against her dungarees and squinting critically downwards. 'Do you think this will fit me? It looks big enough – must have been a Hake-Hackett. They're all built like barn doors, except Felicity. She's the runt of the litter.'

'I've never seen you in a dress!' I said, amazed. Come to think of it, I've never seen her in anything other than dungarees over a T-shirt or jumper, and big boots.

'I need to make an impression, or I'll die a bloody virgin.'

'But Barkis is willing.'

'I can't seduce a vicar when I'm about to embrace the Dark Powers. You can't seduce vicars anyway. It isn't done. You have to marry them, which is impossible.'

'It's not impossible, and he's rather attractive.'

'I don't want to marry, I'm quite happy with my life the way it is, or I will be, once we've got rid of Jessica. No, I just want casual sex, preferably in a place of power, like the standing stones on the moor. Besides, I couldn't have any sort of relationship with a man who thinks Dickens is the greatest British novelist!'

'No, I suppose not. Er . . . you do *know* all about safe sex, don't you, Em?'

'Wasn't born yesterday,' she said indistinctly as she pulled the dress over her head. It fell in loose folds about her and would have been flattering had it not been for the layers of bulky fabric underneath and the boots. 'I'll wear this next Friday, for Father's birthday feast.'

'It will have to be cleaned first.'

'It's clean already – still got the cleaner's tag pinned in the neck.'

'Is anyone else coming on Friday?' I asked. There had to be some reason for the dress.

'Mace North – Father's invited him. Jessie's delirious with pleasure.'

'Big deal.'

'He hasn't accepted any other invitations, though that Whippington-Smythe woman's been shameless. Maybe he only *looks* nervous when I talk to him – you watch him on Friday and tell me if you think he fancies me.'

'I will, but you're flogging a dead horse on that one, Em. Even ugly middle-aged men can pull pretty young girls if they're rich or famous enough, so he's probably got a queue waiting to jump into his bed.'

'I'll put something in his drink. And he's not ugly.'

'I didn't say he was – it was just a generalisation. He's . . . interesting-looking, and he has a very attractive smile.'

'Hmm,' Em said, staring at me. 'Why's he smiling at you? You don't want him, do you?'

'No, I've gone off men permanently, except family, of course. And I don't mind the vicar, he's rather sweet. Otherwise, even casual sex seems pointless now I can't get pregnant any more.'

'What have you got in your jumble bags?' she asked, changing the subject to my relief. I am not a rival for anyone's affections; I've been through the sex/marriage/dwindling sex/divorce cycle already, I don't want to repeat the whole damned thing with anyone else, even on a temporary basis.

'Jeans, and a lot of sea-green stuff. Dresses, T-shirts . . . a dark green suede jacket . . . matching desert boots, sandals . . .'

'Now that definitely *was* Felicity. She had a green phase last year; thought she was a bloody naiad, but it didn't suit her. Too yellow. That's a nice dress.'

'I think it's a nightie really,' I said doubtfully, holding up a wispy green chiffon number. 'But it has got a nice Peter Pan sort of touch about it – frondy.'

'Well, call it a dress and wear it next Friday. When do we ever dress up?'

'Never?'

'We *shall* go to the ball,' Em said.

Chapter 13

Jam Tomorrow

I spent a couple of days washing, altering and mending my new wardrobe – Felicity is a little larger than me, even now I'm starting to fill out a bit. I had to filch one of Bran's belts to keep my jeans up, but I don't suppose he will notice.

The two little girls (who, under Anne's practical influence, have started calling themselves Clo and Febe) helped me to paint a jungle on the inside of the verandah's glass walls in poster paints. It will come off eventually, but give me the right dense green atmosphere to work in until I get enough plants.

I was glad the paints were non-toxic, because Flossie tried licking the glass and smeared several leaves before she decided she didn't like the flavour.

Clo painted a sort of monkey in her bit, and Febe did lots of butterflies and a lizardy thing like a salamander.

I did a snake. The serpent in the Garden of Eden.

Skint Old Gardening Tips: 2

Spider plants have no reason for existence – they are simply a sort of green chain letter.

   1) Place in a cardboard box and abandon them somewhere they will be found quickly: e.g. outside a charity shop just before opening time.

   2) Include the macramé potholders.

   3) Walk away: just feel that relief!

One afternoon Em appeared in her loomingly silent way, followed by Frost, who tried to poke his head into Flossie's igloo and got short shrift.

Since a blast of dank, icy air had fingered its way in with them I deduced that they had come in through the verandah. They'd taken to using the place as a short cut up to the Parsonage after their walks, which was fine, except for the surprise; I'm not big on surprises after the Dead Greg episode.

With my meagre wages from the nursery I'd purchased an economy-sized can of one-coat pale yellow emulsion and was obliterating flowered wallpaper in my kitchen/diner/bedroom.

'I've got you another job,' Em said casually.

'What do you mean? What sort of job?'

'Caitlin's nanny. Mace took her away from the Rainbow Nursery because she didn't like it, and now he's finding it hard to concentrate on writing his play, so he needs someone to look after her in the mornings while he works.'

'But he doesn't like me!'

'I don't know why you think that – and anyway, Caitlin likes you; she said she wanted you. It'll be fine. You can bring her to the Parsonage, and take her for walks and things. You're starting at nine-thirty tomorrow, and he's going to pay you London wages.'

'But Em, he saw me bashing melons the other day – he can't want someone he thinks is loopy. And he can't know about Greg either! You must have forced him to offer me the job.'

'Of course I didn't force him. I just suggested it when I popped in with some melon and ginger jam,' she said, slightly self-consciously. 'He probably thinks you have to bash the melons as part of the process or something. He didn't mention it, anyway. And I don't think anyone round here other than the family know about Dead Greg. It only made your local paper, after all, thanks to that earthquake and the lurid sex-murder trial.'

'Jessica knows.'

'Yes, but I told her if word got out we'd know it was her, and we'd kill her and put the body down the old well, so that's okay.'

The image of a tiny Jessica looking up from the bottom of a well sort of twitched my painting nerve.

'Did you take the vicar any jam?' I asked curiously.

'Not yet ... but I might,' she said, smiling in an unusually Mona Lisa way. 'And one of my advance copies of *Womanly Wicca Words of Spiritual Comfort*.'

When Em and Frost had gone up the Parsonage stairs I

assembled my melon-bashing equipment in the garden. (Ripe ones are *so* messy.)

First, the stand Walter made, Greg-high and spiked to hold the melon still. Then I positioned the fatal kitchen steps and climbed up holding the pan . . .

This time I checked there was no one on the track before I took the first swing.

The blow connected solidly, but the sound was too soggy.

The second landed fair and square too, and it almost sounded right . . .

I set the last one up, climbed back up on the steps, and lifted the pan high, as if it was hanging on the hook. Then I shifted to a two-handed tennis racquet grip to swing it down and—

'What are you doing?' enquired the vicar curiously, his head bobbing up right next to me.

The pan had begun its inexorable swing, missing Chris by a hair's breadth and connecting with that oh-so-familiar-from-my-nightmares meaty 'thunk!'.

The melon bounced off its spike rather gruesomely and rolled away.

'That was the sound!' I said, amazed. 'That was it! And I *couldn't* stop the pan, even though I was afraid I was going to hit you.'

'No, I'm sure you couldn't, not from that height and holding it like that,' he agreed. 'Once it started to swing down, that would be it. Did you mean to hit the melon?'

He sounded interested rather than surprised, so after he'd helped me take everything into the cottage I made some coffee and prepared to Confess All, which I suppose vicars are quite used to.

'I expect people tell you this sort of thing all the time,' I finished.

'Not really,' he answered thoughtfully. 'Still, I hope you are now truly satisfied that you didn't mean to kill this Greg?'

'I am *now* . . . and even the noise was right. It felt – cathartic.'

'Good. Accept that what happened really wasn't your fault, and although it will be hard to live with the memory of it, it was just an accident brought on by his own actions.'

'I only hope his wife, Angie, accepts that too – she was feeling very bitter and vindictive towards me after the inquest, and she's sent me poison-pen type letters threatening to come here and tell everyone about me.'

'Poor woman,' he said charitably. 'If she does, I will speak to her and offer her comfort.'

She might be interested, at that, but I do not think they will both define 'comfort' in the same way.

I sat back in the old wooden rocking chair and everything suddenly looked subtly different, as if it had all shifted in space slightly and become brighter. I felt reborn: a slightly dazed new phoenix Charlie arising from the ashes of her old nest.

'Do you know, Chris, I think I could paint again? I'm going to paint Jessica down the old well.'

'Oh? I understood from Em you only painted the jungle.'

'I do, but Jessica's going to be at the heart of the next one, far, far down a well, looking up.'

He looked thoughtful. 'I expect there's something deeply Freudian about that, but we won't pursue it. I'm glad you're feeling better.'

'Yes, and once I'm painting I won't need another job. Em's got me a temporary one, looking after Mace North's little girl in the mornings while he writes, but I expect the cottage is just a whim. A famous star won't want to hang about in Yorkshire for very long, will he?'

'I rather selfishly hope not,' he confessed, looking glum. 'She – Em – likes him, doesn't she?'

'She does find him interesting,' I admitted, 'but he's frightened of her. I expect that's how she got me the job.'

'Frightened of her? How can anyone be frightened of her?'

I looked at him with dawning respect. 'Yes, but she's a *witch*.'

'She certainly is,' he agreed enthusiastically. 'She's put a spell on me. Did you give her my message?'

'Yes, it's taken her by surprise.'

As long as she doesn't take the actor by surprise . . . although I suppose he would be more suitable for Em's purposes than a vicar, even if I don't particularly like him.

Poor Chris! He's obviously seeing her through the eyes of love – and he's really rather attractive. And I never was keen on the idea of Em embracing the Black Arts – she's so very *thorough.*

But could an alliance between Wicca and Church work? I must speak to Gloria and see what she thinks.

And I've made up my mind that I'm going to tell Mace about

Dead Greg before he finds out from someone else. If he doesn't want me to take care of Caitlin after that, it's fine by me.

Tips for Southern Visitors, no. 4:

In some parts of Northeast England, a man would rather kill himself overtaking on a blind bend at seventy miles an hour than drive a hundred yards behind a woman.

When I went up to his cottage next morning there was a sleek, sporty red car pulled up outside it which hadn't been there before. The actor's car is some low, dark thing.

Caitlin opened the door, her fingers to her lips: 'Ssh! Come into the kitchen – Mummy's here, and she and Daddy are having a talk in the living room.'

Indeed, even as she drew me into the kitchen I heard a husky voice drawl: '. . . buried out here in the cultural desert!'

But there she was quite wrong, for there are lots of blue-blooded Russian émigrés in Huddersfield, all enjoying soirées, the dance, theatre, ballet. A stray Tartar would be quite at home.

'Perhaps I should go away and come back la—'

'*There* you are,' snapped Mace North from the doorway, as if I was hours late. 'Caitlin, go and put your things on and Charlie can take you for a nice walk.'

'It's brass-monkey cold out there,' I said. 'I'll take her down to the Parsonage.'

'Wherever,' he said abstractedly.

'Is that the nanny you mentioned?' said the low, slightly husky voice, and Mace's ex-wife, the actress Kathleen Lovell, peered around him. She looked me up and down critically with huge brown eyes in a gauntly pretty face.

Up to that moment I'd felt quite good in my jumble-sale denim trousers and dark green suede jacket, but now I felt like the hired help. Come to that, I *was* the hired help.

'You're tiny, aren't you? And not so very young – I expect you're glad of the job. Would you like to come to America with us after the wedding?'

As job interviews go, it was a bit sketchy.

'No,' I said. 'I'm staying here.'

'And so is Caitlin,' said Mace with a steely note in his voice.

'Of course – for now,' she agreed. 'I'm just back from Morocco,' she said to me. 'I've been filming *The Return of the Sheik* – you must see it, it's too scary for words! The Sheik is a ghost, drawn back by my golden-haired, voluptuous beauty, but ours is a love that can never be.'

'No, I can imagine,' I agreed.

'That's the last *fat* part I'm going to play,' she added firmly. 'I'm going to lose a stone for the wedding, and then I'll be thin enough for roles in America – you have to be skinny to get *anywhere* over there. My fiancée, Rod – Rod Steigland, you know, the actor? – is going to insist I'm the female lead in his next film.'

'I don't think you've got a stone to lose,' I said, amazed, for she looked even more of a collection of bird bones than Jessica. 'Or even an ounce!'

'Sweet of you,' she drawled. 'But thin is the new fat – it simply isn't good enough. Are you *sure* you don't want to be our nanny and come to America?'

'I wonder if you'd excuse us, Charlie?' Mace interrupted. 'Kathleen and I have got a lot to discuss before she has to leave. Caitlin will be down in a minute.'

'But—' I began, because surely Kathleen would want to see something of her little girl before she went off again? But the door to the living room closed firmly behind them. And then, as is the way with old doors, quietly clicked open again, just a hairline.

A better person might have gone to round up Caitlin, or waited outside. I edged a little nearer to the door, and listened, fascinated. It was like hearing a play on radio with an exceptional cast: the enunciation was *superb*.

'I'd like to have Caitlin make her main home here in England with me, Kathy,' Mace said quietly. 'If you remember, I didn't go for custody because we agreed that we'd share time with her and do whatever was best for Caitlin.'

'Well, we have, haven't we? And you can still see her. I mean, Rod's got a flat in London, you've got a house there, and you come over to the USA sometimes to make films.'

'Not so often – my ambitions have changed in the two years we've been apart, Kathleen. I see my future now mainly play-writing and maybe the odd cameo role.'

'Well, I suppose that's right for you. Go while you've still got what it takes.'

'Yes, but it means I'm the one with the stable home, while you're jetting about from one place to the next leaving Caitlin with a series of nannies. It would make more sense if she lived with me and came to you for holidays.'

'You're just jealous of Rod, because Caitlin likes him! You can't bear the idea of another man being her daddy!' said Kathleen, her voice rising. 'You only married me because I was pregnant!'

'I'm *glad* she likes Rod – I like Rod too, the poor harmless mutt. But I'm still her father, and I don't want her living on the other side of the world.'

'Well, I'm her mother, and you will just have to put up with it!' she exclaimed triumphantly.

'Not if I apply for custody. I know one or two things about you, Kathleen, that a judge might be interested in!' he said, his voice hard.

'Well here's something you didn't know,' Kathleen said with deadly venom. 'Caitlin isn't yours!'

At this interesting moment Caitlin galloped back into the kitchen, wearing her teddy suit and with her wellies on the wrong feet, so I quickly ushered her out of the cottage.

Behind me it had gone ominously silent, until I heard Mace say, in a quiet but carrying voice that brought goose bumps up on the back of my neck:

'What do you mean?'

Then I regretfully had to close the front door.

I began to feel sorry I'd never seen him act in anything.

Em was in the kitchen, and so, to my surprise, were the twins, perched on chairs with their arms up to the elbows in mixing bowls.

Frost and Flossie were in hopeful attendance, lightly dusted with flour.

'What are you making?' demanded Caitlin excitedly, bouncing up and down in her little flowered wellies.

'I'm making rock cakes, and Febe is making gingerbread,' Clo said importantly. 'Do you want to join in?'

I divested Caitlin of her teddy suit and wellies, wrapped her in a pinafore and stood her on a chair.

'You can make chocolate slab,' Em said, tossing digestive biscuits into another bowl. 'Here, take this rolling pin and bash these biscuits to pieces.'

'Where's everyone?' I asked Em as the girls beat the ingredients to death, squealing.

'Father's working. His agent's taken to calling him on an hourly basis, so he's finally shaken off the tart and got on with it. The said tart's gone off in a huff, shopping, but the girls didn't want to go.'

'I thought they liked shopping?'

'Seem to have gone off it – and they wouldn't put dresses on this morning, only jeans. She didn't like that, either.'

'Well, they're only children. You can't have much fun if you're trying to keep expensive clothes clean.'

'Anne's gone for her treatment, but she says she'll tell them some more stories later – and she's bringing them an effing *present*.'

We exchanged slightly incredulous stares.

'Bran's in his room, working – he's nearly fit to go back, I think. It's not long before he'll be home again for Christmas, anyway. Walter's watching the TV, and Gloria's in there too, with the ironing.'

How cosy it all sounded . . . and soon it will be Christmas – at home – without Matt!

'Mace was having an argument with his ex-wife when I came out,' I told her. 'She's beautiful, but even skinnier than Jess.'

'Gloria says Mace's reputation with women is terrible,' Em said.

'Does she? How does she know?'

'*Surprise!* magazine. She gets it every week. She doesn't like you going down there to look after Caitlin so she's going to read your tea leaves, to see if you're safe.'

'Of course I'm safe! I hardly think he's even registered that I'm a woman – just a useful version of the village idiot,' I assured her.

When I took Caitlin home, tired, grubby and with a cake tin of edible goodies for Daddy, there was no sign of the sports car or its glamorous occupant.

In its place was a battered motorbike, and the vicar and Mace were in earnest discussion in the kitchen.

It seemed a bit early for whisky.

It was certainly no time to explain about Dead Greg either, which was a pity, for in my brief absence someone had scrawled 'Murderess!' on the verandah windows in harpy-red lipstick.

Looked like Angie'd arrived.

Chapter 14

In Combat

Tips for Southern Visitors, no. 5:

People will be quite kind to you when they realise you are from the South, because you can't help it.

My painting of Jessica Down the Well is coming along nicely, and I have a little row of tiny primed white canvases awaiting my attention.

Jessie was not at her best this morning: first she kicked up a fuss because the washing she left in the machine last night had been decanted onto the floor, although she should have known from past experience that getting up early to take it out herself was her best option.

Then she made a bit of a scene at breakfast, when the twins showed her the presents Anne had brought them back from town, although they were only new outfits for their Barbies.

The girls' dolls were now fetchingly attired in army fatigues *à la* Action Man.

'They don't do Action Woman yet,' explained Febe earnestly, 'or Anne would have got those, but these fit okay. Anne usually buys men's clothes anyway, especially waistcoats, because you need loose, practical clothes in a war zone. See – my Barbie's wearing a flak jacket.'

'And mine's got army boots on, and when we get home from school, Anne's going to help us to camouflage their helmets with grass and twigs!' said Clo eagerly.

'But Barbies aren't soldiers,' Jessica said earnestly. 'And Action Man is for little boys!'

'But I've just explained – these are Action *Women*,' said Febe impatiently. 'Really, Mummy!'

'But Mummy's always taught you that war is wrong!'

'Yes, but if it happens, someone's got to report it, haven't they?' Febe said sensibly. 'Anne goes on the TV. When she's better she's going back, and then we can see her on the news!'

'Mummy,' wheedled Clo. 'Could I have a Movie Director Barbie?'

Thrown off balance, Jessica said, with relief: 'Of course, darling! That will be much more fun, won't it?'

'Oh yes – then *my* Barbie can be the camerawoman recording Febe's Barbie for TV,' Clo agreed.

'Call your sister Phoebe, Chloe. I don't like these abbreviations.'

'Clo, Mummy. And Phoebe's always going to be Febe now: we've decided.'

That was the final straw and Jessica forbade them to have anything more to do with Anne, a condition impossible to impose in the circumstances.

Father had had enough by then, and said he was glad to discover the twins were not just the brainless, giggling little imbeciles he'd thought them, and then Jessica turned on him and tried to have a row.

Father doesn't like rows, so he scowled and went off into his study, locking the door; so at least he will get some work done today.

'Em, can we have treacle tart and cream tonight?' wheedled Clo. 'It's my favouritest pudding in all the world.'

'And mine,' agreed Febe. 'Mummy, Em calls you the Treacle Tart – is that because *you're* scrumptious, too?'

'No, it's because she's dark and sticky,' Em said, smiling.

Bran, who'd been sitting silently stirring sugar into his porridge in slow motion, looked up and answered the smile. 'Sticky pudding?'

'After dinner,' Em said.

'I don't know what your problem is, Jess,' Anne said, from behind the newspaper. 'You don't want them to grow up thinking being a giraffe-necked blonde bimbo is the height of ambition, do you?'

Jessica is sulking again. Em might be about to win the battle after all.

*

100

I have packed up my black clothes and Gloria is going to take them to a charity shop. I wear my jumble-sale finds now, and a crocheted cardigan in multicoloured yarn that Gloria made for me, in a pattern of daisies in squares.

Other than my cardigan I seem to be moving towards the sea-green and silver spectrum, which I suppose is more suitable to a cool and fishy Pisces than black.

Horrorscopes: what your star sign says about you!

PISCES are cool: watch them slither off on their own business just when you thought you'd caught them in a net of the mundane. But don't worry, there's nothing scaly about them and they always return home to spawn.

Mace was definitely taciturn next morning, but that was all right because Caitlin talked enough for all of us. I don't suppose he is brooding over what his ex-wife said, though, because it was probably something she thought up in the heat of the moment.

He does seem to be a devoted daddy, whatever Gloria says about his reputation, while I cannot say I was impressed by Kathleen's maternal instincts. But clearly she's got some, or she wouldn't want to take Caitlin to America with her.

Mace sort of loomed in the kitchen doorway and glowered while I helped Caitlin into her teddy suit and made sure her wellies were on the right feet.

'Take her out for a walk,' he ordered, like she was a dog.

'That's what I intended doing,' I snapped. After all, *I* hadn't done anything to make him mad – yet. Not perhaps the most opportune time to confess about Dead Greg?

We left him stewing in his own juice (Tartar sauce?) and I took Caitlin up to Ramshaw Heights in the car, feeling in need of the air and exercise and a space in which to compose my explanation to Mace about Greg, before Angie broadcast it to all. It had to be done sometime.

Em is going to try and find out where she is staying, by one means or the other: better not to ask.

She did take the vicar some jam, and he said he'd treasure it forever, though I hope he doesn't because it'll go mouldy. She didn't tell me what he said about *Womanly Wicca Words of*

Spiritual Comfort, but she looked thoughtful when she came home.

I left Flossie behind, snoozing noisily, but with the Parsonage door open at the top of the stairs in case she woke and fancied company. She likes a touch of Frost, in small doses.

At first Caitlin walked quietly by my side through the lightly iced woodland, pulling me to a halt from time to time in order to point out some marvel.

'This,' she announced importantly, 'is rabbit poop, and this is sheep poop, and this is dog poop.'

Feeling some answer was expected of me I said vaguely: 'Oh?'

'But I don't know what squirrel poop looks like,' she went on, satisfied that she had my full attention. 'And there are lots of squirrels here, so there should be some. I wonder where it is?'

'Under the trees?' I suggested. 'Though I suppose they're swinging from tree to tree, or whatever they do, and let fly at the same time, so it will be scattered everywhere.'

Caitlin giggled. 'We could be showered in squirrel poop at any minute! I'll tell you a joke,' she added.

'Go on.'

'What's got a hazelnut in every bite?'

'I don't know. What *has* got a hazelnut in every bite?'

'Squirrel shit!' she said, laughing like a hyena.

I recalled that Sylvia Plath used to walk in the woods at Hardcastle Crags, not so very far away, and write poetry. Either she didn't have her children with her at the time, or she was much better at blanking out small, piercing voices.

We wound our way up along the valley and came out high up where you could look way, way down from the jutting rocks.

'I like you,' Caitlin announced unexpectedly. 'You don't say things like: "Get away from the edge of that rock this minute, Caitlin!"'

Startled and guilty I realised that her wind-whipped slight form was precariously balanced near the edge of a slab of rock.

'Of course, that's the sort of thing I should be saying, isn't it? Only I'm not used to children, so I forget.'

'I'll remind you – after I've done it. I don't go right to the edge anyway, because Daddy let me once, while he was holding my hand, and I felt like I wanted to jump off and whirl round and round like a sycamore helicopter. Only Daddy said I'd plummet straight down like a conker, and when I got to the bottom I'd be spread out like raspberry jam, so it wouldn't be worth it.'

'Er – no,' I agreed.

'And he'd be very angry with me,' she added, as a clincher.

'Does he often get angry?' I asked tentatively.

She giggled: 'Yes, but not with me. Mostly with people on the telephone, and magazines when they tell fibs about him. And Mummy,' she added. 'He's a big grumpy bear.'

'This is a long walk, isn't it? What have you got in your pockets?' I asked, hoping for sweets, even old fluffy ones.

'What's it got in its pocketses?' she screeched. 'I've got *Lord of the Rings* on tape, and Gollum hisses and says that, and when I first heard it I had nightmares every night for a week!'

'I'm not surprised – it's too old for you.'

'No it's not. I could read it now. I can read *anything*. I can read the newspapers.'

'I wouldn't bother. The only interesting women they ever tell you about are in the obituaries.'

Still, that explained her wide vocabulary. Not having much experience with small children I'd assumed all the others at the nursery were a bit dim, but maybe that was just in contrast to Caitlin?

'My brother, Bran, could read when he was two, and he learned French from a set of old Linguaphone records when he was four,' I told her, but she didn't seem noticeably impressed.

'Those people over there are snogging.'

'Kissing. Snogging's not really a nice word.'

'I snogged Joel last week, but I didn't like it, so I'm not going to do it again.'

'It's a pity *I* didn't think of that earlier.'

'Not snogging, because you don't like it?'

"Not doing anything twice that I didn't like the first time.'

'But sometimes you have to do things you don't like,' she pointed out like a miniature philosopher. 'Daddy usually manages not to do the things he doesn't like, but then sometimes it makes other people cross.'

'Yes, that's the price you have to pay.' I held my hand out. 'Come on, let's get back to the car – we've got time to stop for a hot chocolate with whipped cream on the way back if we run!'

*

103

Mace greeted us at the cottage door, and he didn't look any more cheerful than when we left.

He silently handed me a note on horribly familiar blue paper, and stood there, arms crossed across his broad chest, watching me read it.

Light blue touchpaper and retire.

You are trusting your innocent child to a murdering whore! it said, rather predictably.

'Is it true?' he asked, (quite mildly, considering) as Caitlin ran off past him into the house, her teddy-bear ears flapping.

'Which bit?' I said brightly, wishing I'd got in first with the explanation.

'The murdering bit. I can see the possibilities of the other myself, now you aren't dressed like a small perambulating Bedouin bag-wash any more.'

I scowled at him. 'I meant to tell you, but you didn't seem in the mood for conversation this morning.'

'You were going to tell me you were a murderer?'

'Of course not. I didn't murder him, it was an accident – ask the vicar!'

'*Chris* knows about this?'

'Yes, I told him when he caught me hitting melons the other day, although actually I've given it up now.'

'Murder?'

'Hitting melons. You see, I accidentally hit Angie's husband, Greg, with a frying pan, and he died, and Angie – that's who sent you the letter – is a bit upset about it, and she's followed me here. I don't know why she keeps calling me a whore though, because I didn't lead him on – I haven't led anyone on, except my ex-husband, and look where that got me.'

He stared at me. 'I find your conversation curiously oblique, but I think I've got the gist – and,' he added thoughtfully, 'I'm not altogether sure I still fancy that ginger and melon jam your sister Em presented me with.'

'We had to do *something* with the melons. They're very dear just now.'

'Yes, I can see that.'

I sighed. 'Well, I don't suppose you will be wanting me to come and fetch Caitlin tomorrow?'

'Why, you aren't likely to hit her with a frying pan, too, are you?'

'Certainly not! I like Caitlin – even *Em* likes Caitlin. I wouldn't hurt a hair on her head.'

'No, that's what I thought. We will carry on as before, then, and I'll keep my melons hidden when you're around,' he said, with one of his sudden, absolutely demoralising smiles.

I wish he wouldn't do that.

'I told you I'd given melon-bashing up.'

'So you did,' he said, still smiling: a ravaging horde in his own right.

On the way back to the cottage I tried to remember exactly what he'd said about whores and Bedouin washing to see whether I'd been insulted or not.

I would have immediately asked Em's opinion, but Xanthe Skye was sitting in the kitchen with her, eating rich fruit cake and drinking something green out of a Russian tea glass.

I stopped in the doorway. 'Is my aura all right today?'

Xanthe examined the air around me with an expert gaze. 'A bit sultry dear, but no blue.'

'Oh good,' I said, coming further in. 'The sultry bit's probably because Mace's found out about Dead Greg, Em. He's had a poison-pen letter from Angie.'

Dead Greg was clearly no surprise to Xanthe, but of course all the people who *matter* in Upvale will know, they just won't drag it into the conversation.

'How did he take it?' Em asked, cutting me a slice of cake.

I considered. 'Quite well, really, I suppose.' And I recounted what he'd said as well as I could remember it.

Had I known Gloria was within earshot I'd have left the whore bit out. She bounced out of the nearest scullery:

'Cheeky bugger!' she said. 'You don't want to go near that one, he's *wicked*!'

Xanthe sighed. 'He certainly is!' she agreed dreamily.

Gloria gave her a look.

'At least you won't be going to look after his little girl now.'

'Yes I will. I told him Dead Greg was an accident.'

'I hope you told him you're not a whore as well!' she said tartly. 'Or that your sister would be, if he gave her half a chance.'

'That's enough, Gloria,' Em said firmly. 'There aren't any whores these days, everyone's at it, apparently – except me. And I only want to utilise him on a temporary basis, while Charlie is only interested in his money.'

'He's not for either of you,' Gloria said, glowering. 'I know what I've seen in the tea leaves.'

'Earl Grey?' enquired Xanthe interestedly.

Chapter 15
Taken Out

Anne gave me an article she'd written for *Skint Old Northern Woman*, to be published anonymously, which read more like one of her war correspondent reports than anything. But I was deeply touched by it, and felt I understood Anne more than I'd ever done before.

Health Check, no. 2: The Body as Battlefield: One Woman's Fight Against the Big C

As a war correspondent I'm fit and healthy, but battle-scarred. Any threat to my health I always expected to come from outside, but this time I carry a war-wound caused by a traitor within myself: cancer.

The enemy sneaked in and set up an advance position in the form of a small lump in my left breast, hoping to go unnoticed until reinforcements were well entrenched.

However, fortune favours the flat-chested: when you have boobs like two fried eggs even a tiny bump stands out like a beacon.

Even then, I just assumed it was a troublesome cyst – there was nothing impressive about something the size and shape of a petit pois under the skin. But within two days I found myself diagnosed with malignant cancer, and offered a range of exciting clinical procedures.

I opted for a lumpectomy, and with amazing speed was summoned to hospital where the surgeon circled the little bugger and whipped it out, also taking a gland or two from under the arm to check for any spread to the lymph glands.

The arm was sorer than the boob, but the glands showed negative for cancer spread, so it was worth it.

The outlook was good, but six weeks of radiotherapy was advised as back-up, which I accepted. It's no big deal.

Then they offered me the drug Tamoxifen, 'just in case'. You take it for ten years, and when I asked if it had any side-effects they gave me a leaflet to read.

The possible side-effects included hot flushes, skin rashes, genital itching, menstrual disorders, breast pain, hair loss, weakness, muscle and joint pain, and sickness.

This didn't sound like a whole lot of fun, but then I turned the leaflet over and found the possible serious side effects: liver problems, yellowing of the skin and eyes, visual disturbances, feverishness and unusual bruising and bleeding of the skin.

After a brief exchange of views on the matter (I told them to stuff it where the sun don't shine, they told me I was very lucky to be offered the drug at all), I elected to decline it.

Lessons I learned from this experience are: 1) Watch your back (and your boobs). 2) Don't rush into anything, but study your position carefully and weigh up the options. 3) Don't panic – you need a clear head to fight and survive. 4) If you've got all the facts, you are as expert as anyone else and can make your own decisions. 5) Your operation scar's just as much a battle scar as any other, and you don't need to be ashamed of it.

Finally, number six is: Live each day like it's all you've got. I've always done that anyway – today is the only day we can be sure of. Don't waste it.

'Anne,' I said, 'the magazine isn't going to be published at all – I'm just doing this for fun.'

'Yes it is, Em and I will see to that. It's the sort of thing that should be published, if only once.'

'That's right,' Em agreed from the other end of the kitchen table. 'I've got the advance from my book, and Anne's got some savings, and we're putting it into the first and possibly only edition of *Skint Old Northern Woman* magazine – or comic. Susie says it might turn out looking a bit more like *Viz* than *Woman's Own*. I've got lots of pieces written for it already.'

She bent her head back over her cookery books. 'Do you think duck pâte would be good as the starter tomorrow?'

'Do your vichyssoise soup. Everyone likes it, and it's cold, so it doesn't matter what time you eat it,' Anne said.

'Yes, but listen you two,' I interrupted. 'I can't possibly let you pay for the magazine to be published. It won't sell enough to pay for itself, and you might need the money!'

'We think *Skint Old Northern Woman* should exist,' Em said. 'If only briefly. And that's that. The rest of the discussion group are coming round here tonight to help sort out which articles go where, and Susie's bringing her sister, Jen, to help us – the one who works for the small publisher.'

'He's a little man?' Anne asked, interested.

'No, he's small as in not a huge publishing house. But efficient. We can have it out before Christmas.'

'Bloody fast, Em!'

'That's modern technology for you – stuff it in one end, out comes the finished product at the other.'

'I think there might be a bit more to it than that,' I said feebly. 'Besides, you can't have a magazine without pictures.'

'We'll have that painting you've just finished – 'Jessie Down the Well' – on the front cover,' Em said.

'Yes, and Susie's done some good cartoons. That should do it,' added Anne. 'There you are. All sorted, Chaz.'

'You don't think Mace or the vicar is vegetarian, do you?' asked Em, getting back to business.

'Mace looks like a meat eater to me, Em,' Anne said.

'When did *you* meet him, Anne?' I asked curiously.

'Out and about – don't spend all my time in bloody bed. And the vicar came to see me – don't know why. I quite fancied him, but he's got the hots for old Em.'

'Chris isn't vegetarian,' murmured Em, absently thumbing through Mrs Beeton. 'Can I do roast beef and Yorkshire pudding?'

'You certainly can, better than anyone,' I said enthusiastically.

'No, I meant, because of the Mad Cow – that Jessie won't touch it for a start.'

'She won't touch anything with calories in anyway, she's even started saying the bubbles in fizzy mineral water make you fat,' I said.

'And everyone probably thinks we're the Mad Cows already,' sniggered Anne. 'Go for it, Em.'

'Right. And sticky toffee pudding with custard afterwards –

men like their stodgy puds.' She closed the book. 'There. That's that. I'm off to the shops. Shouldn't you be off to get Caitlin, Charlie?'

I jumped. 'Oh yes, of course. I thought we could both paint in the verandah today so I've set the small easel up next to mine for her.'

'There are iced rabbit biscuits in the Beatrix Potter tin – take them down with you. But not the frog ones, they're for Bran.'

'Okay. Thanks, Em.'

'And I'm off to the hospital,' Anne said, pulling herself up.

'The meeting's tonight at eight, after dinner,' Em reminded me. 'In here.'

I didn't try to protest any more: if Anne and Em were determined *Skint Old Northern Woman* would live, then live it would, and I started to feel quite excited.

We see the tip of history's iceberg.
Entombed in the deep belly
the women's mouths move
silently.
From 'Words from the Spirit' by Serafina Shane

I don't know why Gloria felt that I should beware of Mace, because he has never shown the slightest tendency to drag me into his lair and ravish me, which would be slightly difficult with Caitlin in the offing anyway.

I think he is more in danger of Em dragging him into *her* lair: if she makes her mind up she is likely to pounce should she get an opportunity. Still, I think she also finds Chris attractive too, if she can only get over his double handicap of Christianity and the love of Dickens.

Mace did not even emerge from his study when I got there this morning. Caitlin was ready and waiting for me.

I painted 'Caitlin in the Rainforest', and Caitlin painted 'Charlie with Blue Hair'. Time flew past on hummingbird wings, and before we knew it Mace had come knock, knock, knocking on heaven's door, and entered our paradise like a particularly beautiful, but potentially dangerous, snake.

Smooth and fatal, sums him up pretty well, really.

Caitlin proudly showed him her picture.

110

'It's a speaking likeness,' he said solemnly. 'Especially the hair.'

'Yes it is,' Caitlin said severely. 'You aren't looking properly, but Charlie showed me: look at Charlie's hair.'

He turned his oblique, midnight-velvet stare on me, and I shifted a bit under the searching scrutiny.

'It's very pretty – and unusual. Silvery hair combined with dark eyes, eyebrows and eyelashes – different.'

'It's natural,' I said coldly.

Caitlin tugged impatiently at his arm: 'You're not looking properly, is he Charlie? The blue paintwork is reflecting onto it so she's got *blue* hair.'

'You're right,' he said, after another minute inspection. 'And there *is* a blue-green light up one side of her face, from the plants. If she weren't wearing jeans, she'd look like a wood nymph.'

'It's not good enough to look, you have to *see*,' Caitlin said importantly.

I hope *I* didn't sound that bossy.

Mace walked around me and stood close enough to radiate body heat, gazing down at my canvas. 'It's amazing how like Caitlin that is, even though she is so tiny in the middle of it. Clearly Caitlin . . .' he added quietly. 'Herself – there's nothing of me in there.'

'No, she doesn't look like you or her mother,' I agreed. 'Though she has got your eyes.'

Then I suddenly remembered what his ex-wife had said about Caitlin not being his . . . though surely he hadn't believed that?

'Anyone could have dark blue eyes,' he said.

Surprised, I twisted and looked up into his brooding face: 'Well no, they couldn't – didn't you do genetics at school? Besides, yours are a real dark navy blue, and you don't often see that.'

He smiled like the sun coming out over the High Atlas and said unexpectedly: 'I think I'll take you out for lunch.'

'Oh yes!' Caitlin agreed. 'Let's take Charlie!'

'Thanks,' I said, somewhat taken aback. 'But I—'

I stopped and swallowed. Well, *you* try being invited to lunch by Mace North and finding an excuse on the spur of the moment.

And *part* of me wanted to go. I suspect it's the same bit that always wanted to drag the young gardener, Steve, behind the shrubbery.

111

'Were you doing something else?' he enquired, employing the ultimate weapon: the 'I'm going to abduct you on horseback, and carry you off to my tent – you don't mind, do you?' smile.

'No,' I conceded weakly.

Barbarian hordes, sweep me away.

'Get your coat,' Barbarian Horde said practically.

I was *so* glad to see that he wasn't wearing the red duvet today.

'So my little chicken's been going out with that actor,' Gloria Mundi said, parting the silver fronds of my fringe and peering searchingly into my eyes.

'What? Did you?' Anne said, surprised. 'Well, bugger me! Does Em know?'

'I didn't go *out* sort of out. I just had a pub lunch with him and Caitlin. I think he asked me on impulse.'

'Drink this tea,' Gloria said, thrusting a cup into my hands. 'I need to see what's coming to pass.'

'I don't feel like a cup of tea, thanks, Gloria. The discussion group will be here any minute, and I've got to fetch the magazine stuff up from the Summer Cottage.'

She stood over me, though, until I drained the cup, and then spent long minutes staring down into the tea leaves and muttering.

The coven might dismiss her as a mere wisewoman, but I'm sure she knows a lot more than any of them. She just doesn't share it, even with Em.

'Dead Greg's widow's staying at Hoo House with the other loonies,' Em said coming in. 'Inga's up in arms – said I'd made her employ a "muwdwess".'

'Charlie's nicked your actor,' Anne said helpfully.

'Someone dark and strange is entering her life ... bringing change and trouble,' agreed Gloria, taking another doubtful look into the teacup. 'Storm clouds are gathering.'

'That might be Angie. She's naturally dark, she just dyes her hair, and she's certainly strange.'

'I've got *no* hair,' chipped in Walter, who was quietly rocking away by the stove, carving another walking-stick head. 'No bodily hair what-so-ever.'

'And there's the Treacle Tart, too. She and Father have made it up, and they're even more all over each other than before.'

'It's a man,' Gloria said with certainty. She tilted the cup as though some trick of the light might show her something better.

'And I see a child . . . but—' she broke off, frowning.

'What?' I demanded.

'Never you mind.'

'They do a good lunch over at the Stone Cross,' Em said.

'How did you . . .?'

'Freya. In the back room with her lover.'

'You don't mind, do you, Em? It didn't mean anything, they were going anyway, and just sort of took me along. I don't want another man even if Mace is interested in me that way, which he isn't. Anyway, he's a bit scary.'

'He does have a deliciously dark edge to him,' Em agreed. 'That's why he seems so much more suited to my purpose than Chris. I need the love of a Bad Man. We'll see tomorrow night. The way to a man's heart is through his stomach, so I'm going to mix a potion up that will make him appreciate me. Gloria, you're in charge of seeing it gets in the right glass of sherry before dinner, and I don't want any more of that "he's not for you" business, right?'

'Right,' conceded Gloria, with unusual meekness. 'I'll see to that for you, don't you worry. And if you don't want that vicar, I could see that he falls for Anne instead?'

'No,' Em said quickly. 'No, I'm enjoying the novelty of having a Barkis, even if he's the wrong one, and Anne doesn't really want anyone just now. Do you, Anne?'

'No, just want to get fit and back to work. Besides, Red's phoned me up.'

'Red? But you wouldn't have him back, would you?'

'Might. Never trusted him in the first place, but damn good in the sack. I'll think about it.'

'There's that Freya at the door,' Gloria said absently, and I didn't ask how she knew. 'I'll be fetching the ice in.'

I noticed she took my teacup out with her.

We were there until nearly midnight putting the magazine more or less in order, with Jen to tell us what was and wasn't possible.

It was hard work, but I think we've got it right, and Jen's taken my painting of Jess Down the Well for the cover.

Susie's cartoons are great.

Gloria hung around most of the evening, giving me strange,

furtive, sideways looks, so goodness knows what she saw in the tea leaves.

But whatever it was, it certainly wasn't anything romantic, since that part of me has atrophied away to nothing. I confess to faint lustful pangs sometimes when I think of Mace North, but that is more just the last stirring of dying embers, and is balanced out by the slight frisson of terror he also somehow manages to inspire in me.

Probably half the female population of the English-speaking world feels the same way, since without being in any way a hunk, he is still the sort of man women look at and wonder about the body beneath the clothes.

Mmm . . .

When we were tossing filler article suggestions about, Gloria suddenly said she had a winter tip for southern visitors: *Never eat yellow snow.*

Well, thank you for that one, Gloria.

Chapter 16

Going Hairless

On the Friday of Father's birthday, everyone was preoccupied at breakfast, and immediately afterwards went their separate ways. (Rhymers don't do cards and presents, they have Feasts instead.)

Branwell is pretty much recovered, but he has received dispensation from his university to stay at home until after Christmas and put the finishing touches to his Great Work. There wasn't much term left anyway; universities seem to spend more time off than on.

Father abandoned *his* nearly finished book and went out somewhere with Jessica, dropping the girls at school en route. Jessica was upset at breakfast because she had put two pounds on, and wouldn't eat anything at all, just drank black coffee, which Em said she'd probably sick straight back up again if she got the chance. (But I think she was joking.)

I couldn't see any sign of the two pounds either, but I suppose that's sort of like three extra layers of skin all over her little bird bones.

Anne vanished for her mysterious treatment, Emily readied herself for a mammoth cooking session, Walter went off into the dining room to polish all the glasses, and Gloria disappeared into the back scullery to brew mysterious potions.

She still had my teacup from last night in there with her when I looked, with a 'do not wash this cup' sticker on the side. I couldn't make anything of it, except that it was drying out like dark dandruff.

While I was getting ready to fetch Caitlin, Flossie emerged from her igloo and intimated that she wouldn't mind coming too, which was a surprise: extra exercise seems to be paying off.

We set off happily enough, but then some primal instinct made me look over my shoulder just in time to spot Angie, turning the Parsonage corner and starting down the track.

Call me a coward, but I did not feel in the least like a screaming match at forty paces, so I scooped Flossie right up off her flat, furry little feet and ran, bursting into Mace's house unheralded and panting.

Flossie may be a bit thinner and fitter, but she's still heavy.

Mace, elegantly disposed on the window seat with a cup in one hand like a soigné coffee advert, raised a surprised eyebrow.

'Come in, why don't you?'

'Sorry,' I panted, dumping Flossie on the rug. 'Angie – Dead Greg's widow – chasing me.'

Flossie, wagging her tail, ambled over and stuck her wet nose up his trouser leg.

'Brazen hussy,' he said, reaching down to pat her domed and silky skull, inside which precious little went on. 'I don't let girls do that until the second date, and we hardly know each other.'

'That's not what Gloria says,' I commented unthinkingly.

He stared at me: 'I don't remember any Gloria.'

'Perhaps you haven't met her? She's ... she helps ...' I stopped. There *is* no way of describing Gloria and Walter's roles. 'She's Walter's sister.'

'*Two* old retainers? Well, well! And what does Gloria base her estimate of my character on?'

'Tea leaves. Oh – and *Surprise!* magazine.'

His face darkened alarmingly: 'Never mention that evil, slime-spreading rag again in my presence!'

'Why? What's the matter with it?'

We were interrupted by a sudden hammering on the door. 'Come out you murdering witch – I know you're in there!' screeched Angie.

I thought of those long, blood-red talons reaching out for me, shuddered and backed away, but Mace got up.

'What are you doing?'

'Opening the door,' he said calmly.

I darted in front of him clutching at him with both hands. He simply swept me behind him like I weighed nothing, and turned the handle.

I peered around him; Angie, poised for another onslaught at the

116

knocker, overbalanced and fell forward onto the path, where she stared up at him between witch-locks of violently auburn hair.

'Can I help you?' he asked politely.

The transformation from raging, unbalanced harpy to normal-if-drooling fan was astonishing in a science-fiction, shape-changing sort of way. Maybe the aliens were at it again? Probably recruited her at the same time as Matt.

'You're Mace North, aren't you? I loved you in *One Midsummer Night*, and – aargh!'

She flung herself frantically back as a clatter of hooves heralded Elfreda Whippington-Smythe's sudden advent. Her large and expensive horse slid to a stone-rattling halt and stood steaming, reeking and rolling its eyes, vast hooves inches away from Angie.

'Oh Mace,' Elfreda gasped, wrestling with the reins as her mount jerked its head up and down. Her little round boiled-goose-berry eyes under the pulled-down hat zoomed in on her quarry. I don't think she noticed anyone else was there.

'Hef you heard? That Charlie Rhymer's an actual murderess! Inga at the nursery—' She stopped as some elements of the tableaux before her finally registered. 'Oh ... you're there, Charlie?'

I stood on tiptoe and peeped around Mace, who was still holding me behind his back like a secret present. 'Yes, the murderess in person – and this is Inga's guest.' I indicated Angie, momentarily silenced. 'The murderee's widow.'

In the face of a new, expanded audience, Angie gave it her all: 'She killed my husband! She led him on, and then killed him when he made a pass at her!'

'I killed him, but I certainly didn't lead him on!' I said indignantly. 'He sneaked into my house and assaulted me, and his death was an accident.'

'An accident? You hit him with a cast-iron pan!'

'It dropped on his head, and I've got an unimpeachable witness to prove it.'

'If you mean that batty old cow who lived opposite you, she'd say anything.'

'Don't speak like that about one of my best friends!' I said furiously, trying to duck under Mace's arm, but he held me back with muscles like iron.

'I just thought you ought to be warned about the woman

117

looking after your child,' Elfreda said to him stuffily. 'Especially after what she did to Gunilla at the nursery.'

'She didn't do anything to Gunilla. It was the other way around, and *I* have an eyewitness to that one – Caitlin,' Mace said pleasantly. 'But thank you for the warning, Mrs Whippington-Smythe. How nice of you to rally to a helpless man's defence.'

She stared at him, went faintly pink, and kick-started her nag into movement. 'I wouldn't have bothered if I'd known you were under her spell already,' she said nastily, and jolted away like a sack of potatoes. King Edward's.

'What spell? I haven't *done* any spell!' I yelled indignantly, trying again to release myself and get around Mace.

'*Will* you be still?' he said exasperatedly over his shoulder, then turned back to Angie. 'I'm so sorry about your husband, but I'm sure Charlie didn't mean to kill him – it was clearly an accident – and if you persist in trying to blacken her name like this there is a law in this country she can use to stop you. Haven't you got a life of your own to lead, without a hate campaign?'

'Life? No – I *had* a good life, and we were going to Japan after Christmas! And there isn't even a proper pension, and the insurance are hanging back on paying out, and to top it all, the squirrels are an Act of God! And it's all because of that innocent-looking bitch behind you.'

'I don't think you can blame the squirrels on me, Angie,' I protested. She ignored me, her voice rising:

'She hasn't always looked like that, you know. When she killed my husband she looked like the vamp she is!'

'Goth,' I corrected. 'Different thing. I'm sorry about, well, about everything, Angie. Can't you just let it rest and get on with life?'

'Never,' she said, turning away. 'You just wait, Charlie Rhymer. I'm going to make sure your name is like mud, stinking mud, around here.'

'You could get her stopped,' Mace said, pushing me back in and closing the door.

'Anyone who matters around here knows already. The incomers are the only ones who won't have heard yet.'

'Like me? Don't *I* matter?'

'Well, yes, but I *was* going to tell you. Angie just got to you first. You can let go of me now,' I added pointedly.

'I'm not sure I dare – you've got quite a temper.'

'I don't think I even register as a blip on the Mace North scale of temper, and anyway, I'm not angry with *you*.'

He gazed down at me, his grip tightening rather than letting go . . .

'People were shouting, Daddy,' Caitlin said, pushing the door open with a large bag from which spilled clothes, teddy bears and hair ribbons in artless profusion. 'Why are you holding Charlie?'

'To stop her flying off.'

Caitlin giggled. 'Like a fairy?'

'Something like that. Don't you think it's a bit early to pack?' Mace said mildly.

Caitlin was to have tea with the twins and stay the night, while the grown-ups had dinner in a civilised manner – though actually no Rhymer Birthday Feast had ever quite managed that yet.

'Perhaps Charlie wouldn't mind going upstairs and helping you to repack it a bit?'

'If we're not disturbing you?'

'I find you constantly disturbing, especially since you've given up the widow's weeds: but if you mean will it stop me writing, then no. I've come to one of those patches in the play where nothing goes right, and I need a break.'

I stared at him uncertainly, but he was looking so Mr Rochester that I suppressed the impulse to bleat out: 'What do you mean, disturbing?' and just followed Caitlin up to her room, where I repacked her case, and calmed her down a bit – she was wildly excited about spending the night with two big girls like Febe and Clo.

'What sort of clothes should my Barbie take?'

'Practical ones. Clo and Febe's Barbies are not really party animals these days.'

'Ski wear?' she pondered.

'As long as it's not a red duvet, like your daddy's.'

She giggled. 'Daddy calls it his duvet now, too!'

Daddy, six-four of soft, downy vermilion, went out for a walk with us later, thus entirely defeating the reason for employing me to entertain Caitlin in the first place. But he said he needed to stretch his legs and think.

We climbed right up to the beacon, and although I'm not sure how the conversation took such a turn, I ended up telling him all about *Skint Old Northern Woman*; only I called it a comic, since he seemed to have an acute aversion to the word 'magazine'. He said he'd order a dozen copies and send them to all his friends for Christmas.

I do not have a dozen friends. Come to that, apart from family (in which I include Walter and Gloria) Miss Grinch, and possibly Vaddie at the gallery, I'm not sure I've got any at all.

'You need an arts page,' he suggested. 'A sort of "What's On in the North".'

'"What's On in the North That's Worth Parting With Brass to See",' I corrected.

'Did you know there's a sort of natural amphitheatre in the rocks above the stream in the woods?' he asked. 'It reminded me of the Minack outdoor theatre at Porthcurno in Cornwall. You could start a campaign to have summer theatre there.'

'Yes, I know where you mean. It's on Madge's land, too, so her old dad could charge everyone going in.' And out, knowing him.

'You could have local people as the actors, like the Passion Play at Oberammergau.'

'Or a Shakespeare a year . . . in the vernacular!' I enthused. 'I can see it now: "Enter Hamlet – he were a short, stiff man with no hair or eyebrows." Or "Romeo, Romeo, thou art got a right poncey name, flower."'

'That kind of thing,' he agreed, grinning. 'I could direct it.'

'I don't suppose you will be spending that much time here.'

'I intend spending as much time in Upvale as I can, though I'll have to keep my London house on, as well. Upvale and the moors have got to me, in a way Haworth never did.'

'Don't mention Haworth – or the Brontës,' I shuddered. 'My brother and sisters and I are the result of a failed Brontë experiment.'

Then I described Father's attempt to replicate the conditions that had turned the sisters – or, in Father's opinion, the brother – into literary geniuses.

'So he chose a similar area, not too far away as the crow flies, and settled there with my mother. She's Lally Tooke, have you heard of her? She went to America, and she's *very* big on the radical feminist literature circuit – and they had Em and Anne and me. And by then their opinions of the Brontës had turned in opposing directions, Mother discovered that she hated childbirth, and wasn't that mad about children, and she bolted. Father carried on, since it made the situation more authentic, after all, especially after our first au pair had Branwell, and made the numbers up. But none of us was brilliant except Bran, and he is a genius of a different kind.'

'I met Bran in the pub with your father,' he said. 'Well, I say met, but we didn't seem to be speaking the same language.'

'Not many people do.'

'Probably not. I've also had a close encounter with your other sister, Anne. She said she thought I would strip well.'

I choked: 'I think she just means you look like you'd be a good man in a fight.'

'Let's hope it won't come to that – I think she'd win.'

By the time we got back it had been a longer walk than I'd intended, and Caitlin was ready for a snooze before being brought to the Parsonage.

There was no sign of Angie, except for something very rude scrawled across my door in spray paint, which Walter had already half-obliterated with Mediterranean Blue.

'I seen 'un off,' he said. 'I were up the back chopping firewood, and come to see what she were up to. She screamed and run off.'

'Were you still holding the axe, Walter?'

He nodded. 'Aye, that'll be it. Still, t'door wanted another coat.'

'Yes – it'll look lovely, Walter. You're very kind to me.'

He beamed. 'Don't you worry about the mad lady – Em's going to set them three witches on her.'

That should be interesting.

Father wandered into the kitchen, removed several candles from the top of his birthday cake, tossed them into the bin, and wandered out again, muttering darkly.

'I told you he wouldn't like the right number on it,' I said. 'Has anyone told Jessica how many it *really* is? He's wearing well for his age, but he's still getting on a bit.'

'Dining room's ready,' Anne said, appearing. 'Girls are in bed listening to that story tape I got them.'

'I thought Jessica confiscated *Rambo: Tocsin of Terror*?'

'Ho bleeding ho,' said Anne. 'Lion, the Witch and the effing Wardrobe. They've got a load of biscuits, pop, and stuff. Said they were going to have a midnight feast.'

121

'I don't think any of them will last as long as midnight, and let's hope they aren't sick.'

'Em,' I said cautiously, looking at the hem of the magnificent amber velvet gown in which she strode about like a queen: 'I don't think gorilla slippers go with that dress.'

'It's that or boots.'

'No it isn't – bare feet would be better. And you look amazing – it could have been made for you.'

'You've all scrubbed up nice,' Gloria agreed, coming in with a furtive air and secreting something away in the pocket of her pinafore. 'I thought you were going to wear that lovely green dress, Charlie?'

'I think it's a bit much – I couldn't decide. It's very *wispy* for the middle of winter.'

'You go and put it on this minute,' Gloria ordered as the Parsonage doorbell sounded. 'That's your father's guests now.'

'Oh, all right, Gloria.'

Em said: 'You know what you're to do, Gloria, don't you?'

'Don't you worry, Gloria knows what she's doing.' She looked severely at me as I hovered on the stairs. 'Scat!'

I ran down and quickly changed into Felicity Hake-Hackett's rejected Tinkerbell costume and strappy sandals.

There is one thing Felicity and I have in common besides being the runts of our respective families: we may be skinny, but we both have busts. This dress showed more of mine than I thought I'd got.

And thank God I'd already lawnmowered my legs and armpits even though it *was* winter when you're usually glad of the extra warmth in Upvale. Otherwise, I'd have been much, much later.

Skint Old Beauty, no. 1: Going Hairless

One of Nature's most cruel pranks is the way that, after forty, she starts to thin the hair on your head, while over-compensating by causing a sort of angora body stocking to gradually envelop the rest of you like mould.

And, to add insult to injury, there is no cheap, fast, efficient and painless way of removing it. (Or even cheap, fast, efficient and painful.)

One day, we hope, they will perfect the art of a total immersion in body wax from nose to toes, but until then we must suffer.

Now you know why Victorian bathing costumes covered you up like that – and it wasn't for modesty.

One of the Great Mysteries of the Universe is: just where did that three-foot spike of nose hair hide before it sprang from your nostril, fully formed, at an embarrassing moment?

Chapter 17
Surprised

Skint Old Fashion Victim, no. 3
Leopardskin prints and gold accessories complement each other perfectly.

The girls were hanging over the banisters in their pajamas when I went up to the drawing-room floor.

'You look like a flower fairy,' Febe said. 'If there *are* green ones?' she added doubtfully.

'You're *very* pretty,' Clo agreed. 'Mummy said you looked like a little ghoul in those baggy black things you used to wear.'

'*My* daddy says she looks like an abandoned nymph,' Caitlin said. 'Is that good?'

It is, as long as she didn't get it wrong, and he really said 'abandoned nympho'.

'Em's got a pretty dress too,' Febe said. 'The vicar walked into the door-post when he saw her. Even Anne's got her best denim shirt and trousers on!'

'We like to push the boat out at Rhymer Birthday Feasts.'

'Bran had his tea with us – he ate all the biscuits, but he let me hold Mr Froggy.' Caitlin said importantly. 'He says he hasn't time for birthday dinners, he has to finish his book before anyone else gets in his head and interrupts.'

'And Walter was there, too,' Febe said. 'We had our own party!'

'Why has Walter got no eyebrows?' asked Caitlin.

'It was the war. His hair just fell out and never came back,' I explained. My neck began to ache from tilting back to look up at them, so I was quite relieved when Gloria popped her head out of the drawing room and beckoned.

She was holding a tray of sherry glasses. (That's how the Birthday Feast *always* goes – sherry and birthday cake *first*, then dinner.) 'Take that glass nearest you,' she instructed, 'and go and give it to Em while she's talking to the vicar.'

'Right. Will it . . . ?'

'Just open her eyes to his good qualities.'

'I can see most of those myself, from here. And wasn't it his goodness that was the stumbling block?'

'Love will find a way,' she said. 'Better him than that actor – for either of my little chickens.'

'I don't know what you've got against Mace. What *did* you see in the tea leaves, Gloria?'

'Trouble,' she said heavily. 'And that Mace – his first wife drove into a tree and killed herself.'

'*Did* she? How awful! But you can't blame him for that, can you? Poor Mace!' No wonder the poor man was bad-tempered.

'*Surprise!* magazine said she lost control of the car after a row with him,' Gloria said. 'After she found out about the other woman.'

I looked at her. 'But how did she find out about the other woman?'

'From the *Surprise!* Stolen Secrets column – though they can't name names.'

'I wondered what Mace had against women's magazines, and now I know. Was it true, about this other woman?'

'There's no smoke without fire, and that one's still burning,' Gloria said cryptically. 'Look at him!'

I turned; Jessica had cornered him, and he was standing, arms folded, glowering down at her. Tyger, tyger . . .

Then he caught sight of me, raised one eyebrow and smiled. It was the Ravaging Horde bit all over again.

'Here,' Gloria ordered brusquely, giving me a dig in the ribs with her sharp elbow. 'Take that glass to your sister this minute! Bloody tea leaves – I'll show 'em!'

Em and Chris seemed to be getting on fine without any herbal help, so it was easy to give Em the glass while she was looking at him.

They were in the corner, and Chris was leaning over her with one hand on the wall next to her head, in a very masterful way. I'm sure Em was enjoying the novelty, because otherwise she would have released herself in a painful manner: painful to Chris, that is.

None of us except Father actually like sherry, but Em was too engrossed to notice what she was drinking.

I'd missed Father blowing out the candles on the cake, because Anne was now slicing it ... and Gloria was purposefully forging down the room in the direction of Mace and the Treacle Tart, one solitary, twinkling amber glass left on her tray.

Something Wicked This Way Comes.

She *wouldn't* – would she?

She would.

Mace had just lifted the glass to his lips when I said urgently: 'Don't!' and reached out for it – but too late.

He stared at me in mild astonishment.

'Excuse *me!*' Jessica said tightly, having been unceremoniously elbowed out of the way. 'Mace and I were having a conversation.'

'Sorry, was that your glass?' Mace said, relinquishing it to me.

'Yes. Gloria gave you mine by mistake,' I said feebly. 'Shall I get you another?'

'No. I don't really like sherry, though I don't mind sharing this one – with you,' he offered, with that irresistible smile – *and* smouldering dark eyes, so Gloria was right about the fire. 'You look like a creature from another world tonight. Beautiful, fragile, insubstantial ...'

Disconcerted, I found I'd taken a gulp of the potentially doctored sherry myself – then Mace took the glass, turned it around, and drank from the very place my lips had touched, his eyes holding mine.

Do not ask me why this was the sexiest thing that ever happened to me, because I don't know. Take it from me, it *was*.

I was dissolving faster than a love philtre – which is probably what we were drinking.

Whoops.

'Do you feel all right, Mace?' I asked tentatively.

'Yes – in fact, I feel wonderful!'

'Right. Er ... Mace, I think Gloria put a little something of her own concoction into the sherry.'

'I thought it tasted unusual – but pleasant. What does she use? I thought it was only liqueurs that had herbs added?'

'I could have been wrong. Or got the glasses mixed up?' I mused.

127

'It doesn't matter, does it? At least now I've got the chance to tell you how beautiful you look tonight.'

The slow-fuse-burning smile made my spine tingle and my toes sort of curl like Turkish slippers . . .

Jessica, who'd retreated to the other side of the room, was giving me the evil eye, and I don't think she even realised she'd taken a bite of birthday cake. Em's birthday cakes have one hundred calories per crumb.

The blissful moment was rudely shattered. 'You made a right cock-up of that, you daft ha'porth!' Gloria hissed in my ear like an angry wasp. 'He was supposed to be looking at that Jessica when he drank it, not you!'

'But Gloria, wasn't that a bit . . . underhand?'

'Never you mind!'

I was about to tell her that I'd had a sip myself, then stopped. It *was* the tiniest sip and couldn't possibly matter . . . could it?

'Still, maybe . . .' She sighed heavily. 'I'll brew him something tomorrow to cancel out the spell – but you can't go against Fate, I should have known better. Time to start dinner.'

'What's the matter? What was she saying?' asked Mace.

'Everything's fine,' I assured him. And it would be once he'd had the antidote and saw me in my usual persona of boring old Charlie, sometime murderess and part-time children's nanny.

Walter beat the gong with enthusiasm, and we all trooped into the dining room and seated ourselves under the birthday banner, Father at the head of the table, with Jessica sitting smugly at his right like a Borgia bag of secrets.

I don't remember much about the rest of the dinner, except that Mace sat next to me and told me all about his first play, and the one he was writing now, which both seemed to be about guilt, and hasty actions leading to disastrous outcomes. But then, so is life.

Good, dry champagne ran like water, and Jessica drank too much, which is easy to do when there's nothing else whizzing round your bloodstream. She got a bit giggly and excitable. The sticky toffee pudding would have lagged her bones a bit, but she declined with horror.

'Oh no, I really couldn't eat a stodgy dessert!'

'You can't seem to eat anything at all lately,' Gloria said. 'And when you do it doesn't stay down. Happen you're pregnant – unless it's that bulimia.'

'I have *not* got bulimia!' protested Jessica. 'And I'm certainly not pregnant. I had my tubes tied when I had the twins.'

'Then I hope they were tied good and tight, flower, because there's no knot that can't be undone,' said Gloria grimly.

Jessica stared at her, aghast. 'Have you been putting something in my food? Or Em? – she's put a spell on me, so I get pregnant!'

'Don't be silly,' Em said. 'The last thing I want is for you to get effing pregnant and have any excuse for hanging around here.'

'And it's not what goes in your *food* that makes you pregnant,' pointed out Gloria meaningfully.

'Shouldn't think she is,' Anne said, busy surrounding her castle of pudding with custard prior to the initial assault. 'We've all seen the backside of forty.'

'*I* haven't!' exclaimed Jessica.

'That could have been more felicitiously put, but you're right, Anne,' agreed Em.

'Ran, I'm not pregnant, am I?'

'How should I know?' he said irritably, looking up from his dinner plate. 'Does it matter?'

'Of course it matters! It took me a year to get my figure back after the girls were born, and I'm not getting married looking pregnant.'

The pause after that statement *was* pregnant, even if nothing else was.

Ran sighed and put down his spoon. 'Well, I was going to save it for the birthday speech, but the cat is out of the bag now: Jess and I are getting married.'

'What for?' asked Anne.

'We love each other!' Jessica declared dramatically.

'Good home and a meal ticket for life, for Jessie,' Em said, looking grim. 'Unlimited sex forever for Father.'

'Do we have to have this sort of family discussion in front of our guests?' Father asked with some asperity.

Em looked suspiciously at the vicar. 'Did you know, Chris?'

'No, but I think it's a good idea. I think marriage in general is a good idea,' he added meaningfully, trying to hold Em's hand.

She glowered at him, and then absently drained the wine glass Gloria had just refilled, although she's not generally a heavy drinker.

129

'Yes, congratulations,' Mace contributed. 'And on the baby, too, if there is one.'

'There won't be,' Em said firmly. 'She's too old.'

'I am not too old!'

'If there is, it might not be Father's anyway,' Anne suggested.

'If I had a baby it would be obvious who the father was – unlike Branwell and Charlie,' Jess said. 'Just look at them – they could be *anyone's!*'

'I don't know what you're hinting at, Jessica, but not all children take after their fathers,' Em said.

'Yes, there's no Rhymer family birthmark shaped like a bloody strawberry,' Anne contributed. 'Chaz looks just like Mother.'

'But no one seems to know who Branwell takes after!'

Father, who had been ignoring the argument, looked up, frowning. 'I can't remember what Maria looked like after all this time – but no, the boy *has* to have got his brains from me.'

'So that's where they went,' Em said.

'Ho, ho,' Father said, glowering.

'I saw this really good programme on TV the other day,' Jessica said brightly. 'About a new test you can get to prove whether you're the father of your children – and lots of men have found that they really aren't. Have *you* heard of that, Mace?'

There was a small silence. I thought Jessica was just trying to get his attention, but it was an unlucky shot in view of what his exwife had said.

Mace turned and stared at *me*, like I was some kind of traitor. 'You overheard what Kathleen said? And I thought—'

He stopped abruptly, and turned his head away as if he couldn't bear to look at me.

'No, Mace!' I protested. 'I haven't – I didn't . . .'

'Only I always get *Surprise!* magazine on Fridays,' babbled Jessica, 'and today it says in "Stolen Secrets" that you had an argument about Caitlin with your ex-wife, and Caitlin's quite plain, really, isn't she? She doesn't look like you at all. And then it said Kathleen Lovell hasn't been seen since she visited you, so I wondered . . .'

She petered out in the face of the incredulous silence. Open mouth and insert both feet.

'Mace, I did overhear, but I didn't tell anyone – no one at all!' I said urgently, putting my hand on his arm. 'It was obviously

130

something she tossed out in the heat of the moment. Caitlin's yours.'

He sort of shrugged me off, like an insect. '*Surprise!* magazine? *Again?* What did I ever do to them to be victimised like this?'

'Didn't you know about it?' Jessica asked brightly. 'There was a picture of Kathleen Lovell – she's gorgeous, isn't she? – but I still think she's lucky marrying Rod Steigland. And a Christmas honeymoon on a Caribbean island, too!'

'I think you'd better get this gossip rag and show the man, now you've gone this far,' Father said, but Gloria had already fetched her own virgin copy and was thumbing through it.

Em, largely uninterested in the face of her other problems, had been having a muttered discussion with Anne from which I'd only heard odd snippets like: 'evicted from my own home' and 'end of the whole effing family' and 'stay to be treated like a servant' and 'bloody invader!'

This time, when Chris tried to take her hand, Em let him.

'Some Birthday Feast this turned out to be!' muttered Father bitterly.

The magazine article was quite short. Father removed it from Gloria's grasp and read it aloud.

'An anonymous source—'

'Not me!' I put in hastily.

—'said dishy but notoriously bad-tempered actor Mace North had allegedly flown off the handle when ex-wife Kathleen Lovell told him he wasn't really the father . . . blah, blah blah – daughter Caitlin was still staying at his country retreat, but no one's seen Kathleen since . . . blah blah,' Father said, editing ruthlessly. He tossed it aside. 'Load of poisonous rubbish.'

Mace looked up, his eyes dark and steely with anger, accusing me.

'If Charlie'd told anyone, it would have been us, Mace,' Anne said. 'And she didn't. Rhymers don't phone up effing gossip columns. Rhymers don't even *read* magazines with gossip columns in them.'

'I do,' Jessica said.

'You aren't a Rhymer.'

'Rhymers seem to be *writing* their own magazines,' Mace said nastily. 'Perhaps I merit a double-page spread of slime in there?'

131

'Now, now, Mace,' Father said. 'You should read some of the things they say about *me*!'

'Yes, but they're all true, Father,' I said. 'And this isn't.'

'It'll soon blow over. Where's your ex-wife gone, Mace?'

'No idea – she stormed off in a temper. Nearly ran me down. But wherever it is – and I assure you it isn't a shallow grave down in the woods – she'll turn up in a couple of weeks, for the wedding.'

'There you are then,' said Father, losing interest. 'Storm in a teacup.'

He didn't know how true that was.

Then he looked down at Kathleen's picture again and amended, absently: 'B cup.'

I looked at Mace's dark, angry face and wondered ... and a shiver ran up my spine. I mean, he *sounds* civilised, but he certainly doesn't look it, and he *was* glaring at me a few minutes ago as though he'd like to get his hands around my throat.

'I think I read the leaves wrong,' Gloria muttered in my ear. 'And maybe the love philtre's not working. But everything's all right – no problem.'

'Can you give him the antidote tomorrow anyway?'

'Perhaps I better had.'

It was an oddly segmented party after that. Outwardly it ran its usual course, and after a short birthday speech Father pulled out a ring of Christmas-cracker proportions and rather sheepishly put it on Jessica's bony finger, to her unconcealed triumph.

After that, Anne excused herself on the grounds of fatigue and went to bed, and Em suddenly announced that she and Chris were going out for a little while. 'Chris is going to show me the vicarage.'

'Why? You pass it almost every day on your walks,' Father said, puzzled.

'Yes, but I don't pass *through* it,' Em said. 'Come on, Chris.'

'Don't you worry about nothing here, blossom,' Gloria told her. 'Walter and me will tidy it away before we go home, and Charlie can help.'

Mace, who'd been perfecting the art of abstracted brooding, now pulled himself together enough to take his leave. 'Thank you for a lovely evening, Ran, and a delicious meal.'

'You won't get none of those when you're married, Ran,' Gloria pointed out.

'Of course I will. Why shouldn't I?' he said heartily. 'Things will just go on as before.'

So like a man.

'You can go out through the Summer Cottage, Mace,' I said, getting up. 'It will be quicker.' *And* give me another chance to try and persuade him that I really didn't grass on him.

'No, don't bother,' he said curtly. He didn't even glance at me. 'I need the fresh air.'

'Mace—'

But he was gone. And after all, why *should* he believe me – and why should I care? In a minute he would be turning the corner of the Parsonage and walking down the track, still thinking I was the sort of person who would do that sort of thing . . .

I got up, said: 'Happy birthday, Father. Congrats, Jess – hope you're happy,' then shot out of the door, down the stairs, through the kitchen where the dogs slumbered by the stove, and then almost fell headlong down the dark stairwell to the Summer Cottage.

Without stopping I ran out onto the track, but Mace must have moved faster, for he was already ahead of me.

There was only one way to catch him: hitching up my skirts with both hands I cut straight across the rough, steep corner, losing my balance and falling headlong down the bank to land on the track at his feet.

There might have been more dramatic ways of getting his attention, but I can't think of any.

The ground was frozen hard, my cheek stung, and my ankle had twisted. It hurt; but then, so did Mace's hands gripping my arms and hauling me upright.

'You fool!' he exclaimed. 'You could have broken your stupid neck running over ground like that in the dark – and you must have known there was a drop down onto the track!' And he gave me a whiplash-injury-inducing shake, my feet dangling in mid-air like a rag doll's.

'I *did* hear what Kathleen said, but I really didn't tell anyone!' I gasped painfully. Then I gave a sudden galvanic shiver; well, I *was* out in December wearing a wisp of chiffon and not much else, being mildly roughed up by a large, bad-tempered man whose wife had disappeared under sinister circumstances.

He stilled and looked down at me, though it was hard to make out his expression in the moonlight. 'Who else could it have been?'

'How should I know who she's told? Perhaps she told them herself!'

Though he could, of course, be convinced she hadn't told anyone because he had after all buried her in a shallow grave in the valley . . .

I shivered again, and he said roughly: 'You're twice a fool: running after me like that when I'm in a rage, and in just a thin dress,' and pulled me inside his warm, downy coat.

'Could you put me down, do you think?' I suggested, struggling weakly. But when he did, my left ankle was too painful to stand on, and he scooped me back up again effortlessly like so much illicit loot, and strode off.

'I don't know what's the matter with me tonight!' he muttered. 'I *want* to be angry with you, but whenever I look at you, I just can't!'

'It's only Gloria's love philtre – it was in your sherry. You were supposed to fall for Jessica, but you looked at me instead. But don't worry – you can have the antidote tomorrow when she's brewed it.'

'You can't possibly really believe in love potions,' he said shortly. 'And you had some too.'

'Only a tiny sip – too little to matter. You drank most of it.'

'Okay, so maybe she spiked the drinks with a few herbs, but . . .' He stopped, and looked down at me, his expression unfathomable in the moonlight. 'No,' he said firmly.

'It doesn't matter whether you believe in it or not – Gloria's spells usually work. Maybe all that rage cancelled it out? But what's important is that you believe me now, about my not telling anyone what Kathleen said.'

'I suppose I'll have to, since you nearly broke your neck telling me.'

'Then do you think you could take me home?'

'No, we're nearly at my place and I want to see what you've done to yourself first.'

'It's all right – Gloria's probably still there, and she will clean my scratches and do something for my ankle. It's only twisted.'

'That does it – I'm not taking you back until she's gone home! And I thought *Em* was the one to watch.'

'Oh, Em just wanted you as a sacrifice.'

'A sacrifice? She was going to *kill* me?'

'Of course not, don't be silly. She just wanted your body, because you have a dark side and could help her get in touch with *her* darker powers. But actually, none of us wants her to try any black magic, because she does tend to throw herself into things so enthusiastically that there's no saying where it will end. So Gloria and I sort of spiked her drink with the love philtre, too, while she was talking to Chris.'

'Does that make Chris the sacrifice?'

'Willing victim, but not to the black arts, which is a relief.'

'So why did *I* get the potion? And why was I supposed to fall for Jessica? No, don't tell me – to get her away from your father and Upvale?'

'Probably. I didn't know Gloria was going to do it until the last minute, so I'm not sure. Or maybe it was because she got the mistaken impression that you were interested in me, and she doesn't like it.'

'Any particular reason?'

'Something in the teacup, mostly.'

'The teacup?'

'The leaves, but she won't tell me what. I expect she thinks you will use me and cast me aside, or something – after all, she's been reading *Surprise!* for years. I've told her I'm not interested.'

'Thanks.'

'Well, it's so silly of her to imagine *you* would be, isn't it? I'm no pretty young girl, and there must be plenty of those interested in you.'

'Oh yes, I'm a babe magnet, all right,' he said shortly, kicking the cottage door open and walking in with me. 'Fame and money are all it takes.'

I looked up at his distinctive face and said involuntarily: '*And the rest!*' and he grinned, and kissed me like the season for it was about to run out.

I don't know what got into me.

All right, I do; and it wasn't just the love philtre. My secret fantasies about dragging Steve the gardener into the bushes had at some point been entirely replaced with ones involving Mace: I just wasn't expecting them actually to *happen*.

Caution prevailed for – oh, maybe three seconds, give or take one or two – and then was tossed away. I mean, so maybe he *had* done away with Kathleen, but did it seem important at that juncture? No.

Or perhaps it was Gloria's potion working in both of us – or all that champagne?

Who cares? It was now or never . . .

'Now!' I said, an abandoned nymph indeed.

Little did Felicity Hake-Hackett know on which illustrious bedroom floor her dress would end up. How much she would have loved to be the one from whose body it was stripped by impatient fingers; in silence. He's a great one for deep, meaningful silences.

Later, drowsily, I let him clean up the mark on my face and convey me (boneless and almost entirely witless, I fear) back to the cottage.

He deposited me safely in my own bed, kissed me long and hard with one hand planted on either side of my head, and took himself off.

Intense isn't in it.

A note from Gloria was pinned to the side of the bedside cabinet.

Drink contents of glass the moment you return, to avert evil consequences.

The contents of the said glass looked like they'd been dredged hastily from the bottom of the nearest cesspool, and the only evil consequence would occur about a second after I drank it.

The other sort of consequences I haven't had for years; I'm a barren vessel, except for the paintings . . . and Flossie.

I *intended* to go and find Flossie, but I couldn't even raise the energy to switch the lamp off before great waves of sleep completely submerged me.

Chapter 18

Absolution

It was very late when I woke the next day, strangely tired, aching and disorientated.

For a few heart-stopping moments I couldn't remember where I was, then my eye fell on the glass of disgusting liquid on my bedside table, now separated out into a layer of sludge topped by clear green, and it all came back to me in Glorious Technicolor, along with my sanity.

Perhaps my vocation in life is to become a hermit and never leave the house, or speak to anyone outside my family, ever again.

Especially Mace.

Not that *he'd* actually said very much last night, as I recall, after that first kiss – but his actions spoke volumes. (The sort that should be behind locked bookcase doors.)

But it was no good; I couldn't hide forever. Besides, I was feeling guilty about abandoning Flossie of whom there was no sign.

After a shower I felt a bit better, and apart from a graze on my cheek, a few promising bruises, and a tender left ankle, I didn't look too bad either.

And at least it was a Saturday, so I didn't have to go down and fetch Caitlin, for how would I ever face him again after last night's goings-on?

I mean, I'm sure they were entirely due to Gloria's potion, probably helped along in Mace's case by enforced abstinence due to being marooned in the country with Caitlin – and there are not many nubile young starlets in Upvale.

I suppose handsome, rich actor/playwrights have casual sex all the time usually, though, so he will not think any more about it once he's had the antidote.

137

I have no excuse for my actions (except for the enforced abstinence bit) because I only had one tiny sip. It was just irresistible lust and champagne.

Mind you, had I known how good sex could be, Fidelity would not have been my middle name all these years. Either Matt was not very good at it, or Mace is a master of the art. I suspect the latter.

Last night was wonderful (in a 'my God! Did I *really* do that?' sort of way) but it mustn't happen again. Gloria will just have to find a way of giving him the antidote to the love philtre *fast*.

I dressed in jeans and jumper and went upstairs, where I found Flossie curled up with Frost; quite sweet, really. I expect that's where she spent the night, so we are both loose women.

Em was sitting quietly at the table – the whole house seemed strangely quiet – and the only place still set for breakfast was mine.

Unusually, she wasn't doing anything, just sitting dreamily over a cup of coffee.

'Well, madam!' Gloria said, appearing in the doorway and surveying me with her hands on her hips. 'Here's another one who was up to goodness-knows-what last night. It's to be hoped you drank what I left for you, because you need some powerful magic to oppose the likes of that one!'

'It's all right, Gloria,' I assured her, although I fear I poured the disgusting stuff down the loo. 'I – just went after Mace to try and explain that I hadn't told anyone about what his wife said when they quarrelled.'

'Takes a long time, that sort of explanation,' she said drily. 'You don't fool me – I know what I saw in the teacups!'

'Well, whatever you saw, it wasn't entirely Mace's fault. You shouldn't have given him the potion.'

'It would have worked fine except for your meddling.'

'I'm sure I've lost my powers,' Em said dreamily. 'When I look inwards I can't see anything except Chris's face. Isn't that odd?'

Yes, that was pretty odd. I tried closing mine for a moment, and immediately saw a dark, strongly boned face as clearly as if he was— I snapped them open again, to find Gloria looking thoughtfully at me.

'I thought sex was supposed to enhance your powers, Em?' I said hastily.

'Only if she did it as part of the rites,' Gloria said. 'In a place of ancient power. Not just flinging herself headlong between the sheets with a man of the Church.'

'I didn't! We just talked – all night,' protested Em. 'Gloria, you didn't put anything in *my* drink, did you?'

'Of course not, my blossom,' Gloria assured her. 'It must be love.'

'White witchcraft and the Church are not incompatible,' Em said dreamily.

'Obviously.'

'Traditionally, the one has been absorbed into the other. Chris and I think our beliefs can co-exist within a relationship of mutual respect.'

Gloria and I stared at her.

'Have you got one of those, then?'

'Yes, but I'll have to make allowances for the Dickens, and he'll have to make allowances for the ways of Wicca.'

'Are his intentions honourable, though, Em?' I asked.

'I effing well hope not!' she said, sounding more like herself.

'You could get married,' I suggested, examining the covers on the hotplate and heaping a plate with slightly dried bacon, egg and mushrooms. Suddenly I felt absolutely ravenous.

'I don't know – we'd have to find a form of service we could both be happy with. But Chris says vicars aren't supposed to live with someone unless they're married to them.'

'You're going to live with him?'

'I don't know,' she said, going off into another trance.

'I'll make you some fresh toast,' Gloria said to me. 'And some coffee – or maybe a cup of tea?'

'I don't feel like tea,' I protested, but that's what I got, and she stood over me until I drank it, too, then sat down and spent a long time examining the bottom of the cup.

She sighed heavily.

'What?' I said, eating buttered toast.

'It's still there. I knew he was trouble, but what will be, will be. And it might not have been the potion, not if he already loved you,' she mused.

'But he doesn't love me, and I don't love him – as will become quite clear when you give him the antidote. Last night didn't mean

139

anything to either of us. For me, it was just a quick last fling before I become a middle-aged artistic recluse.'

'Out with a bang?' Em suggested helpfully, becoming more alert.

'Thank you, Em. And ... do you think you could take Caitlin back to Mace later?' I asked cravenly. 'Maybe with the antidote if it's ready?'

It would be easier to treat the whole thing as if it hadn't happened if a bit of time elapsed before I had to come face to face with him.

'Only I promised Vaddie I'd take my new pictures over to the gallery today.'

'You needn't worry about Mace being there,' Gloria said, seeing through this. 'He's gone and Caitlin with him.'

'Gone? What do you mean, *gone*?' I asked, stunned.

'To London,' Gloria said. 'That's the sort of man he is, even with a full dose of love philtre inside him! Chancy.'

'Mace collected Caitlin early this morning,' Em explained. 'He phoned first ... I'd just got back,' she added dreamily. 'Chris walked me home.'

'Em!' I said sharply.

'Oh yes – he said he was coming to get Caitlin, and take her to his mother's house in London, because the press had started phoning him at dawn, and they'd be turning up on his doorstep in droves any minute.'

'Didn't he leave any message?'

'He said to tell you he had to go away for a few days, and he'd let you know when they were back.'

'Kind of him. Was that it?'

'Yes, except that he asked to speak to Jessie. What *was* all that last night about Caitlin? Isn't she his?'

'Of course she is!'

And if he could ask to speak to Jessica, he could have asked for me – if he'd wanted to.

'There you are then, Gloria. Love clearly doesn't come into it. He's probably forgotten last night already.'

Em looked at me severely. 'I hope you took precautions.'

'Em, I haven't conceived for years and I'm the shady side of forty; I'm barren.'

'And I left her a brew last night, in case,' Gloria added. 'So that should be that ... if she doesn't do it again.'

140

'I've no intention of doing it again!'

'Yes, but it won't stop her getting Aids or anything, will it?' pointed out Em helpfully.

'Mace has *not* got Aids!' I said crossly.

'He's put it about a bit, according to *Surprise!*' Gloria said.

'I'm not convinced you can believe anything it says in there, and I'm sure Mace isn't the sort of man who would have ... who would have put me in danger of that kind!'

And I was, too: instincts of a barbarian, manners of a gentleman.

Gloria looked doubtfully back into the teacup. 'I'd better get that anti-love potion brewed – he's coming back soon.'

'I really don't care; but I'll miss Caitlin.'

'Perhaps he's gone to find what happened to Kathleen?' suggested Em. 'And did I tell you that Father and the Treacle Tart have gone with him? It was an impulse, but Father's delivering his manuscript to his agent, and Jessica wanted to shop.'

'But the girls? It's term time.'

'Anne offered to look after them. She's taken them out somewhere.'

'Let's hope she remembers to bring them back!'

'They're not bad girls,' Gloria said.

'No, I'm getting quite fond of them,' I admitted. 'And Caitlin.'

'Well, I'm not getting fond of Jessica,' Em said firmly. 'One of us will have to go.'

'Yes, but Father's going to *marry* her, Em, so it looks like she's here to stay. We might *all* have to go – she won't want the whole family round her neck, too.'

Gloria had been out of the room, but now returned and began to smear a cold green paste over my grazed cheek.

'Gloria, I can't go over to York looking as if I'm daubed for battle. Vaddie's expecting *me*, not the Last of the Mohicans.'

'It'll soak in. And you were limping – you can't drive like that. Better stay home, and let me put a compress on that ankle. What did he do to my little chicken?'

Her expression boded ill for Mace, should he ever return. I said hastily: 'He didn't hurt me. I fell down – and it won't bother me, driving. Do you want to come, Em?'

'No. I'm taking Chris up to the standing stones on Blackdog Moor. He hasn't been there yet and it's a powerful spot ... I'll take a flask of something hot, and a few sandwiches.'

Thank goodness it's too cold for anything *else* on the stones besides a chilly picnic, because I do not think Chris has the power to resist Em.

'Where's Bran?'

'Finishing off his manuscript before it goes off to be typed up by some poor creature at the university.'

'Oh well, I'll take Flossie, then. She will enjoy the drive.'

But even Flossie declined to come with me, and retired downstairs to her igloo. Perhaps she is miffed that I left her in the Parsonage kitchen all night?

Skint Old Motoring Tips

The car is not a household god, it is a motorised biscuit tin, and need only have the same criteria: dry, roomy and convenient.

For once, it was actually quite good to be driving over the moors to somewhere away from Upvale.

A day away would let me push my confused feelings about Mace behind a locked door. It would also give me a chance to turn over in my mind what was likely to happen if Father did indeed marry Jessica.

From what he said about nothing changing it is clear he has not thought it through. The day he married Jessica, it would be like shaking a kaleidoscope: the parts would be the same, only they'd all be in entirely different places in relation to each other, some not even touching.

Nothing was *ever* going to be the same again.

Vaddie fell on my paintings with cries of great joy. She loved the 'Jessie Down the Well' series, and when I told her that it would be on the cover of *Skint Old Northern Woman* she ordered a personal copy in advance, and said she'd like a whole stack to put on the desk, sale or return, under the actual picture featured.

I've decided not to sell that one, but give it to Father and Jess as a wedding present, assuming she actually manages to pull it off.

Vaddie said I looked totally different, and actually my change of hair colour and clothes made me look years younger and twice as pretty, which was kind of her. She had a cheque for me from the last lot of paintings she had sold – she doesn't part with money unless you go to her in person and demand it – and after that I went out and bought myself a turquoise cashmere tunic sweater and then, as an afterthought, a rose pink and silver nightie and dressing gown.

Definitely Pisces and slithery, although I'm not sure about the rose colour.

I popped in to see Miss Grinch on my way home, and told her about Angie, and my melon catharsis, and in return she told me all about the goings-on of the new people who'd moved into my house.

They sound like they are providing a lot more entertainment for her than I ever did.

During my absence, Gloria had found a chewed document addressed to me in Frost's basket, which proved to be the final bit of my divorce: I have absolution.

I don't know how long it had been in the basket, and nor do I really care.

I have absolution already.

Divorced Skint Old Northern Woman?
The should I?/shouldn't I? dilemma: some common questions answered

1) Will I be lonely?
Answer: Yes, but probably not any lonelier than you were before the divorce. Buy a dog.
2) I'll never be able to understand the paperwork, the tax returns, the bills ...
Answer: The running costs of an accountant are much less than a husband.
3) Will my married friends still invite me round?
Answer: No.
4) Will all my 'happily' married friends' husbands suddenly make a pass at me?
Answer: Yes. You now have 'Divorced and Desperate For It' stamped across your forehead in a special ink only they can read.
5) Will I ever have sex again?
Answer: Only if desperate. (See question 4.)
6) Will I ever find a new partner?
Answer: What are you, some kind of masochist?

143

Chapter 19

Nuts

We settled down to quite a pleasant and normal week before Father and Jessica returned (by train). Pleasant and normal by Rhymer family standards, that is.

Perhaps searching the woodland nearest to Mace's cottage for signs of freshly dug earth *was* a trifle on the bizarre side, but I only truly accepted this when I bumped into Anne and the twins doing the same thing. (Only the girls thought they were looking for acorns.)

Besides, we're quite high up here, and the ground has been frozen underneath ever since I moved home, even when the surface seems to have thawed out. (Just think of Upvale and the surrounding Blackdog Moor as being in a sort of snow dome, with its own ecosystem. Hence the early snow when other people are having Indian Summers.)

I've been spending almost all the daylight hours painting minute barbarian warriors on horseback being sucked into vortexes of savage greenery, like warped Persian miniatures.

It's very enjoyable. And no, I'm not going to think about the significance at all.

Anne seemed happy looking after the girls, although Em took over one day when Red showed up in order to abase himself.

Once he'd grovelled enough they vanished upstairs. Anne was saying as they went: 'So what's the matter with sodding war wounds? Seen them before, haven't you? One battle's the same as any other bloody battle, isn't it?'

I assume their *entente* was *cordiale*, since although he will be away now until the New Year on an assignment, they will resume their semi-attached state of shared flat-dwelling when Anne's back after Christmas. Her treatment will finish just before, so she will be fully revitalised after one of our family celebrations.

It could be the last, for everything is bound to change when or if Father marries Jessica. The kaleidoscope will shift permanently and we will all be cast to the edges.

The family circle has expanded already to include Chris – since the picnic at the standing stones he and Em seem mysteriously to have become one entity.

Indeed, they are spending so much time together, it makes you wonder if he ever does any vicar stuff at all – not that I know what they are supposed to do anyway.

Still, Em's powers seem suddenly to have returned to her with a vengeance: she was very practical when I told her about my dark thoughts regarding bodies in woods. Having borrowed a copy of *Surprise!* with a photo of Kathleen Lovell from Gloria, she called in Freya, Xanthe and Lilith and sat down to discover her whereabouts.

The unanimous result was that Kathleen is certainly alive, somewhere far away from Upvale. And they all felt that Kathleen was ... well ... *dwindling* was the way they put it.

I hope she has not succumbed to some wasting disease? But no – surely she would have told someone?

It is certainly a relief not to have to look for the body any more.

Lilith, Freya and Xanthe seem quite resigned to Em not joining their coven after all. I don't suppose it will affect their friendship.

And speaking of friendship, Freya has managed to strike up an acquaintanceship with Angie, and invited her to meet the other two at the pub tonight to, as she put it: 'direct her out of her present circle of hate, and into a more profitable frame of mind that will take her orbit elsewhere.'

Mars would be good.

On the Tuesday Branwell finished his book – or, at least, stopped scribbling and took to staring at the pile of manuscript as though he couldn't remember how it got there.

He was extremely averse to the idea of its being taken away so we could post it off to the poor woman at the university whose job it is to type up this scrawl into something readable. In the end Em had to lure him away to visit a second-hand book shop, while I had the whole thing photocopied and returned to his room before he realised it had been removed. Then I sent the copy off; it was clearer and darker than the original, anyway.

Of course, when we get the typescript back he will scribble all over it again, but the end is in sight.

When I got back from the Post Office I found Walter arranging a plant delivery in the verandah. There were six coconut palms, one almost touching the roof.

I only know one person who can afford this kind of extravagant gesture – whatever sort of gesture it is – for there was no message, unless it was something to do with nuts.

I suppose it could just be a final farewell from Matt, in lieu of ducks? But I don't think he has the imagination, and anyway, he seems to have forgotten about me entirely.

So it must be Mace. But what did it mean? Nuts to me? You're nuts? What's got a coconut in every bite?

Friday's copy of *Surprise!* contained what could only be construed as an abject apology and retraction about their alleged Mace and Kathleen item. Of course, when you have only hinted at something it is very hard to hint that really your *first* hint wasn't true, but they did their best.

I expect having Invasion of the Kalmucks in your office does wonders for your powers of retraction.

Father was abstracted when he and Jess got home. I fear inspiration for the next character assassination has struck, although we don't know yet who the victim is to be.

Perhaps he will surprise us by proving that Dorothy actually wrote all Wordsworth's poetry for him, in a literary about-turn; but then again, maybe not.

Jessica was, I think, miffed that the girls hadn't missed her more, though they were delighted to see her back, and quite polite about the gifts she had brought them.

They had had a busy week, and we had not found them any trouble at all: Anne did the school run and subverted them, they had painted with me, and learned to cook with Em, been for dug-earth-spotting expeditions in the woods, played with the dogs, learned to whittle with Walter and helped Gloria coat every wooden surface in the house with home-made beeswax and turpentine polish.

Clo shows an interest in photography, and she and Anne have set up a darkroom in an unused back pantry.

They are perfectly happy, just as we all were, growing up here in Upvale. We are adults long enough – why start too soon?

Indeed, why start at all?

Jessica found solace in having increased her store of worldly goods by about half, which, while lifting her spirits, must have stretched Father's credit card until it bulged at the seams.

Sit in the sun and
hold out your hand.
How heavy the world feels
in your palm.
From 'Words from the Spirit; by Serafina Shane

Jessica has started to try and assert herself around the house already, the engagement ring flashing on her bony finger.

Of course it hasn't *got* her anywhere, but it is a sign of what is to come.

Walter is spending much time in the small sitting room constructing Christmas presents, and Gloria continually thrusts cups of tea into people's hands, especially mine, and fusses after me so much that I have even taken to shutting the door at the bottom of the Summer Cottage stairs and ramming a chair under the handle. (Only I'm continually having to remove it to let Flossie in and out.)

There is still no word from Mace, unless you count the nuts, so it looks like the potion wore off all on its own.

'The vicar just asked me for Em's hand,' Father said on the Saturday, wandering into the kitchen and pouring himself a cup of coffee. 'I told him he could have any of her he fancied.'

'He already has,' muttered Gloria.

'What?'

'You didn't really say that, Father, did you?' I asked.

'Of course he bloody did,' Anne said. 'He hasn't realised the implications yet – too full of himself.'

'What implications?' Father looked surprised. 'Em won't get married. She's a natural spinster.'

148

'Thank you,' Em said. 'But as so often in your life, you are entirely wrong.'

'But are you *really* going to marry the vicar?' Jessica exclaimed.

'I might. We've worked out a reasonable compromise about the service. His bishop won't like it, probably, but everyone round here will be fine about it. Anyway, Chris says he doesn't want to rise in the Church, he just wants to stay here, with me.'

'Implications?' muttered Father, looking slightly dazed. 'And what do you mean, stay *here*: is he moving in?'

I think he's pretty well done that already. I'm surprised Father hasn't noticed.

'No, I meant staying in Upvale. He's got the Vicarage – I could live there.'

'Well, I think you're doing the right thing,' Jessica said warmly. 'When are you going?'

Em gave her a look. 'It's not decided yet, but after Christmas – so you can keep your nose out of everything until after that, since it'll be the last real Rhymer family Christmas. Then the place is all yours.'

'What do you mean, all yours?' Father said, finally getting to grips with the situation. 'You *can't* go, Em! I mean, who's going to run the house, and cook and . . .?' He stopped and stared at her.

'Your *wife*, of course, silly!' Jessica said brightly. 'With Gloria's help of course – it *is* a very big house for just us. But I expect we could shut some of it off, and instal central heating, and showers, and a microwave, and—'

'How can we shut it off? We use it all,' Father said, looking bewildered. He dislikes change nearly as much as Bran.

'She means after Em leaves, and Anne doesn't come home any more, or Bran – though it might be difficult to stop him – and I vacate the Summer Cottage.'

'But why would you all want to do that?'

'Wouldn't be home any more, would it?' Anne said.

'The Vicarage bungalow isn't very big, but Chris says we can squeeze everyone in, and my family is his family,' Em said.

'Tell that to Bran,' I said. 'He'll just turn up in his old room whatever you do.'

'Me and Walter go where the girls go,' Gloria said firmly. 'Big changes are coming: I saw it in the teacups. It's started, and nothing can stop it now.'

'Oh, is that all, Gloria? You had me worried there,' I said.

'That was just the general overview,' she said grimly. 'And you are going to need me the most, Charlie; mark my words. Troubles and changes! And it's all since that Mace North came to Upvale.'

'That's quite unfair, Gloria,' I said. 'You can't blame everything on Mace.'

'Yes I can – I knew he was trouble. He's the dark agent of change!'

'What, like a catalyst?' Anne asked, interested.

'I thought he was an *actor*,' Jessica said. 'Ran, isn't he an actor? Only he writes plays, now too?'

'Shut up, Jess, don't let them sidetrack me,' Father said. 'Of course the family stays here. If Em does want to go – well, that's her own funeral.'

'Wedding,' Em said.

'Jess will keep things going here just the same. There's no need for anything to change.'

Not quite: I think a healthy, fat-free diet will pall on Father quite soon. But perhaps the girls will take over the cooking when they have learned a bit more from Em? After all, she started running the household when she was younger than they are.

Jessica was looking alarmed and thoughtful, but Father, having comfortably decided that things could go on as before, minus Em (the linchpin of the whole house), simply put it out of his head.

Bran hadn't taken it into his head in the first place. Em was deep in thought – probably thinking about the practicalities of cooking in the Vicarage kitchen – and Anne was looking like she was starting to miss her nice, spartan London flat.

'Bloody battlefields!' she said, getting up and walking out; but at least she has a place of her own to go to. I've sort of got settled in my cottage, but I'm sure Jessica will want us all to go.

Father, who'd been calmly eating his breakfast now he'd settled things to his satisfaction, looked up. 'I've invited Mace and Caitlin for Christmas dinner,' he announced.

'But what about Caitlin's mother?' I began.

'Her mother's going to be on honeymoon in the Caribbean until the New Year, and Mace said his own mother doesn't celebrate Christmas – she always spends it quietly in a hotel in Bath.'

Bran looked at him and beamed. 'Christmas?' he said happily. 'Brandy snaps? Snapdragon?'

'Of course, Bran,' Emily said. 'Don't we always?'

'Mouse Hunt? Hunt the Thimble?'

'Yes, this time, but it will be the last Christmas as we know it.'

'Oh, come on, Em!' Father protested. 'Where else would you all go? I don't believe you really mean to marry the vicar!'

'I do.'

'You wouldn't be happy and neither would he. It would finish his career.'

'He doesn't want a career. He wants to stay here, in Upvale with me.'

'Just as well – he won't have any option, once word gets round about who he's marrying. I can't think what's got into you.'

'You shouldn't go inviting single men round to the house, then, you great lummox,' Gloria told him shortly. 'Especially men like that actor. Christmas dinner indeed! He's trouble and change. I saw it in the tea leaves – and more!'

'Speaking of Mace, I nearly forgot,' Father said, feeling in his pocket and producing a slightly mangled envelope. 'He sent you this.'

I took it eagerly, but then he added: 'It's your wages for looking after Caitlin.'

It was, too – nothing else. 'Was there any message?'

'No. He said he'd already sent you one.'

'Caitlin looks forward to seeing you again soon. She's staying with her granny until after the wedding, then Mace is bringing her home,' Jessica said kindly. 'I expect you will see her then.'

'I don't want his money,' I said shortly, stuffing it back into the envelope. Father looked faintly surprised.

Jessica said: 'Is it because he thought you'd told *Surprise!* magazine about stuff? That's all sorted out – he's not angry with you any more.'

'Big of him. And I don't *need* his money. I'm selling paintings again.'

'*And* we've got advance orders for *Skint Old Northern Woman*,' Em said.

'Told everyone I know to buy one,' Anne agreed. 'And Em's book, too. Christmas reading. Presents.'

'Not using *my* telephone, I hope,' Father said. 'Some of your friends live on the other side of the world.'

'Bloody skinflint.'

151

'Advance copies should be here next week,' Em said.

'Good. Drum up some more sales.'

Father nodded at the envelope: 'You did the job, didn't you? Take the money, and if you don't want to do any more, tell the man when he gets back on Sunday.'

'Sunday?' I said, looking down at the envelope and feeling like I'd been paid off. Was I worth the money? He's probably had better, but maybe not so easily.

I'm not keeping it.

Skint Old Beauty: Hair Today, part 2

More bristles than a toothbrush? Finding a solution to the moustache problem.

1) Professional treatment at a salon – but if you can afford that, what are you reading this magazine for?

2) Plucking. This is excruciating, gives you a pink upper lip, and the hair doesn't even give up and stop growing back, like eyebrows do.

3) Shaving: not unless you are sure you never want to kiss anyone ever again.

4) Cream. This one has a built-in Catch-22: if you leave it on long enough to work, you get a rash.

5) Bleach. This gives you a white bristly moustache and also, sometimes, an interesting rash. (See also no. 4.)

6) Wax strips. This leaves hair and wax behind on your upper lip, thus giving a whole new meaning to the phrase 'stiff upper lip'. However, excess wax can sometimes be used to shape the hair into a pleasing handlebar moustache.

Chapter 20

Returns

I spent most of Sunday painting more small, mounted infidels in the verandah.

Just as the light was starting to fade in the afternoon, Mace's low, dark car slid past down the track, with lowdown dark Mace in it.

It didn't stop.

Not that I expected it to, of course – and I *wasn't* watching out for it. It was simply a coincidence that Flossie gave the one sharp yap that was her summons for me to open the door and let her out just as he went by.

Three seconds later the door opened again, and Em walked in, followed by Chris, tastefully (and tastily) attired in motorcycling leathers and dog collar.

'Close the door, you're letting all the warm air out,' I said, putting the brush down again. It really was too dark now to see tiny barbarians; or even whopping great big ones.

'Mace is back,' she informed me, patting Flossie, who had followed her back in.

'I know.'

'Hi, Charlie,' Chris said. 'Hope we're not interrupting you?'

'Not at all,' I said politely; I might block the door down from the Parsonage kitchen to keep Gloria out, but it didn't stop anyone walking in the front. My house is like a railway station.

'Did Mace stop on the way down?'

'No.'

'The bastard!' she said.

'Why? Were you expecting him?' asked Chris, looking puzzled.

'No!' we said in unison, and he recoiled slightly.

'Chris's bishop wants to see him,' Em told me.

'Perhaps he's heard about the engagement, and is going to congratulate you?'

'Someone must have told him about us, but I'm not too sure about the congratulation bit.'

'I expect he'll get used to the idea,' Chris said calmly. 'He will have to.'

'We've been to buy a betrothal ring – look,' Em said, flashing a large, strangely set yellow stone in my face.

'Nice,' I said. 'Where did you get it?'

'Chris had it made for me – a friend of his near Huddersfield has a jewellery workshop.'

'Ah, Huddersfield – cultural Mecca of West Yorkshire,' I said nostalgically. It was ages since I'd been to Huddersfield.

'I'd better go and start dinner,' Em said. 'See you later. Come on, Chris.'

Flossie followed them out and upstairs. She clearly sees the Parsonage kitchen as her spiritual home now, to the point where I'm thinking of moving her igloo up there.

Gloria seized her chance to descend with tea and dire warnings, before leaving by the verandah door, her basket over her arm.

I assumed she was going home early, and went up to see if Walter was still about.

Chris was standing by the Aga stirring something and reading *Hard Times*, so even love hasn't yet cured him of Dickens.

Walter was still there, so I asked him to fix a bolt on the door at the bottom of my staircase.

He didn't ask me why, just did it, regarding his neat handiwork at the end with a pleased smile, while passing a pink hand over his shiny pate.

Apart from Father's study, and Anne's bedroom, Rhymers don't lock doors on each other, but I'd like to be able to if I feel the need . . . Or *don't* feel the need for yet another cup of tea.

Before I got the chance to use it Anne and Em trooped past me, saying they were going out for some fresh air before dinner, which I thought was very odd, especially since they didn't ask me to go, too. Em said Chris was watching dinner, so not to worry.

'It's cold out there,' Walter said, gazing after them worriedly. 'Especially without a hat.'

'Yes, but they've both got lots of hair,' I pointed out.

154

After that we went upstairs and he showed me the walking sticks he'd been carving for the little girls for Christmas – including one for Caitlin, which was a nice thought. Then he hid them away in the cupboard by the fireplace and locked the door, before putting the key under his wig on the stand.

There were shavings neatly brushed into a little heap on the carpet; but then, there usually were shavings around Walter.

Em and Anne couldn't have had much of a walk, for they were already back. Em was talking in a low voice to Chris by the stove, while stirring something into the big cauldron. (Probably the Dickens.) Anne was sitting at the table with a glass of whisky in her hand, marking possible Christmas gifts in *Extreme Terrain: The Catalogue*.

'Drink?' she asked.

'No thanks – I'm just going to go back down to stretch another canvas for tomorrow.'

'Dinner in one hour,' Em said over her shoulder.

'Where are the girls? It's very quiet.'

'Out at a friend's. So's Jess. Bran's doing a jigsaw puzzle in his room, and Father's in the study, snoring.'

I went down, resolutely picked up the envelope of money, put on my coat, and set off down the track in the dusk to throw it back in Mace's face – metaphorically speaking.

Or maybe even literally speaking, for I was still angry enough: laid off and paid off.

By the time I got there, though, I'd remembered Mace's scarier aspects, and my nerve for a confrontation had pretty well ebbed away, though the money still weighed on my heart like lead.

So I sat down on his doorstep and scribbled on the envelope with a stub of pencil out of my pocket: 'I don't *want* your money . . .'

I couldn't think of anything else to say, since that pretty well summed it up, so I quietly lifted the flap of the letter box and slid the envelope through the rectangle of yellow light.

As I straightened up, the door swung suddenly and silently open. Backlit in the doorframe stood Mace like the Demon King, the envelope in his hand.

'Oh no, you don't!' he said, and reaching out a long arm yanked me inside and closed the door.

Still gripping me with one hand he glanced down at the envelope. 'Terse,' he said. 'Admirably to the point. But why not?'

'I – just don't,' I said lamely.

'Why? I'm not paying you off for services rendered, if that's what you think,' he said sardonically. 'I just owed you your wages for looking after Caitlin, and I thought you might need them.'

'Well I don't. I'm selling paintings again, now I'm over Dead Greg.'

'Is it because I didn't write?' he said, gazing at me, brows knitted. 'But I *did* send you a message. Didn't you get it?' His beautiful mouth quirked up at the corners.

'The coconut trees?'

'Of course.'

'To say what, exactly, Mace? Nuts to you?'

'No, to say I'm nutty *about* you. Isn't it evident?'

'No it isn't. I think my first interpretation was right – it was a "thank you and good-bye" present: but you needn't have bothered. I don't think Gloria really needs to bother with the potion she made for you now, either,' I added.

He frowned. 'I don't know what you think you're talking about.'

'The other night – you don't need to feel guilty about it, it was just the love philtre. But I'm sure the effects have worn off now, so we need never mention the whole unfortunate episode again.'

'Guilty? Why should I feel *guilty*? And I told you – I don't believe in magic potions, or Sabrina the Teenage Witch, or the Tooth Fairy, or—'

'You don't *have* to believe in them, they work anyway. And just look at me. *I* only had one sip and I did something totally out of character.'

'I'm glad to hear it.'

'What, that I only had one sip?'

'No, that you don't jump into bed with every passing man.'

'Oh? Well . . .' I looked at him uncertainly. 'You may not believe in it, but perhaps you ought to have the antidote, just in case?'

'Have *you* had it?'

'No – I didn't tell Gloria I'd had any love philtre in the first place and anyway, it was just a temporary blip in my sanity. It's worn off.'

'Has it? So, let me get it straight: *you* only slept with *me* because Gloria'd spiked the sherry with a bunch of herbs picked naked by the light of the full moon?'

156

'Something like that,' I agreed. 'But not naked; she'd catch her death.'

'Why do I not feel too concerned about that?' he asked himself aloud.

'I love Gloria! She's been like a mother to me.'

'I think we have a different understanding of the word "mother",' he said wryly. 'So you believe that *I* only slept with *you* because I'd had a mega-dose of the brew? And you only had a tiny bit, so it's worn off: but if I still fancy you, mine hasn't? Right?'

'Er – yes.' I found his expression very disquieting . . . And the way he was standing so close to me, looking down thoughtfully, even more disturbing.

'So, darling, does that explain why the bottle of whisky your father just sent me, delivered with suspicious cheerfulness by your Gloria, had its seal broken? I thought maybe she'd just had a swig and topped it up with water.'

'Gloria wouldn't do that!' I said indignantly. 'She can help herself to any drink she wants, she doesn't have to sneak it.'

'Including your father's single malt?'

'Yes, of course,' I said, astonished. 'But if Gloria was nice to you – and she brought the whisky down herself . . .'

'As a thank-you for giving Ran and Jessica a lift to London. Mind you, I could have done with it before I set *out* for London, to dull the sound of Jessica's non-stop twittering.'

'Her voice is a bit high-pitched,' I agreed. 'But you are right about Gloria – she must have wanted to give you the anti-love philtre she's been brewing as soon as possible. It won't do you any harm.'

'All's well that ends well?' he said sardonically. 'So I drink the whisky and what? I think you're an absolute dog, and never look at you again?'

'Yes,' I said coldly.

'But how do I know it isn't some insidious poison that will send me white-haired and raving?'

'Because she wouldn't do anything like that,' I said, with more conviction than I felt, because there *were* situations where I'm pretty sure Gloria would . . . but I'm certain this wasn't one of them. 'You'd better drink it.'

'I already have, and so have your sisters. And if it's so harmless, you can prove it by having some too.'

'What – Anne and Em? *When*?'

'Just after Gloria left; that's why I haven't been up to see you yet. My visitors have been arriving in shifts since I got home. Here,' he added, handing me a tumbler of neat whisky.

'A likely story,' I said coldly, and defiantly drank the contents of the glass. 'And why would Anne and Em visit you?'

'Em said she was seeing things clearly now, and she felt Gloria was putting the wrong interpretation on the leaves. She stared at me a long time, but she didn't say much.'

'Her powers have increased since she fell in love with Chris, strangely enough. Did Anne say anything?'

'Not much, just implied that she would break every bone in my body if I hurt you in any way. But I told her that was the last thing I wanted to do – and then we all had some whisky.'

'You all had it? I hope Em . . .' I thought about it. 'No, it won't affect her, because she was falling in love with Chris before she drank the love philtre, so she won't fall out of love with him now. It just sort of hastened things on. And Anne didn't have any in the first place, so it won't affect her, either. But you—' I broke off and stared at him. 'What are you doing?'

'Pouring the rest of it down the sink.'

'But what a waste of good whisky!'

'I like to know exactly what I'm drinking,' he said shortly, tossing the empty bottle into the rubbish bin. 'Right, that's that. So now I'm just my usual self, and you are *your* usual, highly irritating, self, and we start again?' He raised an eyebrow quizzically.

'Yes. Only I'm not going to look after Caitlin,' I said, edging towards the door.

'I don't see why, now you're not afraid I'm going to jump on you. Though of course, there's no guarantee that the real, un-tampered-with Mace might not want to jump on you anyway. And Caitlin's going to miss you.'

'I'll miss her, too – but I expect she will be coming down to see the twins, won't she? We're bound to see each other then.'

'Charlie – I'm sorry I suspected you of having told everyone what Kathleen said about Caitlin,' he said unexpectedly.

'That's all right. *I* thought you'd buried Kathleen in the woods.'

'I've had that test done – the one Jessica was going on about –

158

to see if Caitlin is mine. I couldn't decide if I really wanted to know. Even if I wasn't really her father – well, I don't think anything could alter the way I feel about her. I'm waiting for the results.'

'I never thought she wasn't yours for a minute, and I don't suppose Kathleen did, either, it was just something hurtful to say. Has she turned up yet?'

'No, there's no sign of her.'

'I wonder where she's got to?'

'I don't know. And I haven't managed to get hold of Rod Steigland, the man she's going to marry, yet either. He's still in the States, but he'll be flying over soon for the wedding, so wherever she is she's bound to surface some time. She called a friend just after she tried to run me down, that's where *Surprise!* got the information, so she drove off under her own steam.'

'I really did search the woods,' I confessed.

'Why? Do you think I'm that kind of man?' he asked incredulously, and I looked away.

'Well ... Gloria told me about your first wife's accident, and that you had to marry Kathleen when she refused to get rid of the baby ...'

'Bloody magazines! They take a particle of truth and blow it out of all proportion!' he said angrily. 'It's true I had an argument with my first wife – we married young, and we fought all the time – and yes, she slammed out in a temper and crashed the car. I'll always feel guilty about that, just as I expect you will always feel guilty about being the cause of Greg's death. Is that what you want to hear?'

'But Gloria says you argued because she found out about all the other women.' (And she'd said his reputation with women stank, but I didn't repeat that; his temper looked balanced on a knife-edge as it was.)

'There weren't any other women, Charlie. I'm strictly a one-at-a-time man, believe it or not. The magazines don't tell the truth, the whole truth, and nothing but the truth – and what they said about Kathleen was a damned lie! We had a short affair, and I married her simply to stop her aborting the baby. She didn't want Caitlin, she wanted a career.'

I looked at him; it all seemed pretty sordid to me. Maybe I've led a sheltered life?

'I don't know what to believe. It's all a totally different world from the one I'm used to. And I don't know what kind of man you are, either – except it isn't my kind.' I turned to go.

'Charlie,' he said softly.

'Yes?'

'Tell Gloria not to give up the day job, because her concoctions don't work: you still look pretty good to me.'

I closed the door with a slam and set off up the track in the darkness, engrossed in my thoughts . . . until the night was shattered by the deafening roar of a car engine right behind me.

The headlights were turned full on, pinning me in their twin beams like a frightened rabbit – except that I wasn't a rabbit. I leaped sideways into the ditch just in time, and slid down to the icy bottom.

The car roared past, then pulled up with a squeal of brakes.

As I clambered out, a door slammed.

'I *thought* I would have felt it if I'd hit you,' Angie said regretfully, picking her way towards me in her stilettos. 'Pity. And it's a pity no one round here wants to know anything about what you're really like, not even the local paper. What *is* it with the Rhymer family? Some sort of rural Mafia?'

I got to my feet, gingerly. 'No, the family came from round here originally, so when Father moved back we weren't incomers: we belong. The churchyard's full of Rhymers.'

'I was hoping to add one more!' she said viciously. 'I—'

But that was all she had time to say, before I realised the car tail lights behind her weren't stationary but slowly moving back, and I pushed her into the ditch before landing on top of her.

The car slowly careered onto the rough verge and stopped at an angle, one wheel hanging over us.

'You didn't put the handbrake on properly,' I said, hoisting myself up without being careful about kneeling on her ribs.

'Oof!' gasped Angie.

I climbed out of the ditch for the second time. Angie was still spread-eagled in there. She started to lever herself slowly up.

'The car!'

'I think you've cracked your headlight. If you walk to the farm, Madge's dad will get the tractor and tow you out – for a price. And

160

by the way, I think I just saved your miserable life,' I said, and left her.

I washed and tidied myself up, then went belatedly up to dinner. 'Sorry I'm late,' I said, taking my place. 'Angie just tried to run me over.'

'Women drivers,' Father said absently.

Em stared at me. 'Something will have to be done about that woman,' she said severely.

'Better do it bloody quick, before Gloria hears, or she'll be doing something herself – permanently,' Anne advised.

'I'll phone Freya, Xanthe and Lilith after dinner,' she promised.

'Bran, lift your book up. It's in the soup.'

On the hill
the bracken burns;
the red flower feeds
off beauty.
From 'Words from the Spirit' by Serafina Shane

161

Chapter 21

Home Comforts

Food For Thought:
Men are from Mars . . . so, if some of them make chocolate, they
can't all *be bad.*

I tossed and turned all night, then dropped off with the dawn and
was the last for breakfast; Jessica was just leaving for school with
the girls as I arrived.

Father had finished – he and Em are early risers, no matter how
late they go to bed – but he must have received a parcel in the post,
for he was carefully examining the contents of a small box.

As I sat down with a plateful of calories, he got up and
approached Bran with a cotton bud held out before him like a
scalpel.

'Open your mouth,' he said.

Bran looked at him with amicable blankness, but on having the
tip of the cotton bud pressed to his lips obligingly opened his
mouth and then closed it again firmly as though he'd been offered
a thermometer.

'Open again,' Ran ordered. 'And keep it open!'

Obediently Bran did so, and Father gave the stick a quick twirl
and withdrew it. We watched in some surprise as he placed the
bud into a little stoppered tube and wrote on the label.

'Father, what are you doing?' I asked.

'Never you mind – it's just an experiment,' he said slightly
furtively, then snapped impatiently: 'You can close your mouth
now, Bran!'

Picking up another cotton bud he now advanced on me. 'Right,
Charlie. Your turn.'

'No way!' I began, pushing my chair back, but I would have done better to keep my mouth shut instead, for he dexterously popped in the stick.

'Really, Father!' I said, when I was able. 'What on earth do you think you're doing? You might *ask* before you do that sort of thing!'

'I don't know what all the fuss is about,' he said, adding my stick to a tube in his strange collection box. 'It's just a little experiment.' Then he advanced again with yet another fresh cotton bud.

'Emily.'

Em and Anne shared a glance and said in unison: 'Absolutely not.'

Then Em rose, one finger marking the page in the book she'd been reading at breakfast (*Pagan Origins of Christianity in Britain* by Florisande Cote-Gibbon), and stalked out in silent disgust.

'Don't even effing think about it,' Anne warned, helping herself from a dish of kidneys at the sideboard.

Father sighed: 'Well, you girls aren't as important as Branwell.'

'Already bloody know that, don't we?' Anne said coldly.

He went out bearing his little box, and didn't mention the experiment again, so I don't know what all that was about. He does do odd things from time to time. I didn't let it put me off my breakfast.

Later, Em gave me a set of five power bracelets, each one made of a different semi-precious stone. There was clear quartz for peace and wisdom, amethyst for intuition and intelligence, rose quartz for love and the healing of past hurts, garnet for creativity, and hematite for stability and peace.

She said that should cover all the angles, whatever Gloria thought she saw looming in the tea leaves, and it was a nice thought. Had she given me one as a wedding present, my life would probably have taken an entirely different turn.

'I'm absolutely shattered!' Xanthe Skye exclaimed, sinking into the nearest comfortable chair. 'Freya, Lilith and I spent pretty nearly the whole night, helping that poor, tortured soul, Angie.'

'Tea?' asked Em. 'Or one of Gloria's restorative herbal brews?'

'One of Gloria's but not the nettle. The nettle is too robust for my delicate nature.'

Em put the kettle on, and I said gratefully: 'It was very kind of you all to go and sort out Angie.'

'Actually, we quite enjoyed it – there is such an odd assortment of people up at Hoo House that the vibes can be quite wild! You wouldn't believe the results with the Ouija board sometimes – but *gloomy*, always gloomy.'

'I'm not surprised. Did you use the board last night?'

'Yes – we formed a circle, just us three and Angie. Her husband came through; he told her clearly to let go of her anger and move on.'

'Did he? Where to?'

'Freya tried the crystal, later, and she thinks a cruise is indicated – a long, long cruise. But first she must be purged of all dark thoughts, in order to reap good fortune. And Lilith said she thought her heart line showed a new love interest entering her life before too long.'

'I believe cruise ships are hotbeds for that sort of thing – and to afford a cruise, Greg's insurance money must be coming at last, don't you think? That would be the good fortune.'

'It seems likely,' agreed Xanthe placidly, taking a teaglass of disgusting straw-coloured liquid from Em. 'But, as we told her, only if she closes one door behind her will the next door open into a bright new future.'

She sipped from her glass with apparent relish, then crunched up a peanut butter biscuit with her strong white teeth. 'She was wavering ... then Lilith read her leaves. She's not as good as Gloria, but she saw the Two Ways clearly and it's up to Angie now.'

'Oh, she'll take the money and the man every time,' I predicted confidently.

She drank the last of her evil brew and sat back. 'That's better. And so is your aura, dear – not quite golden, but *better*. Would you like me to see what your future holds for you? I have my Tarot with me.'

I shuddered. 'No, thanks. I'll just take it as it comes, one disaster at a time.'

Widows: Unexpectedly Single

While a widow has much in common with being divorced (see page 9: 'Divorced Old Northern Woman – your questions answered') this is singleness without blame or stigma.

In fact, being a widow is so terribly respectable it can be played as a sympathy card in tricky situations. For example, while your friends' husbands will still perceive you as 'available', they will not persist once you make it clear your heart was buried with your husband.

Of course, your heart may have been buried with your husband, in which case you have my very deepest sympathy.

However, many widows go on eventually to make an enjoyable life for themselves (some even start it from day one) and it is surprising how many perfectly happy and liberated widows there are who take on a new lease of life once the shackles are off.

Provided the life insurance and mortgage angle are fully covered, Skint Old Widow may also be a contradiction in terms.

For the down side, many of the answers to the Divorce article apply here too. But always remember: while there is gin and chocolate, there is life.

Later, a truculent Angie walked into my verandah as I was painting, without so much as a knock on the door – or even a quick graffiti scrawl.

She planted herself in front of me and said aggrievedly: 'I've got to say I'm sorry, and I'm going to forgive you. I'll be leaving Upvale soon and going on a cruise.'

'Good for you,' I said, relaxing my defensive grip on the palette knife. 'I hope you have fun – a lot more fun than trying to run me over, anyway.'

'Sorry I called you a whore. Sorry I called you a murderess. Sorry I tried to kill you,' she reeled off, as if reading down an internal list of Twenty Apologies for the Obsessed.

'That's all right,' I said. 'I'm desperately sorry I killed Greg, and I always will be. Is that it?'

She examined her conscience – nicotine yellow, ragged edges – and found it reasonably clear. 'Yes, I think so. Well, that's that done!'

She shifted tack, looking over my shoulder at the small canvas. This is something I am not terribly keen on even with people who haven't recently tried to kill me.

Something about the painting seemed to strike a chord. 'You having it off with that gorgeous actor, then?'

'No, I've just been looking after his little girl in the mornings,' I said coldly.

'Only he seemed so protective of you, down at the cottage – play your cards right and you might get a consolation prize for losing Matt.'

'Could any compensation possibly be enough?' I said sarcastically, but it just passed her by.

'Sort of getting your own back, though, after him ditching you for that nurse in Saudi,' she suggested.

I turned and stared at her. 'Which nurse? He said there *wasn't* anyone else!'

'Well, he would say that, wouldn't he? But I thought you knew. He asked you for the divorce because she got pregnant, and he's going to marry her – if she can still fit in a wedding dress. God, is she huge! Perhaps it's twins, she's big enough for . . .'

I could sort of vaguely hear her voice going on and on, alarmed and rising, but it sounded far away, probably because I was on my knees on the cold stone flags, and some poor woman was howling: 'No! No!'

It sounded like me.

'Poor old Charlie,' part of me said sadly. 'She's having a bad day, but I wish she'd shut up.'

'Charlie?'

Someone scooped me up, rigid and resisting, and held me in strong, warm arms. 'Charlie, what's the matter?'

'We were just talking, and then she went mad!' Angie said.

'What have you done to her?' Mace's voice said angrily.

'I haven't done anything! I only came to apologise.'

'You must have said *something*!'

'Only that her ex-husband was getting married again – his girl-friend's pregnant. I suppose that upset her, because she never had any – kept miscarrying all the time. But I didn't know she would carry on like this!'

'Didn't you? Well, I think you've done enough. Get out before I throw you out!'

'There's no need to be like that when I came round here in all good faith to apologise. And after all, she *did* kill my husband!'

There was the tapping of high heels and a slammed door, but it all seemed to be happening somewhere else, beyond all that awful sobbing.

I cried myself out, curled up on the bed in Mace's arms, while he stroked my hair, and murmured soothing things ... and eventually I stopped sobbing on a hiccup, and lay there, feeling exhausted, but much better.

After a while (and a lot of nose-blowing) he brought my flannel and washed my face with cold water, as though I were the same age as Caitlin. Then he fetched a bottle of champagne (which he must have brought with him) and two glasses, and we lay on the bed and drank that, as the afternoon light faded into dusk.

It was terribly cosy: the lion *shall* lie down with the lamb.

'What are we drinking to?' I asked after a bit. My voice was interestingly husky – quite sexy really – but I didn't suppose it would last.

'The test results – Caitlin's definitely mine. I wanted you to be happy with me.'

'Oh Mace, I'm so glad! And I'm sorry about that scene. I think I must have been bottling lots of things up for too long, and they all sort of exploded at once. I didn't mean to cry all over you.'

'I'm just glad I was here for you.' He tightened his arms around me. 'Charlie: as well as the good news about Caitlin, I also came to swallow my pride and tell you I think I love you.'

'What do you mean, *think*?' I demanded before I could stop myself.

'Well, I've never felt quite like this before,' he said, sounding puzzled. 'I don't know what it is about you, but you've somehow managed to get right under my skin, so now whenever I think of the future, you're there, too. But it's also been slowly dawning on me that if I marry you, I'm going to have to take on board the whole Rhymer clan as well. It's a big commitment.'

Marry me? Is the man mad?

'That's all right,' I assured him soothingly. 'I'm not going to marry you.'

He relaxed his hold a bit and gave me one of his smouldering stares: 'You're *not*?'

'No, of course not! It wouldn't work – I don't want to live in London, and also I simply don't think I could take all the effort involved in trying to look good all the time for the role of Mace North's wife. Too boring and exhausting. There was a Regency dandy who killed himself simply because he couldn't take any more of the buttoning and unbuttoning. I think I'd feel just like that.'

'But you *do* look good all the time. You're a beautiful water sprite, come to drive me mad. Besides, I'm going to spend most of my time in Upvale, though my house in London is very nice, with a big, private garden. You'll like it.'

'I'm not going to see it,' I said firmly. 'I've done the marriage bit, and now I'm going to stay here where I belong, and paint, and maybe run the magazine if it takes off, and be happy.'

'You could marry me and still do all that – and we can share Caitlin,' he offered, persuasively.

'But would I be happy as the third wife of the actor Mace North? I don't think so!'

'Better the last than the first, darling,' he pointed out.

'Really Mace, you must be mad wanting to marry me! I wonder if you could be impervious to Gloria's antidote because of your Tartar blood? But then, if it was that, I suppose the love philtre wouldn't have affected you in the first place.'

'My Tartar blood is about to rise to the boil if you don't say you love me ...' he muttered, kissing me. 'Or maybe it's rising anyway.'

'Cooee!' called Gloria down the stairs. 'Are you there, Charlie? Would you like a nice cup of tea, my little chicken?'

Mace sprang up from the bed with a muffled curse, kicked the door to the bottom of the stairs shut, then shot the bolt.

'Mace, Gloria will think—'

'Gloria will be quite right,' he said, advancing purposefully.

Mace stretched his muscular frame out to straighten the kinks left by my little bed.

He always looks so gorgeously graceful I still expect those camera trolley things to whiz in and out at odd moments. Mind you, it would have been pretty disconcerting if they'd done that during our recent odd moments – if we'd noticed.

'I'll have to go,' he said reluctantly. 'Tomorrow's the opening night of my new play in London, and I'll have to be there. Then I can bring Caitlin home – but right now I'm going to go straight back to the cottage and finish writing the last act of my next play, even if it takes me all night!'

This man clearly has his own private energy source, because I feel as limp as a boned herring.

'And the first batch of *Skint Old Northern Woman* is coming sometime this week!' I remembered, feeling even limper. 'We've got lists of advance orders already, and Chris is coming round in the morning to help us get everything organised – we're a bit amateur.'

'I'd come and help too, if I didn't have to go to London. Still, at least I'm sure now that Kathleen will turn up for her wedding, because Rod phoned earlier from the States and said the wedding organiser would know where she was.'

'Of course – *someone* must be in charge of it!' Weddings don't arrange themselves, after all.

I sighed as he got up, and said wistfully: 'Do you have to go home now?'

'Afraid so. Besides, it will give you a chance to think about me while I'm gone, and maybe miss me. There are advantages to marrying me you may not have thought of yet, too, like if your father's marrying Jessica, couldn't you marry me simply to get your hands on my cottage?'

'That would be mercenary,' I said, shocked. 'Besides, I could go and live with Em in the Vicarage if it came to it, only it's awfully small. I can't really imagine Em being happy in such a little kitchen.'

'Well, my cottage isn't huge, but it's bigger than the Vicarage. You think about it.'

The cottage is likely to be way down the list of his assets I think about while he's away.

He pulled a fleecy dark top over his head, then picked up a heavy leather coat lined with rather outrageous fake fur.

'What happened to the duvet?'

'Nothing – I'm just having a change. Do you like it?'

'On you, yes. On anyone else, I'd say they were a raging queen.'

'Well, I'm not.'

'Evidently.'

'I think I'll leave by the Parsonage and make my peace with Gloria,' Mace said thoughtfully. 'Maybe have a word with Ran, too, if he's in. What would be the best way to make an impression on Gloria? The sort that doesn't involve being transformed into a toad?'

170

'Say you've come specially to take the super-strength love-potion antidote she brewed up at home last night, and if she asks you to drink a cup of tea after that, do it.'

'And it definitely won't be hemlock?'

'No – though I wouldn't mention ... well, what we've been up to.'

'I don't usually issue bulletins. But I thought I would tell your father my intentions are honourable, in case Anne and Em try to kneecap me.'

'He won't know what you're talking about – he doesn't even realise you've ever had any *dishonourable* intentions. And when you've drunk this new version of Gloria's concoction, you probably won't,' I added firmly.

'Don't bank on it,' he said, kissing me.

He opened the stairway door and came face to face with Flossie, who was sitting on one of the steep steps trying to remember whether she was going up or down.

'Hello!' he said, and she got up wagging her tail, licked his face, and went back upstairs ahead of him.

He didn't come back down. Gloria probably ushered him firmly out after he'd spoken to Father – *if* he spoke to Father; for surely he must have been joking?

After a while I dozed off.

When I woke up again it wasn't as late as I thought, and after washing my face – which looked normal if a trifle feverish – I went up to the kitchen.

Em was there alone, though I could hear Gloria belting out 'Three Little Maids from School' in Father's bedroom, and Walter's 'heh, heh, heh' laugh from the small sitting room where he was watching children's TV.

'Where's the body?' I asked.

She looked up and grinned. 'He took the cup of poison from Gloria with his own hand, and drained it in one.'

'Did anything happen?'

'Well, he didn't suddenly smite his forehead and exclaim: "Yes, I see it now – she looks like the backside of a donkey, and has the intelligence of a cushion." In fact, he looked exactly the same, only more so.'

'More so?'

'Sort of determined on a course of action. He said he was off to

171

see Father next, but Gloria gave him a cup of tea first. She told him she'd put bromide in it, but she was only joking – I think. You haven't been at it again, have you?'

'You needn't make it sound like I'm a rabbit. I had a rather traumatic visit from Angie and Mace was just comforting me.'

I told her what Angie'd said. 'And I don't know why it should upset me so much, because I thought I was over all that: I mean, I accepted I wasn't going to have a baby years ago. But Mace was so sweet, and just held me for ages, and wiped my eyes, and hugged me and—'

'Spare me the rest. There was something very significant about the way he slammed closed the door to the stairs.'

'You heard that, did you? Yes, there's something significant about all his actions – it's because he's an actor, I think, but also he's just sort of naturally graceful.' I sighed.

'He's not coming back for dinner later, is he?' Em asked. 'Just so I know how many to cook for – I'm doing individual syllabubs.'

'Coming back? No, of course not. He's suddenly got over his writing block, and he says he's going to finish the last act of his play tonight, no matter how long it takes, because he's due back in London tomorrow. It's the first night of his latest play, then the wedding, so he will be able to bring Caitlin home after that – assuming Kathleen turns up, and agrees to it.'

'So he does mean to come back to Upvale?'

'He did. I don't know how he'll feel after a bit more time in his own theatre world – or about me, after the potion kicks in.'

'*If* it does.'

'Em . . .'

'What?' she said, sieving sugar in glistening cascades.

'You know the five power bracelets you gave me?' I asked. 'Well, the rose quartz one exploded spontaneously, and there are tiny beads all over the place.'

'Probably the heat,' she said drily.

'But that's the one for love!'

'Precisely.'

'Do you think it's significant?'

'Yes, but like Gloria and the tea leaves, I can't decide which way. I'll get you another one.' She set out a row of little glass dishes, and spooned syllabub into them. 'I must put two of these

172

in the fridge for the twins to have later – I promised, because they're going to a birthday party after school.'

Then she picked up a small packet and read: '"Super-Lite Mousse: The No-Calorie Dessert."'

'Is that the Treacle Tart's?'

'Yes, she's bought loads of them, and Super Soup-Lite, and I am to serve her one instead of my fat and calorie-laden concoctions.'

'Is that what she said?' I watched as she emptied the packet into a bowl, poured in double cream and began to whisk.

I examined the packet. 'It says water here, Em, not cream.'

'I know.' She added a bit of sugar, poured the mixture into a little dish, and garnished it with angelica to distinguish it from the rest.

'There. It looks almost as good as the real thing, doesn't it?'

Em was ladling soup by the time Father came in, looking baffled: 'They're all at it! Mace just waltzed in and asked me for Charlie's hand in marriage. Have they all been reading Jane bloody Austen? Is your Red going to turn up next, Anne, singing "It's A Nice Day For A White Wedding"?'

'Not effing likely.'

'What about you, Bran?'

Bran looked up questioningly.

'Going to get married, are you? Got a girl?'

'Isis.'

'You can't have a relationship with a figment of your bloody imagination!'

'Language!' said Jessica primly. We all looked at her.

'Isis Cadwallader. Student. Postgrad.' Bran looked from one to another of us as though trying to pick up faint and fuzzy signals. 'Speaks eight languages.'

'In bed?' asked Anne, interested.

'Yes,' Bran said. 'Miss her a bit,' he added thoughtfully.

'Well, as long as she doesn't turn up and ask me for your hand,' Ran said.

'She's got two of her own,' Bran said seriously, propping his book up against the recumbent figure of Mr Froggy and losing interest in the conversation.

'Mace must have been playing a joke on you, Ran,' Jessica said. 'He couldn't possibly be interested in Charlie – he could have anyone!'

173

'He probably has,' Gloria muttered, hacking viciously at a crisp new loaf.

'No, he seemed serious – said he found her compellingly irresistible.'

Everyone turned and looked at me.

I shrugged. 'We haven't found a cure yet. Gloria's won't work, for some reason, though perhaps the new one will, in time.'

'What do you mean?' Jessica interrupted. 'What cure? And have you been having it off with Mace, you dark horse?'

It forcibly struck me that poor old Jessica is always bobbing along on the surface of our lives like a cork, and she is, and always will be, one sub-plot short of a novel.

'You're such a romantic,' Em said to her sarcastically.

'And you've got it the wrong way round,' Gloria told her. 'He's after my Charlie – but he's only good for one thing, you mark my words, blossom.'

'Bet he's good at that, though?' Jessica said enviously, then caught Father's eye and subsided.

'He's a bold one!' Gloria said rather admiringly. 'Said he'd come for the cup of poison and drank the anti-philtre right down in one go. Then he took a cup of my special tea to take the taste away, smiled at me, said a handsome dark stranger had just entered my life bringing change, and then off he went to see Ran.'

'So, what did you say, Father?' Em asked.

'I said to ask me again when his last wife had turned up safe and sound, and he said he would. Providing she's not in bits, I've no objection, I suppose. But I thought Charlie would have had enough of all that marriage stuff. Have you been dosing the poor man up with love potions, you lot?'

'*I* haven't. And thank you, Father, but your gracious approval won't be necessary – Mace drank one of Gloria's love philtres by mistake, but he's resistant to the antidote. We think it's the Tartar blood or something. Shouldn't the new antidote have worked immediately, Gloria?'

'Yes. He's impervious.'

'Load of rubbish,' Father said uneasily. 'Er – you didn't give any of it to anyone else, did you. Gloria?'

'Oh, do they work?' asked Jessica eagerly.

'No,' Gloria said flatly to both, and slamming down the bread-knife went out muttering.

'Oh, well,' Jessica said, disappointed. 'I expect it's just a temporary infatuation then, Charlie. You should marry him while you can!'

'No point. I won't leave Upvale ever again, but he will soon tire of it and go back to London permanently. We come from two different worlds,' I added tritely. 'We've nothing in common.'

'If pagans can marry vicars, artists can marry actors,' Em said. 'Marry him, and bend him to your will – we will all help you.'

'Come on, does he look bendable to you? And name me an actor who's been married to the same woman for more than five minutes.'

There was a long, thoughtful silence.

'Anyway, I don't want to live *his* life, I want to live my own. I'm going to stay in Upvale, and paint, and maybe the magazine will sell so many we can publish it regularly – say six issues a year or something. I'll be happy and successful, which is the best sort of revenge on Matt that I can think of.'

'Reminds me,' Anne said. 'Jen rang. The first five thousand copies of the mag. are arriving tomorrow.'

'Five *thousand*! Don't you mean hundred?'

'No.'

'My God – where are we going to put them?'

'Anywhere except my study,' Father said firmly.

'How about the back sitting room? The one we don't use because of the little poltergeist thing?' Em suggested.

'Do you think she'll mind?'

'Probably glad of the company. I'd sit in there myself sometimes, except she's always so bloody miserable and restless.'

'Which little poltergeist thing?' Jessica said, looking scared. 'I thought you said that room was never used?'

'Oh it's used, all right, but not by us.'

'Have to get organised: promotion, packing, labelling,' Anne reeled off efficiently.

'Chris is going to help. He's coming round tomorrow when he's seen the bishop, and he's bringing his computer. He says he can print out the address labels on it, and he's going to do the book-keeping,' Em said.

'What if his bishop sends him away?'

'He won't go – he belongs here in Upvale now, with us?'

'There!' Father said with satisfaction to Jess. 'I said everything

175

would go on as usual. The bishop will defrock Chris, and he can come and live here with Em. There's no need for her to leave: problem solved!'

'Not with the Treacle Tart as stepmum, it bloody well isn't,' Anne said.

Chapter 22

First Cuckoo

Mace arrived just after the first batch of *Skint Old Northern Woman* was delivered, strode in like a conquering emperor, and kissed me right in front of Em, Anne and Walter, who were all helping to shift the magazines into the back room.

Bran had been helping, too, but had wandered off with a copy and hadn't come back. Probably analysing it.

Mace was wearing the fur-lined leather coat, with a checked cotton Arab kaffiyeh tied around his neck. Instead of looking poncey and affected, he gave the impression he'd just dismounted from his shaggy pony and parked his scimitar at the door before popping in for a quick tea-and-ravage.

'I've finished the play – three o'clock this morning – now I'm on my way to London,' he said, favouring me with one of his intense 'slow fuse heading for the dynamite' smoulders. 'This is just to remind you that I'll be back.'

He released me, and while I tried to reinflate my lungs began moving cartons of magazines himself, rather faster than we had. 'I'll take a box of these with me, if that's okay. I'll settle up for them when I get back: if you trust me?'

'We'll bill you,' I croaked, then cleared my throat and added, hardening my heart: 'In case you decide *not* to come back.'

'Oh, I'll be back, darling - count on it.'

'Do you want to be nude centrefold in the next one?' asked Anne hopefully. 'Give your services for free?'

'I always do,' he said, grinning. 'And I'll think about it.'

'Heh! Heh! Heh!' laughed Walter, seeming to find this amusing for some reason. 'If he don't want to do it I could be your pin-up,' he offered generously. 'I've got no bodily hair what-so-ever.'

'Well, that would certainly be *alternative*,' Emily said. 'Or how about Chris, in just his dog collar and motorbike boots?'

'Too kinky – the Church wouldn't approve,' Anne said seriously.

'I don't think the Church are going to approve of his marrying me, either,' Em said.

'Chris has been summoned to see his bishop this morning,' I told Mace, as he stacked the last of the boxes. 'We don't know why, but we think he must have heard rumours about Em.'

'Them ones about sacrificing chickens and funny crosses are all lies,' Walter said stòutly. 'Our Em never would hurt a fly.'

Well, she wouldn't hurt a dumb *creature* . . . though dumb people are another thing.

'If Chris and I can work out a form of marriage that respects both our beliefs, I don't see what the Church has got to stick its nose in for,' Em said mutinously.

'Perhaps you and Anne could hammer out some form of agreement for Charlie and me?' Mace suggested. 'A peace treaty, so we could live adjoining lives, like friendly territories, overlapping at the edges here and there. The odd little border skirmish . . .' He reached out and ran a finger down my cheek until it reached my lips, which quivered suddenly in a very SueEllen way, all on their own. 'Meanwhile, I'm off to London, where hopefully I'll discover Kathleen all in one piece, so satisfying Ran, at least, that I possess the qualities of a potential son-in-law.'

'We already know Kathleen's all right,' Em said, looking thoughtfully at him. 'We've seen it – by various means. But if the Treacle Tart marries Father, we *all* might be looking for a new home: so marry Mace, Chaz, and we'll come and live with you.'

'I don't see why *I* have to sacrifice myself so the family can stay together!' I protested.

'Oh thanks!' Mace said. 'Don't mind me.'

'Yes, but Mace is probably filthy rich,' Anne pointed out. 'Aren't you, Mace? You could afford to buy a bigger house, with room for us all?'

'I could, but . . .'

'This *is* the only really big house in Upvale,' Em said.

'Well, he could have an annex built on his cottage?' I suggested. 'And everyone probably won't want to come at once anyway, unless its Christmas or something.'

'So, are you going to marry him?' Anne asked.

'No, of course not. What would I do that for?'

They turned as one and looked at Mace.

'Pretty obvious reasons, I should think,' Em said, after a minute.

'Bloody right,' Anne agreed.

Gloria came in with a tea tray, and gave Mace a scathing head-to-foot inspection. 'It's you, is it?'

'It was last time I looked,' he agreed. 'I'm off to London, though – I've a first night to attend – but I'll be back after Kathleen's wedding, with Caitlin.'

'Why bother? You've played your part,' she said sourly.

'Life's a play, and all the men and women in it but the players ...' he misquoted cheerfully, his pretensions not looking particularly depressed. 'I refuse to be First Villain – I'll be back. Would anyone like any shopping done in London? Christmas presents?'

Em felt in her dungaree pocket. 'If you want a challenge, I've got Bran's Christmas present list here.' She looked down and read: '*Three Hundred and Fifty-Nine Definitions of Meaning* by Gottfried Flauncy Gresham. Published in 1959, probably had a print run of five copies.'

'Hasn't Bran put anything easier on the list?' Anne demanded. 'We'll never effing find that!'

'Jelly beans? Harry Potter? Liquorice smoking set and chocolate cigars?'

'That's more like it.'

'I might as well give the book a go,' Mace offered, and scribbled down the title before giving me another look of extreme (if blistering) intensity and striding off, his shorn black locks ruffled by an invisible hand.

'You lay off him!' I said to the air, which quivered sulkily like a heat haze – only in this case, a *chill* haze.

'You can't blame her for trying,' Em said.

'Yes I can.'

The window shutter banged twice, rather petulantly.

Unfortunately, Chris's bishop did not want to congratulate him on his intended pagan/Christian nuptials with Em, merely to point out the gaping gateway to Hell grinning at his feet.

After that, Chris said, he fully and frankly expressed his own feelings on the matter to the bishop, which is probably how he got sent to Upvale in the first place, it being The Land Time Forgot.

'I'm taking early retirement, just as soon as they find a temporary replacement,' he told us as we sorted out our magazine dispatch depot. 'I won't have remarks like that made about the woman I love.'

'Oh? What did he say?' Em demanded eagerly.

'My lips are sealed,' he replied firmly, looking resolute under his Wyatt Earp moustache.

Seeing Em was considering unsealing them with the paperknife, I said hastily: 'But won't you have to move out of the Vicarage, too, Chris?'

'I'm afraid so. But not out of Upvale. I have a small private income of my own, enough to buy a small cottage. But I hate to reduce Em to that level, after being used to all this space.'

'Oh, anywhere that hasn't got the Treacle Tart in it sounds wonderful to me at the moment, Chris,' Em assured him. 'And you can move in here with me until we sort things out.'

'Not until we're married,' he said firmly.

'But—'

'Bloody straight-laced vicars,' commented Anne.

'He is not!' Em said hotly. 'He—'

'Em,' Chris said, and she stopped and looked at him.

'Oh, all right.'

'The attics?' I suggested. 'There are lots of them empty. Or why not get married quickly, if you've worked out a compromise ceremony?'

'We could, if my friend can get away for long enough to officiate,' Chris said. 'Em doesn't feel she can come any further into the church than the front porch, so we can have a simple ceremony there, and then we can all go up to the standing stones and Em's friends can say a few words.'

'Yes – just a general sort of blessing you know – nothing *extreme*,' explained Em, which relieved my mind a little.

'And then we can have a party!' Anne said.

'If we did it just before Christmas, we could combine the celebrations with that,' Em suggested.

'But what will your father say if I just move in?'

'Nothing,' Anne said. 'You're here most of the time now, anyway, aren't you? He's got used to you.'

'Ran said he had no objection to us marrying now, Em, providing you didn't die in childbirth,' Chris said, returning after bearding the lion in his den. 'Has he always had these morbid ideas?'

'That was bloody *Charlotte!*' Anne said. 'Honestly – you wouldn't think he'd written a book about the Brontës, would you? If anyone was going to die in childbirth it would be Charlie, not Em.'

'But I'm not the one marrying a clergyman.'

'And I'm not having effing children,' Emily stated. 'Date stamp's up.'

'That's all right, I don't want to share you,' Chris said.

'Why not? I share you with your effing motorbike!'

'Are you jealous of my motorbike?' he asked, pulling her close and kissing her.

A small avalanche of magazines cascaded down behind them like a waterfall.

'She doesn't like it, Em,' Anne warned.

'Who doesn't like what?' asked Chris, confused.

'The poltergeist thing. She never likes it when you're happy. She's a miserable bugger.'

'Oh?' He looked a bit taken aback. 'Should I say a prayer, and see if it feels any happier – or goes away?'

'If you like,' Em said unconcernedly. 'If you say one every time you come in here, she might get fed up and leave voluntarily, but she's not doing anyone any harm.'

'Right,' he said uncertainly.

Skint Old Fashion Victim, no. 4

Some time around forty, our fashion sense withers away to a whimpering pinprick, and we make major clothes-buying mistakes.

Although we can see in the mirror that we don't look the same as we did at twenty, somehow we still expect the same clothes to suit us.

This is the time when we buy sheepskin jackets that double our bulk, (and the only thing that looks good in a sheepskin is a sheep) glitzy ankle socks, and diamanté Alice bands.

Due to gravitational pull, our bums and boobs have begun their slow but inexorable continental drift southwards, so leggings and boob tubes are out.

However, you will slowly start to forge a new and unique personal dress style once you've overcome this initial catastrophic phase.

You will know you are over the worst when you buy something thinking: 'I don't give a stuff if that's fashionable or not – it's just so comfortable.'

Since Chris found out about the invisible occupant of the sitting room, I've caught him in there once or twice muttering and sprinkling water about. And actually the atmosphere does seem to be warming up, so maybe she's gradually vanishing from the scene. Or perhaps she simply doesn't like all the new technology: Chris's humming computer, and the printer doing the labels, not to mention the packing of magazines into slithery plastic postal packets, which has all been going on pretty well non-stop.

I don't know how Madge has done it, but it seems like every WI member in the country has ordered a copy for a start, and all Anne's friends and acquaintances have too. (Probably too frightened not to.)

I simply don't have time to think about Mace more than thirty or forty times a day ... and night. It's exhausting; he's certainly such stuff as dreams are made on.

In fact, now he's gone it does just feel like I had a really, really wonderful fantasy involving some gorgeous but unattainable person, who you know really wouldn't behave in the least like that to you in real life. (And it would petrify you if he *did*, anyway.)

I expect things are settling into a more familiar perspective for Mace, too, now he is back with his rich and famous friends, in his posh London town house. I should think a few more days of drinking London water would flush even the most resistant love philtre out of his system.

He hasn't totally forgotten us, though: a reporter and photographer from one of the Sunday papers turned up to do an interview – and who else could have told them about *Skint Old Northern Woman*?

Father was a little aggrieved that they hadn't come to interview *him* this time, and insisted on being in on the photograph at least. Jessie did, too, but we drew the line there since she'd done absolutely nothing to help: I mean, even Clo and Febe have been putting in time packing magazines into packets.

Other than this, there has been no *word* from Mace, though on the first day of Christmas, my new love sent to me – a banana tree.

Figure that one out.

One morning, after the usual brief tussle with Frost, Father retired to the end of the table to read his mail muttering darkly, though I think it's very clever of Frost to realise that the post belongs to us at all: nobody trained him to fetch it in.

There was only one thing in the post for me, and Frost had to drag that in separately – a stiff envelope like you send photographs in, containing – yes, photographs.

I puzzled over them, for most seemed to be photos of the Parsonage interior … especially my bedroom before Jessica seized it, and the little triangular bathroom off it with the fireplace, and rolltop bath with lion feet. ·

There was also one taken inside what looked like a tropical house at Kew, and a note from Mace: 'This is my London house – thought you might like the way I'm re-modelling some of the interior rooms. The workmen have put the conservatory up, working literally night and day, which hasn't pleased my neighbours …'

I looked up. 'It's from Mace. He's making part of the inside of his London house look like the Parsonage …' I looked down again, frowning. 'But he can't have done all that since he got back, can he?'

'And why would anyone *want* to do that?' Jessica said, puzzled. 'He's got one of those lovely, huge old terraced houses in a quiet square, I've seen it in a magazine.'

'He borrowed a book of photographs of the Parsonage interior, ages ago: mentioned it to him in the pub one night,' Father said. 'The one that peculiar American did. *Ranulf Rhymer: In His Place*. I expect that gave him the idea.'

Em passed the photos round to Anne. 'I expect he's just doing one or two of the rooms up to make you feel at home, Chaz.'

'What do you mean, feel at home?'

'So you're happy there, when he has to be in London,' she explained. 'We had a little chat when he came up to see Gloria. He told me he ordered the work done last time he was in London, after the Birthday Feast. Then he had the conservatory remodelled, and he says the garden is very lush and quite private, with a gazebo and a big pond with fish.'

'But that means that he was expecting me to . . . I mean, all that time ago when I—' I broke off, confused. I'd accused him of treating me as an easy lay, when all the time he'd been turning his London house into a home from home for me? I looked at the photos again.

'I can see now it's not the Parsonage – it's sort of Essence of Parsonage meets . . . well – Comfort, I suppose.'

'Yes,' Em agreed. 'He said he wasn't going to sacrifice central heating in the interests of authenticity.'

'Don't bloody blame him,' Anne said. 'Got it in my flat.'

'I like chopping wood and stoking fires,' Walter said. 'It keeps me nice and warm. I feel the cold, I do, because I've got no bodily hair what-so-ever.'

Em said: 'I told him we'd have central heating if we could afford it, only Father always spends too much on tarts and booze – but we'd have open fires as well. And real sockets for the electricity, not two-pin ones with battered old adapters, like we have now.'

'Yes, aren't those dangerous?' Jessica said. 'The ones in my room look like Bakelite.'

'They *are* Bakelite. The whole place is a death trap,' I said.

'Yes, but I'd know if it was going to burn down,' Em said. 'And it would show up in Gloria's tea leaves pretty spectacularly, too.'

'I've never seen a fire in the tea leaves,' Gloria said. 'Not unless you count what Charlie's lit under that Mace, what can't be put out with any potion I can brew.'

'The whole house wants so much spending on it, it's ridiculous,' Jessica said. 'It would be much better to sell it, and have a cosy little modern house in the valley with all mod. cons. and a built-in kitchen. The show house on the Mango estate is lovely.'

'Sell it?' echoed Em.

'Better for bloody who?' Anne asked.

'Ran, why don't we have the house valued, just out of interest,

184

to see what ...?' she began to wheedle, but then stopped and stared.

Ran, a strange and interesting shade of ash, was gazing down at his letter as though transfixed.

Then he looked up and gradually focused on Bran as though he'd never seen him before.

'You're not my son,' he said slowly, in a strange voice. 'I sent the cotton buds away for analysis, and you're not my son!'

'I know,' Bran said, dribbling honey onto his toast.

'What do you mean, you *know*? How can you know? I didn't know till this minute when I read the letter!'

'Mother told me.'

'Mother? Which mother?'

"I only have one of those,' Bran said patiently. 'Maria Podjecki. Professor Podjecki.'

Father's mouth opened and closed silently, like a rather handsome halibut. 'Professor?' he managed to say eventually.

Bran nodded. 'Anthropology. Came to see me in my first term. Pops in sometimes if she's over for a conference. Smoked salami and schnapps. Don't like the schnapps,' he added.

'You never mentioned it!'

'No? Sorry,' he added vaguely, since we were all looking at him. 'Should I have done?'

'But – I've been supporting you all these years, and you're not even my son!' Ranulf dropped his head into his hands and groaned.

'You mean that's what your little experiment with the cotton buds was about? Having us tested out to see if we were the genuine article? Well, I wonder where you got *that* idea from!' Em looked unlovingly at Jessica.

'Devious old sod!' Anne said.

'It does rather make a mockery of your "Breed Your Own Brontës" experiment, Father,' I said.

'Unless he's one of the Nurture rather than Nature brigade,' Em suggested. 'In which case, it doesn't really matter, does it? It doesn't matter to me who Bran's father is either – he's still my brother.'

We all agreed with that except Father, who was still staring down at the letter, turning it over in his big hands as though there might be a retraction on the back: 'Ha, ha! Fooled you!'

'I thought it was odd that Bran didn't look like the rest of you. I mean, Em and Anne are the *image* of their father, but Charlie and Bran—' Jessica broke off. 'Are you all right, Ran?'

'Oh my God!' Father said. 'I missed the second page – the second result – Charlie!'

'What?' demanded Jessica avidly, leaping up and peering over his shoulder. 'Oh my God! Oh no! I can't believe it!' She looked up, transfigured with excitement. 'Guess what? Charlie isn't Ran's either!'

'I want to speak to Lally Tooke,' I said into the receiver for the tenth time, tracking my impossible mother across the American continent.

'Well,' said a voice doubtfully. 'She's vury, vury busy just now. May I ask who's calling?'

'Her daughter.'

That's one thing I can be sure of, anyway.

'Her daughter in England, Europe?'

'Has she got any anywhere else?'

'I don't rightly know, ma'am, but if you hold right on, I'll go see if I can put you through.'

After several interminable and expensive minutes (at the man formerly known as Father's expense) Lally's voice said: 'Hello? Which one of you is it?'

'Charlie. But don't ask me my surname, because I don't have the slightest idea *who* my father is.'

There was a pause. The line hissed like a muted python. 'You know . . . ? Does Ran know?'

'It was Ran who told me. He got some kind of kit and tested me and Bran.'

'Bran?'

'Bran turned out to be not Father's either. Funnily enough, he already knew, but it just hadn't registered as being of any importance. His mother's been in touch with him for years – she's Professor Podjecki now.'

'Oh, I knew that – I took an interest, because of thinking Bran was your half-brother. And actually, we met once in Prague.'

'Mother, who *is* my father, if Ran isn't?'

She paused. 'I wasn't sure if you were Ran's or not. Either way,

186

you were a mistake, because I was about to leave when I fell pregnant, and I had to put it off until after you were born.'

'So who was my father?' I repeated. I didn't want to go into her reasons for abandoning us again, although acute selfishness and enlightened self-interest become something totally other in Mother's books.

'Have you heard of Brendan Furness?'

'The *poet*? It wasn't!'

'Must have been. He rented a house nearby, to get back to his roots because he'd hit a writer's block, and he was quite a bit older than me, but terribly, terribly sexy, with big, sad dark eyes, although politically *totally* incorrect on women's issues.'

'Yes, Maria thought he was attractive, too. That's who she told Bran his father was.'

'The old goat! He had a heart attack and died the year after you were born – and no wonder!'

'This is my father we're talking about!'

'Yes, but he didn't know it, and he'd have run a mile if he did. And he was terribly clever and famous, so I don't know what you're worrying about. Look, I'm giving a reading in ten minutes, I'll have to go and get ready ...'

'Don't you want to know how Ran's taking this?'

'You just let me know if he throws you out,' she said, 'and I'll send you a cheque. How is your divorce settlement doing?'

'Ducked,' I said, but I was talking to the air: she'd slithered off. Mother is a Pisces, too.

'Did you get her?' asked Em, who was heading the crisis meeting taking place down in the kitchen.

'Somebody bloody well should,' Anne said. 'Bran, I can't believe you never said anything!'

Bran smiled, but that might have been because of the hot chocolate topped with whipped cream Em had just put in front of him.

There was one each; clearly this was a time for desperate measures. Flossie had a blob on the end of her black nose, and was trying to get her tongue out far enough to lick it off, her eyes like colliding planets.

'Yes, I got Mother, eventually,' I said, sinking down onto a chair and wrapping my strangely cold hands round the glass cup. 'Bran, you and I have the same father.'

187

'He's dead,' Bran offered. 'Dead Poet's Society. Only we can't keep society with dead poets – except through their poetry.'

'Quite,' Anne said. She wrinkled her brow: 'So, you and me and Em have the same mother, Charlie? And you and Bran have the same father . . .'

'It means Charlie's related to all of us by blood, Bran's related to Charlie through their shared father, so . . .' Em paused, thinking.

'We're all still family,' Anne finished.

'Of course,' Em agreed. 'It doesn't matter who fathered who now, does it? We are *one*. We are the Rhymers.'

'Like a tribe,' agreed Anne.

I was feeling better. They were right.

'But poor Father – I mean, Ran?'

'Shut himself in his study – shut the Treacle Tart out, and serve her right, the interfering bitch,' Anne said.

'He must be terribly upset.'

'His *theories* are terribly upset. For the rest – well, he'll get used to the idea.'

'But he might not want to have Bran and me here any more.'

'We will just have to see. And it might be immaterial, anyway, since the Treacle Tart doesn't want *any* of us here any more. He's going to find himself playing effing Bungalow Bill in Mango Valley if he doesn't put his foot down.'

Skint Old Health

For reasons that should be obvious, never leave lying about those alarmingly suppository-like waxy-pinkish plastic corks from cheap wine bottles.

Their inadvertent application would mean an embarrassing trip to the nearest Accident and Emergency department. (And possible entries in both The Lancet *and the* Guinness Book Of Records.*)*

Father looked dreadful this morning, but that was mostly because he'd been shut up in his study on a bender since yesterday's postal revelations. He let Jessica in sometime, though, because she wasn't round to wake the girls up for breakfast. Anne went and fetched them down, in the end.

However, when he did finally emerge, he kissed my forehead,

patted Bran on the shoulder, and said, heavily: 'Well, well – you are still my children, after all; but it's been a shock. And if that old sod Brendan Furness was still alive, I'd have his balls.'

'Ran, please – not in front of the girls!'

Febe and Clo giggled into their porridge.

'Ran and I are going to look at the show house together on the Mango estate, this morning,' Jessica said brightly.

She'd found time to polish her surfaces and attire herself in a skimpy top and tight, short skirt, though I always think those bras that push up the skin of your chest and then slam it together in the middle are a mistake. From the side she looked like a narrow-chested pouter pigeon.

We all stopped eating and stared at Father.

'What does it matter to *me* where I live?' he said, sighing heavily. 'I'm a broken man, with no son to carry on the family name . . . no grandchildren of my own . . .'

'Jessica had better have her tubes unknotted then, and you can try again,' Anne suggested.

Gloria stuck her head out of the pantry: 'I know what I know!' she said, which was neither illuminating or helpful.

'You can't sell the Parsonage!' I said.

'Why not? He'd get lots of money for it, because it's so big!' Jessica said brightly. 'He can't really afford to keep it up – *or* to keep all of you . . . but then, he doesn't need to, does he? Em can go and live with Chris, Anne's got a London flat, Bran's away at his university – he could live there, he doesn't have to keep coming back – and Charlie can marry Mace: I mean, I know it wouldn't last if she did, but she can get a big settlement when they divorce and buy her own place. Or maybe she'll get the cottage.'

It's amazing what goes on in that tricky bundle of wires she calls a brain. 'I'm not going to marry Mace, not even for purely mercenary reasons! I'm going to be happy and successful on my own.'

'Without a *man*?' she asked incredulously.

'Yes,' put in Em. 'And she doesn't have to marry Mace to have a home. She can always live with Chris and me, and so can Bran.'

'Not when they defrock Chris and turf him out of the bloody Vicarage, though,' Anne pointed out.

'De-leather,' I corrected. 'And he said he would buy a cottage –

though I thought you were trying to persuade Chris to move in here, Father, so you didn't lose Em?'

'I don't know what I want any more,' Father said brokenly, although I noticed he'd managed to put away a gargantuan breakfast as usual. 'I'm a broken reed.'

He went out with Jessica and the girls, so they could visit the new estate after they'd dropped Clo and Febe off at school.

I wonder if that house in Passionfruit Place is still for sale?

Chapter 23

To the Bone

'I've found Kathleen,' said Mace's deep, knee-quiveringly beautiful voice. 'Or rather, she's turned up.'

The line crackled like cellophane. Em, who'd just handed me the receiver, struck a 'be still my beating heart' pose, hands to her palpitating bosom.

'Shove off, Em,' I said, and she grinned and went back upstairs.

'What? Can you hear me, Charlie?'

'Just about, Mace. Em brought the cordless phone down, but it doesn't work very well here. Did you say you'd found Kathleen?'

'Rod found the wedding organiser, and she gave us the phone number, but by then Kathleen had turned up at Rod's place anyway.'

'But where had she been?'

'Some sort of fat farm, trying to lose nonexistent weight – and funnily enough, it turned out that Caitlin knew all the time, except I'd kept it from her that we were worried about where her mother was.'

'Of course!' I exclaimed. 'She was going on about losing weight to get American film parts when I met her at the cottage, don't you remember? And the coven did say she was dwindling! I bet she's not as thin as Jessica, though. We're thinking of using *her* rib cage as a dish rack.'

'I haven't seen her, just spoken on the phone. Rod said she looked great, but then, half the actresses he works with these days are walking skeletons, so his eye for normality's warped.'

'So are *you* used to being with thin, immaculate women,' I pointed out. 'And *I've* no intention of reducing myself to emaciation point – or going in for liposuction, facelifts or even bikini waxing – I'm staying au naturel.'

191

'You don't need to lose weight – you go in and out in all the right places – and I like you just as you are, *especially* au naturel,' he assured me, and I could hear the wicked smile in his voice. 'I wish you were here now, so I could show you how much. And I'm not the only one who misses you: Caitlin talks about nothing but Upvale and the Rhymers. She's dying to get back as soon as the wedding's over and she's done her bridesmaid's act – and so am I.'

'Will Kathleen let you bring her back, though, without a fight?'

'Yes, under certain conditions. It's all been a bit tricky. She was mad with her so-called friend for passing on to *Surprise!* magazine what she'd told her in confidence about our custody argument, because now the newshounds have got their eye on her. But I got together with Rod, who's a really nice guy, and he's persuaded her that she should do what's right for Caitlin – whatever Caitlin wants. And Caitlin's made it abundantly clear that she wants to come back to Upvale. She'll see Kathleen as often as possible, of course, but she can do that in the holidays and when Kathleen's over here.'

'How awful for Caitlin to have to make the choice, though: her mother or her father!'

'Oh, there wasn't any real contest, darling, but it wasn't the thought of living with *me* that swung it, it was life with the Rhymers.'

It didn't seem quite the right moment to tell him that actually, technically speaking, I wasn't a Rhymer any more.

'Kathleen's been offered a major part in Rod's next film, which has focused her small attention span on other things. She loves Caitlin in her way, but her chief worry if Caitlin stays with me is what the press will say about it. So she's come up with a solution – a PR exercise: she wants *you* to come to London and bring Caitlin home to Upvale straight after the wedding.'

I nearly dropped the phone.

'Me? Why *me*? I thought *you* were going to bring her?'

'I'll drive her home, yes, but Kathleen wants to show the press that she's reluctantly letting her make her home with me and her beloved nanny—'

'I didn't know she had one,' I interrupted, astonished. 'It's the first I've head of it!'

'She means you.'

'*Me*?'

'Yes, you.'

'But you're making me sound like an old retainer!'

'That's the whole idea. A touching scene after the reception, where she hands Caitlin over to Nanny. "I only want what will be best for my little girl," says film star Kathleen Lovell . . . Well – you can see how it will be.'

'You're very cynical!'

'I've been around long enough to know the score, that's all. What I didn't tell Kathleen is that soon you'll be looking after Caitlin permanently in your capacity as Mrs North.'

'The third?'

'And last.'

'There's no guarantee of that, though, is there? If I was mad enough to marry you, one day you'd wake up and see boring old Charlie Rhymer and trade me in for a new model. I've already done all that stuff, I'm not going through it again.'

'If you're still waiting for the magic potion to wear off, forget it. You've got so far under my skin you're now part of me, and I want you for keeps. And better to be the last Mrs North than the first, don't you think, darling? Did you get my message?'

'Yes – I'm bananas.'

'*I'm* bananas about *you* – I have to be or I wouldn't have turned my house into Homage to Haworth via Upvale Parsonage. Did you get the photos? I walk into some of the rooms and forget where I am; and the conservatory is like a chunk of Kew. Do you want a fountain and fishpond in there, as well as in the garden?'

'You're wasting your money,' I said severely, thinking what a long time it seemed since breakfast and Revelations One – and an even longer time since I'd seen Mace . . .

'When you come down to collect Caitlin you'll see it, and you can tell me what you think,' he suggested enticingly.

Just as well he couldn't tell what I was thinking at that moment.

'I've got some coloured brochures from a tropical plant supplier full of things like pineapple plants and palms, and I don't know what to order,' he added, my very own private serpent in Eden.

'I'm very busy with the magazine,' I said, weakening. 'We've been working till all hours packing and labelling, and a Sunday paper came and photographed us, and they're doing an article about it. Was that your doing?'

'I may have mentioned it to one or two people. And I'm sure Em and Anne and Chris could manage without you for a couple of days, when they know I need you to come and fetch Caitlin. She's dying to get back, and if you don't do what Kathleen says, she might change her mind – she's very mercurial – and whip her off to America instead.'

'But if my photo's in the paper with a caption saying something like: "Charlotte Rhymer, daughter of biographer Ranulf Rhymer, pictured in the office of her new alternative women's magazine *Skint Old Northern Woman* ..." and then I suddenly appear in *Surprise!* or somewhere in the guise of a nanny, aren't people going to notice?'

'Dark glasses and a nanny-type felt hat,' he said. 'I'll arrange it. And take it from me, Kathleen will be occupying central stage of any pictures, and you will be firmly in the background.'

'Yes, but what if they find out I'm really Charlotte Fry, the Pan Murderess?'

'It was a domestic accident, and no one except the local paper reported it at the time, did they?'

'Well, no.'

'So, how would they find out?'

'Only if someone told them, I suppose ... and Angie's gone home to pack for her cruise.'

'So, what's the problem?'

I dithered.

'Mace, I *do* miss Caitlin, but I'm sure Kathleen could find someone else to bring her here, and—'

'No. She said you or no deal. She took a fancy to you, for some reason. You don't want me to tell Caitlin that you won't do it, do you?' he added persuasively.

'Well, no. We all want her back here. I just don't – I mean, I've never been to London.'

'I'll send a car, and you can stay here overnight; you'll feel at home, because I've recreated your old Parsonage bedroom. Then my mother will have Caitlin's things sent over – she's off to her usual hotel for Christmas – and when you've collected Caitlin in a taxi from the reception at the Savoy, I'll drive you both back. Bring that green dryad dress and I'll take you to see my new play. It seems to be a success.'

'Congratulations,' I said rather absently, my mind racing. Did I want to spend a night alone with Mace in London? (Yes! Yes!) Did I want to be seen at the theatre with a well-known actor and playwright, wearing a chiffon nightie from a jumble sale? (No!)

And if he took me to the theatre he was bound to see at last just how much of a fish out of water I was among his sophisticated friends . . . so perhaps I'd better do it, and sooner rather than later? Gird my loins in floaty sea-green and prepare to disillusion him?

I wavered. 'You just want me to see you crowing on your own dunghill, don't you?'

'I'd rather be Cock of the North,' he said cheekily, but I think he's shaping up to that quite nicely already.

In the end I gave in and agreed to stay one night, but more because he was showing signs of being about to drive all the way back up here just so he could drag me out and carry me off personally. (Not that this idea didn't have a certain attraction too.)

I will tell him when I arrive about my not being a real Rhymer after all, though unlike Matt, who set such store by it, Mace has enough fame for both of us.

It is odd to realise I do not have a right to any name except, I suppose, Matt's, should I get the mad urge to start calling myself Charlie Fry at this late hour. And even that is not really my own, and forever now connected with Dead Greg.

Looking down, I discovered I'd covered the notepad in front of me with 'Charlotte North' in big loopy writing.

'You big, loopy pillock,' I told myself severely.

Chris's temporary replacement had arrived (so amazingly quickly they must be convinced he's thrown his lot in with the Devil and is about to hold satanic rites in the parish church) so he is now devoting himself to the running of *Skint Old Northern Woman*, at which he is very good.

If it becomes a regular thing – and it just might – perhaps he could become the editor?

They certainly don't need me at the moment, and Anne and Em positively urged me to go to London to see Mace on his own ground. I don't know what's got into them.

'After all,' Em pointed out persuasively, as she sewed a button onto her dungarees while still wearing them, 'he's shown he's serious about you, doing all that work to turn his house into a home from home. You could give the man a chance.'

And even Gloria said I might as well go – it would make no difference now.

Well, in the end I thought: what the hell? Feel the fear and do it anyway, if only to stop the arrival of ever more banana trees! I will need a verandah annex at this rate, and will be entitled to call myself Charlie Del Monte.

I was waved off in a large car, the back of which was bigger than the Parsonage pantry, though I was divided from the driver by an impenetrable wall of glass. (Not that this wouldn't be a good idea for the pantry, too, when Gloria or Em are in it brewing potions.)

Anne loaned me a large rucksack, into which I packed my green Hake-Hackett outfit, turquoise cashmere sweater and the pink and silver nightie and dressing gown purchased in York and so far unworn: my encounters with Mace have so far been of the spontaneous kind. (He is clearly the kind of man who starts first time without the choke out.)

Jessica loaned me a pashmina to go over my green dress, but otherwise I do not have many clothes, so jeans will have to do. Let's hope they are acceptable nanny garb, but I can't help thinking they are going to look very odd with a nanny hat and shades.

I took a bottle of Father's best whisky as a present, undoctored this time. Em gave me a picnic hamper, and a huge cold box full of food for Mace, in case no one was feeding him properly down there. She said he needed his strength keeping up, but she didn't say for what.

She also affixed a little silver Chinese good luck charm to the zipper of my handbag and made sure I was wearing my power bracelets, including the new, much chunkier rose quartz replacement one she'd bought me.

Jessica insisted on spraying me liberally at the last minute with her Happy perfume, so I left in such a fug I had to have the windows right down for the first hour, and it must have seeped through the partition too somehow, because the driver kept coughing.

Still, it is reassuring to know that whatever happens to the rest of me, my wrists and handbag will be enjoying a really good time.

*

196

Skint Old Bookworm, no. 2

It is a little-known fact (because no one ever mentions it) that the Brontë sisters were all midgets. A visit to the Parsonage museum at Haworth, where some of their clothes are on display, reveals that they were not much bigger than the Tooth Fairy.

Chapter 24

Strange New Powers

Skint Old Fashion Victim, no. 5

Those in the know get their footwear from the sort of discount shoe warehouses where they string them together in pairs like kippers and toss them over racks.

For the persistent, there are good makes at market-stall prices, and you can build up an Imelda Marcos-sized collection for the cost of one pair of Jimmy Choo's.

There is though, as always, one snag: discount devotees can always be recognised by the two tiny punched holes in the heels of their shoes where the string was threaded.

The driver, Trevor, was quite friendly once I'd persuaded him that opening his little glass partition and all the windows for a short while would be the quickest way to get rid of the eye-watering perfumed fug.

When we stopped for lunch he declined to share my picnic, preferring a burger meal in the motorway café, but afterwards he showed me photos of his four children and serenely smiling wife. (Though don't ask me how you can look serene with that many offspring.)

After this I fell asleep in the back of the car, due to a potent combination of perfume fumes, exhaustion from not having slept much the previous night, and over-indulgence in food from Em's picnic hamper. Oh, and the half bottle of red wine she'd thoughtfully included might have had something to do with it, too.

By the time I woke up it was dusk.

'Primrose Hill,' Trevor said, jerking a thumb at what I'd taken to be a stretch of countryside, then turned down a street of little shops and into a square of big, terraced houses set round a garden, and we were there.

'What was that perfume called again?' he asked as we pulled up. 'Only I quite like it now it's faded a bit, and I thought I'd get some for the wife.'

'At last I have you in my power!' hissed Mace melodramatically, curling the ends of an imaginary moustache and leaning against the closed front door.

I smiled nervously – but the house *was* very quiet. I stood in the hall among my varied luggage, feeling like the new governess in one of those Gothic romances.

'We're not alone here, are we?'

He straightened and smiled, looking more like himself, which was just as alarming in its way. 'Yes. Did you think I'd have a retinue of servants lined up to greet you on the steps, with Mrs Danvers at their head? A cleaning service comes in on Mondays, and that's it. I can cook, too,' he added, 'even if I'm not in the same league as your sister Em.'

'She's sent you some food – it's in the large hamper and the cold box, and there's quite a lot of my picnic lunch left in the small basket. Oh, and there's a bottle of father's whisky as well. Not doctored this time,' I added hastily.

'Just as well – what I've got's incurable, and I'd hate to waste another bottle of good whisky. I thought you had rather a lot of luggage for one night, though,' he added. 'If you tell me which ones you want, I'll show you your room first, so you can tidy up and come down when you're ready.'

Ready for what? I wondered. After all, I'd agonised about spending the night with him and now here I was, alone and in his power, and so far he hadn't even kissed me! Didn't I deserve some compensation for being about to make a fool of myself in front of his friends?

I followed him upstairs, and he paused in front of an open door and said: 'This is mine – if you want me for anything in the night.'

'Unlikely,' I said coldly, but I peeped in as we passed.

Mace's room had a sort of Moroccan palace look to it, something to do with the rich colours and canopied bed. It suited him anyway; as I suppose my little replica Parsonage room suited me, like a shell round a snail.

Looking round it was odd. It was like – and yet not like. Everything was softer and thicker and more luxurious, and the bathroom off had a shower over the little bath, and a heated towel rail, and radiators.

'It's amazing,' I said, wandering around touching everything as though it might suddenly vanish like fairy gold.

'I just wanted you to feel at home, Charlie. I thought it might tempt you to come here with me sometimes.'

'But Father said you'd borrowed that book about the Parsonage interior ages ago before you met me.'

'Yes, he mentioned the book and I realised it was just what I needed for the stage sets for my first play – sort of austere but functional, old-fashioned but with the odd modern convenience standing out like a sore thumb, you know?'

'I certainly do,' I said, back in the bedroom fingering a satin eiderdown like a lilac cloud while my feet sank into the carpet.

The colour was all it shared with the rough cord matting in my old bedroom.

There was soft lighting, and a little desk as well as the rather Shaker-style white painted furniture. I opened the wardrobe and discovered a long, navy gabardine mac with a belt and back pleat, and a polystyrene head sporting a mouse-brown bobbed wig, a navy felt hat like something out of a wartime film, and a pair of round-lensed tinted spectacles.

'I think I've found your dressing-up clothes, but your secret's safe with me,' I said politely.

'*Your* dressing-up clothes – it's your nanny outfit. I borrowed the coat and hat from the props department, but the glasses and wig I bought. I thought they'd give you just that air of drab efficiency you might otherwise have lacked.'

'Thanks.'

I closed the door, and turned to look at him, feeling puzzled and rather touched. 'Mace, you've gone to a lot of trouble – and it might have been for nothing.'

'But I liked imagining you here, and I was vain enough to think I could persuade you. And I want you to feel happy when you are here,' he said.

'Actually, it's more like home than home is now that I've

lost my room to Jessica. Aren't you afraid I might take up residence?'

'No,' he said seriously. 'No, I'm not afraid of that.'

Our eyes met, and he gave me one of his more ravishing smiles; but he still made no move to touch me and I was feeling . . . well, *piqued*, I think you might say.

'I thought you might like to see my play tonight. An old friend's invited himself along, too, with his wife, but we can shake them off afterwards, and come back here for a late supper from Em's hamper.'

'That sounds lovely,' I lied. I expect I might have enjoyed it, too, but not dressed in my jumble-sale finds, and with his London friends. But still, wasn't that part of the point of my coming, to show him how incongruous I am in his usual setting? That it wouldn't work? 'I'm looking forward to seeing your play.'

Well, at least that was true.

He looked pleased. 'Are you really? Then I'll leave you to get ready while I stow away that mountain of food and drink Em's sent. There's lots of time before we have to leave. And by the way,' he added as he turned to leave. 'Note the door does lock, and the key is in it!'

I looked out of the window at the dark, quiet square, where the big trees filtered out the street lights into filigree patterns on the damp pavement, and puzzled over what Mace had said and done – or not done – since I got there.

By the time I'd unpacked and had a leisurely shower I'd come to the conclusion that for some strange male reason, because I was alone in his house with him, he'd decided to behave like a perfect gentleman.

I admit, that's not quite what I expected.

Alternatively, he's playing hard to get.

Adjusting the neck of the green dress to a point where it strained modesty, I picked up Jessica's pashmina and went down to see what the lion was doing in his den.

Walking into the theatre on Mace's arm, wearing my jumble-sale wisp of chiffon, I wondered if I was in a dream or a nightmare.

Mace, six-four of immaculate dark suiting, *was* a dream, but his friend Gavin's wife, Krystal – a tall, beige tapeworm of an ex-model – had given me to understand that I was hopelessly out of fashion to the point of being bizarre, without actually putting it into words.

However, when we got inside I could see that my dress wasn't any weirder than a lot of the other outfits, and then Mace introduced me to several of his friends who didn't seem to see anything amiss either. Most of them were really nice, and quite ordinary. This may have been because they *were* ordinary, but since I didn't know who was famous and who wasn't I just treated everyone the same, which seemed to work perfectly well.

The only dodgy moment came when I was left briefly alone with Krystal and another woman came up to talk to her, trailing a man with her like a fashion accessory.

'Sonya – and Alistair! how lovely!'

'Krystal, darling – all alone?'

'Yes, but only for a minute – Gavin and I came with Mace North.'

Not only did she not introduce me to them, the two women talked to each other like I wasn't even there.

I've never been snubbed before.

After a minute I looked across at Alistair, a tallish, slightly vacuous-looking man with a rather nice, pudgy face, and smiled.

I got off with him, and it was *amazingly* easy: I smiled, he moved nearer and said he hadn't seen me around, had he? He was sure he wouldn't have forgotten me. I said no, I was Charlotte Rhymer and usually lived in Yorkshire, but I was there for the evening with Mace North, and we were just getting on like a house on fire when Mace, with no more than a brusque 'Excuse me!' reappeared and dragged me away.

'What do you think you were doing?' he demanded, crossing his arms and glaring down at me. 'He's a married man – where's your sense of ethics? Or were you just trying to make me jealous?'

'I was only flirting!' I protested hotly. 'And I wouldn't have done it if his wife and Krystal hadn't snubbed me – though he has got a rather nice, teddy-bear sort of face,' I added provocatively.

'Unlike me?'

'You're more Conan the Barbarian than cuddly toy.'

'I don't know if that's good or not,' he said, frowning, 'but I do know that if you flirt with anyone else, it's over the shoulder and back home.'

I bet he would, too.

'We Rhymer girls know how to deal with caveman tactics like that,' I said with dignity.

'Charlie . . .'

The bell went, and people suddenly started to move. 'Come on,' he said, slipping his hand around my waist and almost sweeping me off my feet. 'The curtain's about to go up.'

We were in a box, which made me feel as if I was on show, although I don't suppose anyone was interested in the rest of us with Mace there; he was definitely worth looking at.

My God, he's beautiful when he's angry.

Once the play started I forgot anything else for, as well as his more obvious attributes, he can certainly write: it was sharp, witty and completely engrossing.

I was still bound up in it when we left the theatre, so I didn't notice the photographer until a series of bright lights went off right in my face. I stopped dead, blinded, but Mace kept right on walking, taking me with him.

I only hope the green dress doesn't come out in a revealing Lady Di manner, though perhaps they will airbrush me out, or something, because I'm not anyone.

When we stopped to let Gavin and Krystal catch us up, Krystal was looking furious, but I don't know if that was pique because she missed being in the picture, or because I flirted a little bit with Gavin in the interval, just to see if it worked on him, too.

We parted outside. Mace excused us from going on, saying I'd had a long day (although Krystal didn't seem that enthusiastic about Gavin's suggestion that we all go on somewhere together, anyway), and whipped me off in a taxi, which he seemed to conjure out of thin air.

'So,' he said, sitting back with a good foot of space between us. 'Is flirting something you make a habit of? Charlie?'

'I wasn't asleep,' I said, snapping my eyes wide open again. 'And no, I didn't even realise I could flirt until tonight.'

'Of course you can do it. You had them eating out of your hand, and Krystal and Sonya are probably giving their husbands hell at this very moment.'

I yawned. 'It was their own fault, they should have been nicer to me.'

'Just how nice did you want them to be?' he snapped.

'I meant Krystal and Sonya should have been nicer, not the men,' I explained, 'but I'm sorry if they have got into arguments because of it . . . they were nice. Most of the people I met tonight were nice.'

'Well, I don't know why you should sound surprised about it!'

'Mmm . . . but some of them were quite well known, weren't they? And I'm not anyone, really. I don't fit in your world.'

'Why not? The theatre world's full of oddballs.'

'Thanks.'

'And if you don't fit into my world, I'll make it fit around you.'

'But Mace, everyone will think you are mad! I think you are mad! I'm not anybody. There's no reason . . .'

'Of course you are somebody – the artist daughter of famous biographer Ranulf Rhymer, editor of a new alternative magazine – the article's coming out in the paper on Sunday, by the way – beautiful, unusual, maddening . . .'

'I still don't think people will know what you see in me; and neither do I. I must have the charm of novelty, but it'll wear off.'

'No it won't. It's not love philtres or infatuation or senile dementia or anything else: it's love. And it doesn't matter what other people think, does it?'

'I suppose not, though I thought it did before tonight. But I suppose people are just people when you get down to it. Some are nice, some are boring and some are swollen-headed and full of themselves.'

'I hope that last one wasn't aimed at me?'

'No – you seem surprisingly normal, considering.'

'Considering what?' he demanded, but fortunately we had arrived home, and the first thing I did was kick off my sandals and head for the kitchen.

I might be exhausted – it seemed like a century had passed since this morning – but I was also ravenously hungry. Mace set the table with candles, and opened champagne, and we demolished a large part of Em's supplies, after which I felt like a new woman. (But not necessarily a better one.)

Mace is a very champagne sort of man, I think: dry, crisp and given to the odd occasional explosion.

I'm more like the peaty single malt whisky we had afterwards; though actually, as it turned out, a blended one would have been closer to the mark.

'I'm glad you've stopped being all dog-in-the-manger about my flirting,' I told him, sinking into a rather billowy sofa and tucking my feet under me. 'Because I've got something I want to tell you.'

He stared at me for a moment then threw himself down next to me and pulled me into his arms. 'I'll show you dog-in-the-manger,' he muttered, kissing me.

I kissed him back with some enthusiasm, which might or might not have been due to the combination of champagne and whisky, but after a minute he stopped and frowned down at me. 'I really wasn't going to do that.'

'Well, stop doing it, then; I did say I'd got something I wanted to tell you.'

'But is it something I want to hear, like "I love you, Mace"?'

'No, it's something I found out recently – about myself. But I think you ought to know and . . . well, I want to tell you about it.'

He settled back with me in his arms, and all the lights suddenly dimmed to a romantic glow.

'How did you do that?' I demanded, sitting up.

'Magic,' he said, pulling me back.

I was glad of the dim light, actually, because telling him all about Ranulf not being my father, and all the rest of it, upset me much more than I expected, and Mace had to comfort me in the way he does best.

One thing sort of led to another, but had I behaved like a lady I'm sure he would have carried on behaving like a perfect gentleman, whatever weird masculine reasons he was doing it from.

However, he is pretty perfect just as he is.

Chapter 25

Much Travelled

Skint Old Philosophy
We are the first generation capable of choosing not to become
our mothers.

Mace found me planning out the conservatory next morning
wearing only his dressing down, and had there been more ground
cover I don't suppose I would have been wearing that for very
long, either.

'Mace,' I protested, fending him off with a tropical plant
catalogue, 'the neighbours can see us.'

He released me reluctantly. 'Then you'd better order enough
plants to turn the place into an impenetrable jungle while I go and
find some breakfast.'

'Maybe I'll go and put some clothes on first. I only meant to
have a quick look in here in the daylight, but I got carried away.'

'I'd like to get carried away, too, but it's late, and I've got to go
and collect Caitlin's things from Mother's house before you do
your nanny act at the Savoy.'

'Oh God – is that where the reception is?'

'It's all arranged. Someone will show you where Kathleen and
Caitlin are, there'll be a couple of quick photos, and then you get
back in the taxi and come here.'

'And then we can all go home?'

'Then we can all go home,' he agreed, smiling. 'But first, we've
got to go to Mother's.'

'*We?*'

'She just phoned up. She wants to meet you.'

*

207

I don't know about *meet* me – it was more like I'd been granted a short, royal audience.

Mace's mother was a tall, strong-boned woman with cropped white hair and the same slightly slanting dark blue eyes. She was wearing cord trousers tucked into short laced boots and a jumper that had seen better days.

'Well,' she said, surveying me doubtfully through the first of a series of rank cigarettes, 'You're a shrimp, aren't you? Still, at least you're not skinny – and they do say size isn't everything!'

I looked helplessly at Mace; all he'd told me about his mother was that she'd always spent at least half the year travelling abroad, wherever the fancy took her, both before and after she was widowed. He hadn't told me what she was like.

'Go away, Mace,' she ordered. 'Put Caitlin's stuff in the car, and I'll send Charlotte down to you in ten minutes.'

'So,' she said, as soon as he'd gone. 'Mace has told me all about you. Met your father – man's a handsome fool.'

'He's not really my father,' I confessed. 'I've just told Mace that actually it was someone else.'

'Oh?' She lit a fresh cigarette from the stub of the first and blew smoke rings. I hoped they spelled out SOS and Mace would come back and rescue me. 'Does everyone know?'

'Only the family, and we've only just found out. My brother Branwell has the same father: Brendan Furness, the poet.'

'Mmm. Know the family, and at least he's dead, so no messy ends. So, has it broken you all up? Destroyed this strange Rhymer clan Mace's been going on about, and Caitlin's itching to get back to? Speak up!'

'No,' I said slowly. 'No, if anything it's made us closer. Stronger.'

'Good, because it's attractive to Mace, this family business,' she said, striding about the room. 'He never had one. I travelled, did my own thing – wasn't fashionable, but hell, you only get one life! Hubert – Mace's father – did his own thing too. Handsome, boring man – big mistake. I should never have married, though the money was useful. Mace had a nanny.'

That explained a lot.

'He wants a family – that's why he married that actress when she got pregnant – she trapped him nicely! But now he seems to want you, too.' She looked at me again. 'So, do you love him?'

'What?' I stammered. 'Well, yes, but – I mean, I didn't want to. I don't want to get married again, either. And anyway,' I added, becoming indignant, 'you obviously didn't want to do the home-making wife bit so you should understand that neither do I. I've already had one go, and I didn't like it. It wastes too much time and I've got other fish to fry.'

'He's got money,' she said abruptly. 'He's got fame, he's got looks. All he wants from you is for you to be yourself and let him love you. You go away and think about that. Maybe I haven't been the perfect mother, but I'd like him to be happy now – and you seem to be what he wants.' She turned away abruptly. 'There, I've had my say.'

As I was leaving she added, over her shoulder: 'By the way, Mace gave me a copy of *Skint Old Northern Woman*. Liked it.'

'I'm so glad,' I said coldly. 'I like it too, and I think my readers might think it a bit of a cop-out if the editor suddenly married your son, don't you?'

'No,' she said thoughtfully. 'Having met you, I think you're dyed-in-the-wool skint old northern woman all the way through, and nothing's going to change you.'

Kathleen looked vaguely at the mac, round glasses, and fringe of mousy hair sticking out from under the hat. 'Charlie? You look different.'

Caitlin, after an amazed scrutiny, threw herself at me, giggling hysterically. She was clearly overtired, overexcited and over-wrought, so I picked her up, meringue dress and all. Her little face pressed against mine felt worryingly hot.

'Just a few quick snaps,' murmured Kathleen, arranging us with a series of small tugs. 'Now, if Caitlin leans forward towards me . . .'

As Mace predicted, Kathleen was centre-front to the camera lens, kissing her daughter in a fond farewell.

The photos should be deeply touching though, because Caitlin's raised, flushed face is running with tears – only I know they're really overexcited tears of hilarity at Nanny's appearance, not regret.

'Can we go now, Charlie?' she demanded after a few minutes of this. 'Mummy, is that it?'

'Yes, darling,' Kathleen said. 'The whole wedding was a *Hello!*

exclusive. Now, give Mummy a kiss goodbye – I'll have to get back to the party.'

'No,' Caitlin said firmly. 'There's been too much kissing already.' And she turned her head away.

'She's tired, Mrs – Mrs Steigland,' I said, just remembering in time who she'd married. 'It's been an exciting day for her. Shall I take her away, now? In fact,' I said, looking cautiously down at Caitlin's suddenly sober, and slightly awry expression, 'I think she's going to be sick!'

Kathleen took a step back: 'Oh darling – I told you not to eat two lots of crème brûlée! Yes, do take her away, Nanny, and – er, Mummy will phone, darling . . .'

Fortunately there were no photographers to see when Caitlin threw up behind a convenient pillar outside, only a disgusted doorman and two arriving guests, and although the taxi driver was reluctant to let us get into his cab, I assured him that should Caitlin feel that she had to chunder again, she could do it into my handbag.

Well, maybe it wasn't strictly speaking *my* handbag, but the staid clasp-top leather job Mace had borrowed with the nanny outfit.

Fortunately this extreme measure didn't prove necessary, Caitlin having recovered her colour, but not her bounce, by the time we got to Mace's house. He carried her in, half-asleep, and put her straight on the sofa for a little nap.

She looked like a rather flushed and dishevelled cherub.

'She'll probably feel better by the time we are ready to go,' Mace said.

'I think she felt better as soon as she'd thrown up,' I said.

'Too much excitement for one day, but at least she doesn't get car sick, and she looks tired enough to sleep most of the way there.'

I yawned, and itched under the wig. No wonder Walter never wears his! 'I'll go and change out of this awful outfit.'

'Do you want any help?' he offered, a gleam in his eyes. 'Only you look pretty grim in that uniform, and I'd enjoy helping you remove it.'

'No thank you,' I said primly. 'Caitlin might wake up.'

I sincerely hope he doesn't have a nanny fixation, after practically being brought up by one, because I have no intention of ever donning this get-up again.

Chapter 26

Dazed and Confused

Back in the Parsonage kitchen with Anne and Em, Flossie on my knee, I described my adventures.

Well, *some* of them – the ones that didn't need an X certificate.

It was late, and Mace had dropped me at my door and gone straight on down to the cottage, with Caitlin fast asleep in the back of the car in her child seat, tucked up in a bunny rug. She was still wearing the crumpled meringue dress, but at least she hadn't been sick again.

The house was quiet; Chris was staying down at the Vicarage, Father and Jess had gone out, and the twins were in bed. Bran was quietly sitting at the far end of the kitchen table, doing a big jigsaw puzzle of an Alpine scene.

It had been an action-packed trip in more ways than one, and I felt exhausted and sort of stunned by the experience. Jet-lagged. It was good to sit there with a mug of cocoa in my hands and a plate of Em's macaroons in front of me, fondling Flossie's silky ears.

'So how's Mace, Chaz?' Anne asked. 'Is he absolutely shattered too?'

'He's not the man I took him for if he isn't,' Em remarked.

'Mace behaved like a perfect gentleman,' I said evasively, not mentioning that unfortunately *my* behaviour hadn't reached the same standard.

'Bad luck, Chaz,' Anne said sympathetically. 'Maybe the potion's worn off then?'

'No it hasn't. He still wants to marry me, though I don't know why. I mean, things are all right as they are, aren't they?'

'Apart from the fact that you may not have a home of your own much longer,' Em said. 'Jessica and Father must have seen every house for sale in Upvale.'

'Have they? But I'm sure he can't be serious – he wouldn't really sell the Parsonage?'

'Jessica's been working her wiles on him. He's started to say how cosy it would be with just the two of them, and the girls, presumably, in a little home of their own.'

'That doesn't sound like Father. And it can't be that small, either, because of all the books, and a study so he can work.'

'And a big bedroom, with lots of effing wardrobes,' Anne added.

'Let's not think about it until after Christmas,' Em said. 'We'll make this the best Rhymer family Christmas ever; and Chris and I are getting married the day after tomorrow.'

'Oh Em! Is it all arranged?'

'Three ceremonies in one day – register office, church porch blessing and then a little rite up on the moors with Xanthe, Freya and Lilith. Chris says he wants to be sure he's covered all the angles.'

'I think that should do it. Is it just family?'

'Mace and Caitlin can come if they like, and I don't mind the twins. That Jessica will come whether I want her or not. Then Chris is moving in here with me while we look for a place of our own – but not an effing Mango Home.'

'Oh Em, if only you and Anne hadn't put all that money into *Skint Old Northern Woman*, you'd have much more to spend on a cottage now!'

'It's taking off. Going to be a cult thing, I think,' Anne said thoughtfully. 'Get our investment back.'

'Yes, and it could give Chris a job too, in case he's at a loose end now he's retired. And then Charlie can concentrate on writing the articles for the next one, and her painting – and Mace.'

'It will certainly be good to get back to my painting again: I've got an idea, a new theme.' It was the combination of Mace, and the lush greenery in that outrageous conservatory ... 'I met Mace's mother. She's mad.'

'Well, we can't effing talk,' Em said. 'What was Mace's house like?'

'You'd like it, Em. Parts of it are just like the Parsonage, only comfortable, and the conservatory has a little domed glass roof, and a fountain. Oh, and the garden is long and surrounded by trees and bushes, you could be in the country!'

'So you quite liked it then?' Anne said drily. 'What about London?'

'Mace's part is more like a village, with a little shopping street, and a park. We didn't go anywhere else except the theatre – someone took our photo coming out – and he introduced me to lots of people. Some of them looked a bit familiar, so I expect they were actors and stuff,' I said vaguely. 'They were all quite friendly and sort of ordinary, except for a couple of women who snubbed me, so it was all right. If they don't delete me from that picture of Mace, though, you will probably be able to see right through my nightie.'

'If so, let's hope it says who you are,' Em commented. 'It'll give the magazine a bit more coverage.'

'If you can see through Charlie's dress, she'll probably gets lots of effing coverage,' Anne said. 'What's in the carrier bag, Charlie? Prezzies?'

'One present – for Walter.'

I fished out the bobbed nanny wig, like a flaccid ferret, and the polystyrene head. 'Mace got the wig to go with the nanny disguise, in case anyone recognised me – the article on the magazine's about to come out. He didn't want it back, so I thought I'd gift-wrap it for Walter for Christmas. What do you think?'

I arranged the wig on the head, and they studied the effect.

'It's quite Good King Wenceslas, isn't it?' Em said. 'He'll love it. I tell you what, I'll make a wreath of gilded artificial ivy and berries to go round it. That will finish it off.'

Bran, who'd been slapping jigsaw pieces into place with great speed, now looked up and said: 'Finished.'

'So it is,' Em said. She looked at her watch: 'One hour and twenty minutes, Bran. I think that's a record. Are you going to turn it over and do the other side?'

'No. Might go up to the pub.'

'Well, Ran and Jess are there, and Walter.'

Bran went off to find his coat, and once he was out of earshot I said: 'Mace managed to find a copy of that book Bran wanted – I don't know how. It's in America, but it's coming Federal Express, or something.'

'Well, bugger me!' Anne said.

*

213

Skint Old Bookworm, no. 3

If the bestseller charts and the literary prizes were judged on the actual numbers of books sold by the authors, Mills & Boon writers would occupy most of the top places. However, these can safely be left out of the equation, since they are only writing for women, a mere half of the world's population.

Em had a white wedding. It snowed.

Fortunately it was just a light sprinkling, enough to make everything look pretty, but not stop Chris's friend, another motor-biking vicar, from getting here to officiate.

Em looked lovely in the tawny velvet gown, with a dark cloak for warmth, loaned for the occasion by Freya – very *Wuthering Heights*, although actually Em is more Heathcliff than Chris.

Love kept her warm; the rest of us dressed like Nanook of the North or Hell's Vicars – or teddy bears, in Caitlin's case.

We drove in a small procession from venue to venue, ending with the bumpy track up to the standing stones, then we all retired back to the Parsonage, where Gloria and Walter laid out a buffet prepared by Em, and we all had a party.

I rather got off with the visiting vicar, using my newly acquired skills, until he noticed Mace glowering at him and sheered off; but it was quite encouraging, what with that and the two men in London, because at least *they* hadn't had any love philtre and yet still obviously fancied me.

Perhaps the love philtre didn't have anything to do with it, and Mace really did fall for me? Only when I look at him, tall, dark, handsome, brooding and way out of my league, I just find it very hard to believe.

Later, Father, Chris and Mace got their heads together in a corner, having what looked like a very serious conversation: but being men it was just as likely to be about something totally trivial, like sport. Or the pros and cons of marriage – Jessica had gone distinctly orange-blossom and yearning as the day wore on.

'That Mace!' Gloria said, bobbing up beside me suddenly like a cork as I watched the three little girls chasing each other around the room, flushed and overexcited, their home-made wreaths of gilded bay leaves slipping over their eyes. 'He wasn't the dark man with the child, bringing trouble and dividing the family, like I saw in the leaves – I don't *think*. It must have been that Brendan Furness. He was dark, and he brought trouble, turning out to be your dad, and all.'

'He hasn't broken up the family though, has he?' I pointed out. 'We're still together. If anyone breaks us up, it's clearly going to be Jessica, because Father is putty in her hands; and since he found out about Bran and me he seems to have lost all power to resist her.'

'You must all stay here in your place; not let that Mace lure you off to London with him again.'

'*He* seems to want to stay here, too, and marry me, but I don't see the point of marriage any more. I don't really see myself housekeeping in his cottage either, do you? Such a waste of time when I could be writing magazine articles and painting!'

'I need to read your leaves again,' she muttered thoughtfully. '*And* his.'

'Gloria just made me drink one of her disgusting cups of tea,' Mace complained later. 'It hardly goes with champagne and good brandy, does it? Then she said I was "a great streak of nowt", and went off with the cup.'

'Oh good. I'm glad she's getting to like you, now she knows you better.'

'*I* wasn't glad to see Chris's friend getting to know *you* better,' he said darkly, putting his arm round me and pulling me close. 'I'm jealous as hell. Is that what you wanted?'

'No, of course not,' I assured him, though actually it was still an enjoyable novelty. I wonder if that extreme Goth look frightened men away before? Or perhaps it was just that I hadn't thought to try flirting? 'I don't see why either of you find me interesting. I'm not young or particularly pretty, or sophisticated, or—'

'Don't fish for compliments; you're beautiful in your own strange way – and unique – that's why I love you. You aren't like anyone I've ever met before.'

'I don't suppose Em or Anne are like anyone you've ever met before, either.'

'But I haven't fallen in love with either of them – only you. You are what I've been searching for always, only I didn't know it until I found you,' he said poetically.

I was putty in his hands. A voice that beautiful could make baked beans sound like the food of the gods.

Caitlin panted to a halt in front of us and stared from underneath her lopsided festive wreath.

'Daddy, you've got your arm round Charlie!'

Mace put his other arm round Caitlin. 'It's because I'm trying to persuade her to marry me.'

Caitlin peered across him at me, her eyes wide: 'Are you going to marry Daddy?'

'I don't know.'

'I think you ought to,' she said firmly. 'Then Anne and Em and Bran and everybody will be *my* family too, won't they? And I'll belong here.'

'Yes, but wouldn't you mind my marrying your daddy?'

'Not really – he won't love you as much as he loves me, but he does like you a lot, really.'

She bestowed a kind smile on us and skipped off.

I stared after her. 'Isn't the stepmother/stepdaughter relationship supposed to be excruciatingly difficult?'

'Only when they hit adolescence, I think, and then they're so awful it all hardly stands out against the rest. Anyway, now you've received royal dispensation, are you going to say yes?'

'No – I still don't think it would work long-term, Mace, so there isn't any point.'

'Why not? What do you really *want* out of life, Charlie?'

'To stay here in Upvale, and be successful with the paintings and magazine – which it looks like I'm going to be – and for the Parsonage to stay the same, with my family around me. Only nothing ever does stay quite the same, does it?'

'No. Your family's changing already, now Jessica and Chris are becoming part of it. And what about *me* now you've turned me upside down? Do you want me?'

'You know I do, but . . . well, I want to live *my* life, not be a minor satellite orbiting yours.'

'I think it's the other way round – *I'm* the one being sucked into orbit around Planet Rhymer, and there's no escape now.'

'Daddy,' Caitlin said, reappearing. 'We have to come back on Christmas Eve, Em says, for dinner and Snapdragon and Hunt the

Mouses. And I can come tomorrow too, and help Febe and Clo and everyone bring in the holly, and the ivy and mistletoe, and make decorations, and do the tree.'
'Snapdragon?' he queried, looking down at me, eyebrow raised.
'Mouses?'
'You'll see,' I said.
'Time to go home to bed,' Mace said, picking Caitlin up.
'You've got a busy day tomorrow – you've got our tree and decorations to put up too, don't forget.'
'I'll get lots of holly,' she said sleepily.

When everyone had gone I retired to my chaste couch, and there discovered an early Christmas present, tied up in gay wrapping paper and gold cord.
The label on it was from Gloria.

Open this first thing tomorrow: not before, not after.

Another spell?

Chapter 27

Present Magic

After I opened Gloria's present next morning, as per instructions, her magic had such a powerful effect on me that by the time I shook off the spell and went upstairs with Flossie everyone had had breakfast and gone, except Anne and Em.

Anne was still sitting lazily over a cup of coffee, since she's finished her course of treatment and so doesn't have to rush out every day to the hospital, and Em was making Christmas stollen at the other end of the table, hence the delicious, spicy aroma.

'We'd given you up,' Em said. 'Thought you might have gone down to Mace's, or something.'

'No. I was a bit . . . a bit occupied,' I said distractedly. 'And I'm not very hungry so I'll just have some toast.'

'You'll have more than toast,' Gloria said, suddenly popping her head in from the scullery. 'You need to keep up your strength. Am I right?'

'I don't know how on earth you knew, when I had no idea,' I told her.

'No idea about what?' Em demanded, looking up.

'Gloria gave me an early Christmas present last night – a pregnancy kit. And I've just done it, and it's positive.'

'Bloody hell, Chaz!' Anne exclaimed.

'Well! And you asked *me* if I knew about safe sex,' Em said. 'How pregnant are you?'

'I've no idea. You know how erratic my periods have always been – probably why I've always found it difficult to get pregnant. It seems ages since my last one, but I sort of thought I was heading into an early menopause.'

'Not yet, my chicken,' Gloria said. 'You're much too young for that.'

'But aren't I a bit old for pregnancy? And I don't even feel pregnant. I wonder if the test was wrong?'

'No, it's right,' Gloria assured me. 'I could see it in the leaves.'

'Oh well,' I said, sitting down. 'There's no point in getting excited. I expect I'll just lose it like the others.'

'Not this one you won't,' she assured me.

I looked at her hopefully. 'It says I'll have the baby in the tea leaves?'

'Yes – it was there all along, only when it came out about that Brendan Furness being your real dad I got confused and thought he might be the dark stranger bringing trouble and a baby, and nothing to do with Mace. But I kept looking again, and it's still there.'

'You'll have to tell Mace, it's only fair,' Em pointed out.

'I can't! He only married Kathleen because she was pregnant! I don't want him to think he has to marry me.'

'Since he wants to marry you anyway, that doesn't matter, does it?'

'I don't think he really does – I'm just a whim. I seem to have some sort of novelty value for him, though I don't know why, and it can't last.'

'You're a bloody expensive and long-lasting whim, Chaz!' said Anne. 'Face it – the man *loves* you.'

'And he could have anyone, but he's chosen you,' Em pointed out. 'Is it because he's been married before? Anyone can make a mistake.'

'Mistakes – he's had two previous wives, don't forget.'

'*You* were married before, too.'

'But only once!'

'Well, you aren't operating a "two strikes and you're out" policy, are you?'

'No . . .' I agreed. Everything just seemed too much to take in at the moment. 'Let's just keep this to ourselves for a few days – I'm finding it all hard to get my head around. And until I get over the three-month stage I'm really not going to really believe it's going to happen.'

'All right,' Anne agreed.

'You must tell Mace on Christmas Eve, though,' Gloria insisted. 'That's the right time.'

'Is it?'

'Yes,' confirmed Em, looking up with that familiar, far-seeing, 'the lights are on but there's nobody home' expression. 'Mace is going to make decisions on Christmas Eve that will affect us all.'

'Changes are coming,' agreed Gloria.

'They certainly are,' I said, looking disbelievingly down at my still-flat stomach.

I mean, if they call mothers over thirty elderly, what are they going to call *me*? Geriatric?

'Hurry up and eat your breakfast,' Anne said. 'The girls will be down in a minute, ready to go for the Christmas tree. We're picking Caitlin up on the way.'

'Yes,' agreed Em. 'There's lots to do. I've got all the sugar mice to make for the hunt later, and I need some string for the tails, and more silver balls for the eyes. Oh – and Bran says will someone take him shopping for his Christmas presents?'

'I'll do that then, and get the stuff for the mice,' I offered.

Bran may be last-minute with his present-buying, but he solves it by going into one shop and buying the same thing for everyone.

The year it was a cobbler's and we all got small shoe-cleaning kits in tins was particularly memorable, but the year of the chemist was even more so.

'He's on the phone,' Em said. 'Can't you hear him shouting?'

There was a far-off bellowing going on, now I came to think about it, but I'd just sort of thought it must be Father, as usual.

'Won't hold it next to his ear in case the bloody demons pop into his head,' Anne explained.

'I thought that was just mobile phones?'

'So did I, but it seems we were wrong. His girlfriend phoned up.'

'Isis? You mean she's *real*?'

'Sounded real. They started talking some weird language or I'd have left the door open so we could have had a listen.'

'I'd better put her on the present list,' I said. 'Let's hope Bran chooses something easy to post this year because it'll have to go straight off.'

'Done all mine,' Anne said complacently. 'Order one day, arrive the next. Sorted.'

'Speaking of orders, I'd better just see how the magazine's doing,' I suggested.

'It's okay – Chris has it in hand,' Em assured me. 'You'd better start writing issue two: it's taking off.'

A strange letter arrived from Matt, who had apparently been sent all the magazine cuttings of me in London with Mace, and the newspaper article about setting up the magazine with Anne and Em.

Angie must have sent them as a last spiteful gesture before setting off on her cruise.

Matt seemed to be insinuating that I'd been underhand and devious in being happy and successful without telling him, and I should be paying maintenance to him, or something.

However, as I learned recently, what I actually signed was a clean-break divorce agreement, giving me no further right to Matt's money and vice versa. Not even a duck.

There is something deeply satisfying about Matt knowing that not only have I set up a successful business without him, but I am going out with a man who is so far up the desirability ladder he's fallen off the end. Had I wanted revenge, this is surely the best sort.

He also included a threat to tell Mace (and the newspapers) that I'd killed Greg, so I sent him a 'publish and be damned' note back: Mace knows, and no one can say it was anything other than an unfortunate domestic accident – or not without being sued by my personal Barbarian Horde.

Now, had anyone noticed that the mousy little nanny hovering in the background of one of Kathleen's wedding feature photographs was me, that might have been a different kettle of fish. But even I can't recognise me in that outfit.

Skint Old Cook

When buying lemons for gin and tonic, buy large unwaxed ones, slice them thinly, and freeze. This way when you add them to a drink you get both ice and lemon instantly, and it is economical since you never have green-furred lemon halves on saucers at the back of your fridge.

Christmas seemed to hurtle towards us, a whirl of activity and excited children; and excited me, too, nursing my secret to myself.

It's just as well Chris is now running the magazine efficiently, for after the article about *Skint Old Northern Woman* was published, with a photo of 'the three daughters of Ranulf Rhymer, the biographer' ('Botticelli's Three Effing Graces,' as Anne put it), we were swamped with orders and enquiries. People now want to subscribe regularly, so we're having to do a bit of long-term planning. I've started writing new articles for the next one.

I'm also painting like mad, too: a London gallery saw the article, and wants to show my work, though what they will make of my current 'Adam and Eve' series, goodness knows. Still, thank goodness for Chris's managerial skills.

You know, it feels like Chris has always been one of us – he's just naturally fitted in, and Em looks terribly happy. We're all doing an ostrich thing about what will happen to the family after Christmas, because it looks increasingly like the unthinkable is going to happen and Father will sell the Parsonage and move into a smaller place with the Treacle Tart.

Mace and Caitlin are here every day, too – in fact if you took a film of the Parsonage and the bit of track leading to Mace's cottage, and speeded it up, it would probably look like an ants' nest. Sometimes Caitlin goes off with the girls and Mace and I get a bit of time together. It is difficult otherwise, because I won't spend the night at the cottage with Caitlin there, and he can't leave her and come here. But he hasn't mentioned marriage for days.

He's probably seen how impossible it would be, and decided to settle for what he can get – which I'm afraid in my case is almost anything he asks for. And he's already given me the best Christmas present in the world, even if he doesn't know it.

Why does everyone insist that I have to tell him? He'll start going on about marriage again, even if he *has* changed his mind. It seems a pity . . .

We've now had a delirious postcard from Angie, who'd flown out to the Caribbean to start her cruise, and a birth announcement from ex-spouse and wife number two, but no duck. (Still, there were no veiled threats either, this time.) It didn't upset me as much as Mace thought, but I let him comfort me again in the way he does best.

Nobody does it better.

The Christmas landslide swept us all along to Christmas Eve, and

223

paused for that still moment when even the house seemed to be holding its breath on the edge of something momentous.

The Parsonage was garlanded, bedecked and scented with fir and spices. Presents were wrapped and piled under a huge tree, and Walter stoked every roaring fire in rotation, because there was no skimping on firewood at Christmas.

The night before Christmas Eve we all went down to Mace's cottage to add some finishing touches to his decorations (and, from Em, some edible gifts to his larder) so it now looked, and smelled, like an extension of the Parsonage.

Chris had closed the magazine office for the holiday, leaving the diminishing little poltergeist thing as caretaker, and was down at the church helping his temporary replacement with the celebrations.

Em communed with her kitchen, performing traditional rites of her own, and on Christmas Eve manufactured an excuse to get everyone out of the house for an hour while Gloria hid the sugar mice.

Then six o'clock came, and the Rhymer family and guests assembled for what we all knew in our hearts to be the last Christmas in the Parsonage.

Chapter 28

Snapdragon

As always, one of the oddest things about the Christmas Eve party was seeing Walter with a flossy white beard, eyebrows and hair; but then, bald Father Christmases are not traditional.

He has to take the beard off to eat his dinner, and on one memorable occasion his eyebrows kept dropping off into the food.

Mace and Caitlin would be going back to their cottage tonight after dinner followed by the Mouse Hunt and Snapdragon, but coming back tomorrow morning. Mace wanted me to stay too, but I wouldn't: this Christmas morning it should be just Mace and Caitlin, the stocking, and three million presents.

Not that she didn't seem to have a lot of presents under our tree, too.

While we were all drinking mulled wine and eating a Christmas cake depicting Stonehenge under snow, with Druids, set in a garland of gilded oak leaves, the girls ran in and out shouting out how many presents they had under the tree, and begging to open just *one* now.

'Mouse Hunt!' Father announced loudly, putting his empty glass down. 'The one who finds the most wins the chocolate mouse. Come on Jess!'

He seized her hand and she looked surprised. 'But isn't it just for the children, Ran? I mean—'

'Children? No – why should they have all the fun?' Dragging her with him he rushed out into the hall and flung open the door of the grandfather clock.

'Aha! One!'

'Come on, Mace,' I said. 'Not finding any is a true mark of shame.'

'Don't you Rhymers have an unfair advantage? You will know where they all are from previous years.'

'Oh, Em and Gloria always find more new places – and this year there are fifty, because there are more of us to find them.'

The others, swept along by Father's enthusiasm, had left the room on his heels, but I tarried long enough to remove a green mouse from the music box on the mantelpiece, and two more from behind the fire dogs.

Mace, getting into the swing of things, beat me to the slightly warm one in the light fitting.

We had a good number by the time we passed Em in the kitchen (there never are any in there – it's too under her feet) and descended the stairs to my cottage.

'Will there be any down here?' Mace asked.

'Not usually, but there might be this year,' I told him, resolutely bolting the door at the bottom of the stairs. 'There, that should hold the others off if they think of it.'

'Oh?' he said, a gleam in his eyes. 'Isn't that cheating, or did you have something else in mind?'

'I've got a couple of things to say, Mace.'

'And I've got something to say to you, too, darling – or *break* to you before dinner, when your father tells me he intends to spill the beans.'

'Spill the beans?' I echoed, forgetting my own news. 'About what?'

'You first,' he ordered. 'And this had better be a confession that you're dying to marry me after all!'

'No-o . . .' I said, avoiding his dark eyes. 'No – I – it's . . .' I took a deep breath and took the plunge. 'Mace, I'm pregnant.'

Mace stopped lounging elegantly against the table and stared at me. 'Pregnant? My God! Charlie – but you told me you couldn't – that you were—'

'Barren? I know. And I'm sorry, Mace. I did think I was.'

He strode across the room and seized me. 'Sorry? What the hell are you sorry about? It's wonderful! Aren't you pleased?'

'I'm still stunned. I can't believe it, or that it will be all right. But Gloria and Em both predicted it, and that the baby will be fine.'

'Darling, of course it will be all right!'

'It's not only that I'm afraid of losing it like the others, whatever Em and Gloria tell me; but I'm past forty, which is old for a first baby. And there's a higher risk of something being wrong with it.'

'There's more chance of everything being *right* with it.' He looked searchingly down at me. 'My secretive little Undine! So, how long have you known?'

'Only a few days,' I assured him hastily. 'Gloria knew first, and she bought me a pregnancy test. I still don't feel any different than usual, which is partly why I didn't want to tell you yet. Only, Em and Gloria both seemed to think I should tell you *tonight* for some reason.'

'Not tell me? Of course you should bloody tell me! I'm the father, aren't I?' he demanded hotly, his arms tightening around me.

'Of course, but you *had* to marry Kathleen, and I didn't want you to think I was trying to force your hand.'

'But Charlie, it's the other way round this time – I want to marry you, and you won't even stay overnight at the cottage with me!'

'Because of Caitlin. It wouldn't be fair to her to suddenly appear in your bed one morning – and then disappear when you got tired of me.'

'Which would be never – so she's going to have to get used to it. In fact, when we are married she's going to think it pretty odd if we *don't* live together.'

'I don't know what to do any more,' I said helplessly, putting down my handful of hot, sticky sugar mice.

'Just as well I do, then. Let me tell you *my* news: I've bought the Parsonage from your father, lock, stock, barrel and Rhymers. I'm moving in, and the only people moving out are Ran, Jessica, and the twins – and then only as far as my cottage. We've done a sort of house-swap.'

My knees buckled slightly and he held me up, close against him, which made it even harder to concentrate on what he'd just said. 'You and Father have been plotting this behind our backs? How could he do this to me? The devious old sod!'

'Tut, tut,' Mace said. 'Is that any way for a dutiful daughter to speak about her father?'

'He isn't strictly speaking my father; and how can you expect the rest of us just to fall in line with your arrangements?'

227

'Why not? Isn't it the perfect plan? The Parsonage continues being everyone's home just like before, except I thought Em and Chris might like a private suite in the attics, so they can be on their own when they want to be.'

I pushed him away as much as I could (which wasn't very far) so I could look up at him. 'Is this just a negotiating move? You can't *possibly* want to take on the whole clan!'

'It's more of a coup. Think of the advantages, Charlie – we can turn the Summer Cottage into the *Skint Old Woman* offices and Chris can run it, full time. Em continues her reign over the household, but they'll have their own private spaces too. You can write for the magazine, paint in your verandah, and generally continue leading your odd Charlie Rhymer existence, and Anne and Bran can come and go as they please. The twins will be near, which Caitlin will like, and even Ran can use the house as a bolt hole if Jessica gets too much for him. What do you say?'

Not a lot – the ground seemed to have been efficiently and ruthlessly cut from beneath my feet, and if I didn't grab Mace I was going to fall an awfully long way . . .

'What about Gloria and Walter?' I said weakly.

'I included them in with the family – they will stay here, won't they, if you all do?'

'But Mace . . .'

'I do have one condition, though: you have to come with me to London sometimes, because then I'll have you all to myself. I have a fantasy about you and me in the conservatory . . . all that lush, tropical greenery . . . the hot, steamy air . . .'

The air seemed to be getting a bit hot and steamy *now*. But it's interesting that it's not just me who fantasises about dragging people behind bushes.

'So what do you say, darling?'

'I think I've been overwhelmed by superior fighting forces.'

He was just overwhelming me again when the verandah door burst open letting in a cold blast of air and several people.

'Cheats!' Anne said. 'We had to run round in the cold and get the key out of the frog!'

She unbolted and threw open the door to the stairs, and the girls rushed down followed by the two dogs.

There was a crush of bodies in the little room, and then it

emptied just as suddenly again – including, I noticed, the mice I'd put down on the table.

'Oh dear. I'm going to get the booby prize for Least Mice,' I said ruefully.

'Which is?'

'I get to wear the reindeer headband and fluffy tail all through dinner. But I can take the flashing nose off to actually eat.'

'I can hardly wait,' he said.

Party Games: Snapdragon

Snapdragon is an old English custom that well deserves reviving, since it is highly dangerous but still legal. It makes an exciting finish to a Christmas meal, the adrenaline rush aiding digestion.

Involving the same technique as igniting the Christmas pudding (and there is something so *deeply symbolic about setting light to the finale of a meal the woman of the house has spent the entire day producing) you simply pile a great heap of raisins onto a fireproof dish, pour alcohol such as brandy over the top, and set light to it.*

Everyone then tries to snatch a raisin without burning their fingers or setting fire to themselves.

Tip: have a lid large enough to cover the whole plate, a fire extinguisher, and a fire blanket to hand, for those unforeseen moments.

Father won the Mouse Hunt, which put him in an excellent mood for dinner, though everyone except me was laden with sugar mice anyway.

Mace said I looked cute in the reindeer headband, but I noticed his lips kept twitching whenever he looked at me. Personally, I was still in a state of numbed shock from his deviousness (and Father's) and so was everyone else when we got to the sherry trifle and Father told them all about his and Mace's plans.

I've never known a family gathering be so silent for so long. Then Em and Anne turned as one and looked at me.

'I know – Mace just told me downstairs.'

'Bloody good tactics, Mace!' congratulated Anne. 'Surrounded and out-manoeuvred, Chaz.'

'Mahomet came to the effing mountain – nice one,' agreed Em. She looked thoughtfully at Mace. 'That seems ... very satisfactory.' Then she turned and gave Chris a poke in the ribs with her elbow, and he choked on his wine. 'But don't you ever hold out on me again, Chris, or I'll be wearing your guts for garters. Right?'

'Right,' he agreed, his eyes watering. 'But I was sworn to secrecy, because Mace wanted to sort it out and then tell Charlie first. It seemed to me the perfect solution all round.'

'*I'm* to live in Mace's cottage?' Jessica said slowly, as she caught up with the plot.

'You said you wanted somewhere small with all mod. cons.' Ran pointed out. 'Well, the cottage has it all – and a study for me. But I'm warning you, Jess, if you don't let Em teach you how to cook, the wedding's off!'

'Cook? I *can* cook!'

'You can wash a lettuce leaf – but I'm not a bloody bunny! You learn to cook, I'll set the date for the wedding.'

'If it means getting her out of the house, I'm game,' Em said grimly.

'No, don't, Mummy! We want to stay here too,' wailed Febe. 'We don't want to go and live in a cottage, it isn't fair!'

'No,' agreed Clo. 'Em doesn't mean it. She's only joking, aren't you, Em? Please say we can stay here!'

'No, you can't,' Jessica said rather snappily. 'You are my little girls, and you will live with me and Ran.'

'The cottage is lovely,' I told them. 'There are little bedrooms tucked into the roof, and you can come and stay here in the Parsonage whenever you want to.'

'Yes – keep your attic rooms here – share you out,' agreed Anne. 'Come and go as you please.'

Caitlin, who had been nodding off into her trifle, her lap full of mice, said: 'Daddy? Where am *I* going to be?'

'Here, of course, with me and Charlie, and everyone.'

'Oh good! So you are going to marry Charlie? And I can be a bridesmaid again?'

I said 'No!' just as Mace said, 'Yes.' We looked at each other.

'You better had, Charlie,' Ran said, 'after all this swapping over and stuff. The man's gone to a lot of trouble for you.'

'Yes, but—'

'Haven't you told Mace your news yet?' demanded Em.

'Can we get down now?' interrupted Clo. 'We're all full, and we think there are some mice we haven't found.'

The children vanished, while everyone looked at me like I was about to produce a rabbit out of a hat.

This was not an announcement I ever expected to make – and especially not while dressed as a reindeer.

'I'm – well, *Mace* and I are—'

'Charlie's having my baby,' Mace announced proudly, like I'd just accepted a particularly lavish gift. (Which I suppose, in a way, I have.)

Even Bran was staring at me, the string tail of a sugar mouse dangling from his lips.

'Em and Gloria don't think I'll lose it this time.'

'You certainly won't, my chicken!' Gloria said from the end of the table,

'Freya said she saw you with a baby ages ago, in the crystal, but she didn't like to say anything,' Em added.

'Yes,' agreed Anne. 'And you said Lilith predicted happy outcomes to old issues in the cards, didn't you? She's certainly having an issue!'

'Did anyone happen to see *me* with Charlie and the baby?' enquired Mace with suspicious meekness. 'Or don't I come into it?'

'You already came into it – nothing but trouble, you are!' Gloria said. 'It said so in the leaves all along.'

'It must have said something else, too. Like: "they lived happily ever after"?'

'Yes – bound to have,' enthused Anne. 'Jane Austen said a large income was the best recipe for happiness she ever heard of, and Mace is bloody rich! So didn't it mention that in the leaves, Gloria?'

She sniffed. 'It might have: but I didn't want my Charlie taken away from Upvale again, with her child that should be born here.'

'I'm not going to take her away, or not for more than a couple of weeks at a time, anyway. You know she can't stay away for long – she wouldn't be happy: I understand that.'

Gloria sniffed, and gave him a dour look; but she is starting to like him, I can see.

'In fact,' Mace went on, 'the only trouble *I* seem to have caused is through you trying to avoid the trouble *you* think I might cause.'

We all looked at him: and actually, when you think about it, he is quite right.

'Isn't it all in the interpretation of what you see? I hope Charlie was troubled by me – she certainly drove me mad. And I went to a lot of trouble to win her. Isn't that trouble enough, Gloria? Aren't there any "happy ever afters" in there?'

'There might have been,' she conceded reluctantly, then got up. 'You'd better have a nice cup of tea. And Charlie.'

'I've suddenly gone off it,' I told her firmly.

'Champagne!' announced Ran. 'Walter, fetch it in, there's a good man. And we haven't had the fortune cookies or Snapdragon yet!'

Mace and Chris exchanged a startled look across the table: 'You don't think we've had enough excitement for one day?' suggested Chris tentatively.

'It's Christmas Eve,' Father said, as if that were an answer. 'We always have fortune cookies and Snapdragon. The champagne was for toasting the house exchange, but we can toast the baby too.'

'Time for Snapdragon?' asked Bran hopefully.

'Bran, take that string out of your mouth before you swallow it,' Em said. 'And save the rest of the mice for tomorrow, or you'll be sick, like last year.'

'Have you Rhymers ever thought of doing things the same way as everyone else?' Chris asked despairingly.

'No, what would be the fun in that?' Em said, astonished. 'This is our way – and yours, now, too. After all,' she added, 'you and Mace and Father have worked out what *you* want, and now you'll just have to go along with the family way of doing things.'

My fortune cookie said that my *chi* was flowing in a creative direction, but it's a bit late with the message, because it's already done that.

When the lights went out and the raisins in brandy were lit, I missed my turn, because Mace took the opportunity of pulling me to the back of the room and kissing me until I was breathless. But then, I'd been burnt already.

We found Caitlin asleep on the bottom step of the stairs, and Em went to find a soft blanket so that Mace could carry her home without waking her.

'So what happens on Christmas Day?' he asked me, looking slightly apprehensive.

'We get up, have breakfast, and open our presents. Then you and Caitlin come up and we play Hunt the Thimble for an hour or so, to work up an appetite for Christmas dinner, which is at about two. And we have the works, with a flaming pudding afterwards, and home-made crackers. Then we take the dogs out for a walk, and come home, and play some quiet games. Then it's a sort of tea-cum-supper, and by then we're all usually exhausted and go to bed early. Only Gloria and Walter go home after Christmas dinner and have another Christmas dinner in their house and watch TV.'

'It might take me a year to recover from all that – and *you* shouldn't get too tired either.'

'Tired? I'm not tired in the least!' I said indignantly.

He smiled, and hoisted Caitlin into his arms. 'I am and I've still got a Christmas stocking to stuff.'

'At least she's asleep,' I consoled him. 'I'll let you out downstairs.'

I kissed her flushed cheek, tucking the soft blanket around her.

'Goodnight, you devious actor you,' I said, giving him a kiss over Caitlin's head.

'I'll tell you something, darling,' whispered Mace confidentially on the doorstep. 'I prefer you as a reindeer!'

And he strode off, laughing, into the night.

I'd forgotten I was still wearing the headband and fluffy tail.

After he'd gone I went and looked Undine up in the dictionary, and apparently I am a water spirit that has obtained a human soul by bearing a child to a human husband. (Either that, or I have a preoccupation with running water, especially urine – but I think not.)

Next morning Caitlin ran past me into the house squealing with excitement and trailing a pillowcase full of presents behind her: not that there weren't a sackful more waiting for her.

She thundered off up the stairs to the Parsonage, while I closed the verandah door before letting Invasion of the Infidels sweep me into his arms.

'Mace, if I marry you, you must promise me one thing,' I told him seriously.

'Anything,' he agreed, with one of those devastating smiles.

'Then just don't turn into an alien, like my first husband did.'

'Did he do that? Must have been a defence mechanism.'

'What do you mean? Are you insinuating that I—'

'You are an impossible woman, but I'm not turning into anything except a devoted – and probably jealous – husband. If that's alien, you'll just have to get used to it.'

'I think I can live with that.'

'I'm not giving you an alternative, darling,' he said, pulling me even closer and kissing me again.

What could I do? I'd done my best to resist, but clearly in a situation like this it's every woman for herself!

With a sudden staccato rattle, a cascade of rose quartz hit the flagged floor and ricocheted against the windows like hailstones.

'What the hell was that?' he exclaimed, raising his head.

'Oh, nothing important,' I told him dreamily. 'Just my love beads exploding again.'